The Adventures of
Oreo

The Adventures of
Oreo

Fabiana Salgado

Library of Congress Control Number: 2020917820
ISBN: Hardcover   978-1-5065-3415-2
                Softcover   978-1-5065-3416-9
                eBook   978-1-5065-3414-5

Print information available on the last page.

Rev. date: 15/09/2020

To order additional copies of this book, contact:
Palibrio
1663 Liberty Drive
Suite 200
Bloomington, IN 47403
Toll Free from the U.S.A 877.407.5847
Toll Free from Mexico 01.800.288.2243
Toll Free from Spain 900.866.949
From other International locations +1.812.671.9757
Fax: 01.812.355.1576
orders@palibrio.com
820106

Contents

Chapter 1

The Beginning

My life started in the dark, pitch dark. I heard other pups like me yipping and squealing, and I could sense a dog *way* bigger than me too.

A few weeks later, I opened my eyes… holy moly. I was flabbergasted and amazed! My mother, the super big dog, was there, along with my three sisters and two brothers. Adding us all up, that made six of us.

We were in a kennel, like a big cage, and lots of people in white coats were looking through the bars at me and my family.

Time passed. I don't know how much.

The people started to reach in to grab us. I'm surprised my mom even let them. Someone carried me out a door. So many smells for the first time! The green stuff below smelled the best of all. The scents of other dogs drifted toward me. Some were big, some were only a tad bigger than me, (or smaller, which surprised me seeing as I was only a few weeks old) and a lot of people in uniforms. They put us down in a giant cage, just for us.

As soon as they put me down, I sniffed the green stuff.

It's called grass, my mom said. The people had brought her along, too.

I like grass, I thought. And to prove it, I started rolling around. My sister took that moment to stumble onto me.

Pinned ya! she declared.

Yeah, yeah, yeah, I grumbled, admitting defeat. *Now get off me.*

She ran off after another pup. She was running already! And *pretty* well too! I tried it out. I stumbled a little at first, but managed it a second time.

Ruff!

Huh? I turned around. A fluffy dog with caramel-colored fur and a white chest was sticking their nose through the bars of the cage. I ran over.

Ruff! she sounded female.

I got close to her nose. *Yip!*

She stretched out her tongue and licked my snout. Startled, I sneezed. Before I could get revenge, she ran off. A growl built up in my throat.

Pups! Come! my mom called.

We'll finish this later… I grumbled before wobbling over to my mother.

After feeding time, the people put us with dogs our size. My mom stayed close by. I looked around for the snout-licker. There she was!

Hey! I barked, standing in her way. *Don't think I forgot about you!*

Oh, please, for some stupid reason pups like you can never forget, she said sassily.

And in case you didn't know, pups like me also love getting revenge, I lifted my rump into the air, ready to pounce, and growled.

She started backing away, but a group of pups tackling each other got in her way. She was cornered.

A millisecond before I pounced, I was grabbed by one of the people in uniform.

Darn people getting in the way of my revenge! I struggled in the woman's hands. She plopped me into another cage next to my mother, who was there already. My siblings got dumped in after me. They also left a bowl of… something... for my mom.

Nooooo! I clawed at the bars. *I have to get my revenge!*

Get revenge another time, one of my brothers said. *Or at least quieten down.*

My other siblings murmured in agreement.

They have a point, my mom said. *You should get some sleep.*

Revenge another day… I muttered. But I *was* pretty tired. I yawned and flopped down into a pile of my sisters and brothers.

Good night sweetie, my mom licked me and curled around us.

After a few weeks of this routine, during which the snout-licker and I made up, we started eating like our mother and drinking water.

One morning, after eating breakfast, the people picked us up. They usually took us outside, but we went through a different door this time.

Where are we going? I looked up at the young lady carrying me. I had learned from her conversations with the other people that her name was Sally. Of course, she couldn't understand me.

We emerged into a small building. There was a gate that kept little kids away from us. A person in uniform was explaining something to them.

A bunch of tiny humans squealed as they put us down.

Nope, I cowered behind my mom. *Too much noise.*

3

My siblings joined me.

"Please, quiet down!" the person told the people staring at us. "The pups have never been around so many people. They might get scared by all the noise."

The bigger humans, probably the adults, shushed their children. It worked.

Go ahead, mom urged. *Say hi.*

I walked slowly and cautiously towards the gate. I could hear one of my sisters or brothers following.

"Here we go," the uniformed person picked me up. "This one seems to enjoy introductions. Gentle hands, please."

The first child looked about nine years old. And, thankfully, pretty responsible too.

She put her warm hand on my fur. "Aww, she's so cute!"

"Definitely," her mom said.

"He's a boy," the person carrying me corrected.

"Oh," the girl looked strangely disappointed. "Can I see a girl?"

I got put back in the cage and was replaced by my sister. Replaced!

After the girl carried my sister for a while, the uniformed person put her back in the cage and said, "Okay, guys, say goodbye."

Goodbye? I tilted my head in confusion.

My mom whimpered.

"Sorry, Molly, but pups get adopted fast," the person told her.

I'm so confused, another one of my sisters said.

My mom took a deep mental breath. *Your sister... the humans are taking her with them. They are her new family,* she explained sadly.

What? the "adopted" sister said. *But you're my family.*

I know, but dogs are supposed to be with humans. It's just how it is, my mom said.

I suddenly felt a crazy need to protect my sister. *No.*

It doesn't work that way, honey, my mom said.

4

Well, it does now, I said. *Humans shouldn't be able to separate us from each other. It's not fair.*

Yeah, my other sisters said in unison.

He's right, one of my brothers joined in.

True, the final brother ended.

Well, try if you must, our mother looked at the person reaching in to grab the "adopted" sister.

I got in between them and barked my loudest bark yet. That startled her. "Silly puppy," she pushed me aside. But, luckily, Brother One was there to back me up. They had formed a shield around the sister, ready to protect her. I followed suit.

"Okay, guys, stop it," she sounded angry. "Y'all can't just stay here forever. You need a home." She tried picking us up at the same time, but we were fierce.

"Hey, Daniel!" she called. "Could you get these pups out of the way for me?"

"Sure," another man walked in. He picked up a small travel cage and started shoving us in. Soon, I was the only one left. He reached in to grab me.

Lord forgive me, I thought. I snapped at him and growled. He jumped back, and my siblings escaped. We reformed our shield and started barking and growling.

"Ugh," the woman scowled at us. "I'm sorry, but could you give us a few minutes? Thanks," she told the people. She opened the door to the kennels. "Get in." We did. She grabbed a bunch of leashes and collars off a rack and clipped one on all of us. All except the "adopted" sister. She hung us up on a hook on the wall and picked up the sister.

No! I pulled, but I wasn't even close. Neither were my siblings.

I realized something. She hadn't hooked my mom.

Momma! She turned to look at me. *Please, don't let her go!*

She hesitated. The human was about to go through the door.

Woof! The human halted. My extraordinary mom ran in front of her and growled.

"Pat, I got a code 72 over here," she said into a walkie-talkie.

A man with a net hooked onto a stick came in. I saw what he was going to do.

Mom watch out! I warned. But I was too slow. The man threw the net over my sweet mother's head and pulled her down.

"Where should I take 'er?" the man asked in a deep voice.

"The pound. She's too aggressive," the woman said.

The pound sounded bad, really bad. We were about to lose two members of our family.

Little did I know that my clever sisters had been gnawing away at their leashes and now they'd chewed though them enough to break them and escape. Which is what they did.

All together, they leaped at the people's arms, one went for the man, the other took the woman.

The people yelped in alarm.

"What the heck?!" he exclaimed.

The "adopted" sister dropped out of the woman's arms.

"That's it!" the woman yelled. "Take these stupid dogs to the pound!" she stormed out of the room.

The man gave us a nasty grin.

Chapter 2

New Human?

Twenty minutes later, we were in the back of a truck. It was dark. We were all separated into different cages. My siblings started to whimper.

Shhhh, my mother said somewhere to my left. *It'll all be over soon, I promise.*

This is all your fault, one of my brothers said accusingly, he seemed to be in front of me. I realized he was talking to me. *If you hadn't told us to protect our sister, we would still be in that wonderful place.*

Yeah, what were you thinking? one of my sisters asked.

I opened my mouth to speak.

It doesn't matter, my other brother said angrily. *Now we're going to the nasty, sad, not wonderful pound.*

We sat in silence. I sighed and lay down in defeat.

This is all my fault, I thought. *I'm such a dumb pup.* I sniffled.

Hey, the almost adopted sister whispered, *thanks for, you know, standing up for me back there.*

Yeah, you're welcome. It got you sent to the pound, I whispered back.

I prefer the pound over getting separated from my family, my sister said. *You especially.*

I smiled. *You sure 'bout that?*

Definitely.

Thanks, I said.

Don't mention it, my sister said.

The truck stopped moving. The man, Pat, opened the door, and light shone in. We started yipping.

"Shut it!" Pat said. "Bruce, help me out!" he called.

Bruce ran over.

"You take the mother, I'll take these rascals," Pat ordered.

Bruce picked up our mom's cage.

Mom? one of my sisters said, tilting her head.

Don't worry, I'll be fine, mom said. Which was strange, because surely, they were putting us together… right? *Take care of each other.*

That freaked me out. *What? But we're going to be together.* Now I had my doubts. *Right mommy?*

I don't know hon, she said sadly. *I love you guys.*

Brother One sniffled. *We love you, too.*

"Where should I take her?" Bruce asked.

"Aggressive block," Pat replied. "These should go with the growing pups."

"Roger that," Bruce said, walking away.

Pat picked up a cage with an unnecessarily big lock and started piling us in. We tumbled around in the cage until he stopped and opened a door to another, bigger cage. He dumped us in and closed it.

"Have a nice life," he let out an evil laugh and disappeared into another room.

Now what? my almost adopted sister asked no one in particular.

Don't know, I admitted. The floor in our cage was cold, it didn't have a bed, blanket, or anything. Just a bowl of water.

Sister Two lay down in a corner. My siblings joined her.

I looked outside our cage. Beside us were more pups. Most were asleep, and some were whining. I sighed and lay down in front of the door. I heard my brothers snore, and my sisters soon after. I couldn't sleep.

At dawn, a lady came in and took a pug away. "You're getting a home, you poor thing," she whispered.

The pug saw me staring after him. *Good luck. Hope you find a home soon,* he told me.

Thank you, I said.

In the morning, after taking a brief nap, somebody came into our cage with a bowl of food and put it down. It wasn't like the food we had before, but still, it was something.

Many sad months passed this way.

One day, a boy in a football jersey was roaming around our area. He had pale skin, brown hair, and matching brown eyes. The boy stopped at our cage and looked at a card on it.

"Eleven months old?" he said in disbelief. "Where's your mom? Shouldn't she be with you?"

Where's yours? I growled softly in warning.

"You poor thing," he crouched next to the bars. He smelled sad and tired. I took a cautious step forward.

"I'm not going to hurt you," he said. He curled his fingers around a bar.

I sniffed his hand. He looked about twelve years old.

"Of course, I can't take you with me," he said. "My mom would kick you out."

I licked his hand. He grinned. "But I'll see what I can do."

After petting the rest of my siblings, he left.

The next day, a family came to see us. A father, mother (Lucky), two teenage sisters, and a ten-year-old brother.

"Aww, this one's cute," one of the sisters said, petting Sister One.

"You fine with a girl, Luke?" the father asked the boy.

"Sure," Luke answered.

An employee appeared out of nowhere. "You want her?"

The girls giggled as my sister licked them.

The parents smiled. "Yep," the father said.

Good luck, I nuzzled my sister. My other siblings did the same.

Same to you, she said.

The employee picked her up and put her in the boy's arms. They took her away.

Turns out people *love* Bernese Mountains. Both of my brothers and Sister Two got picked up. Only my almost adopted sister and I were left.

It was evening when a young couple came by.

"The girl is so sweet," the female said.

"Yeah," the male said. "Excuse me," he called the employee.

I don't want to leave you, my sister told me as she walked over.

It's okay, I thought of the football jersey boy. *I have a feeling I'll get adopted soon either way.*

She nodded. The lady picked her up.

I was the only one left. It was extra cold at night because I didn't have my siblings to snuggle with.

Once again, somebody came and gave me food.

In the afternoon, I could hear the boy talking frantically, coming this way.

"Please!" he pleaded to a lady he was walking with. "I'll do everything!"

"He gets *one* chance, that's it," the lady, who was probably the boy's mom, said.

"Yes!" the boy cried gleefully. "Thank you!"

Soon, the employee was giving me to the boy. I licked him; he laughed.

My new home was enormous. It had five floors at least.

"Remember our deal," Mom said. "If he makes a mess; we take him back. And DON'T let him into the office."

"Yes ma'am," the boy said.

"I'm going to work," Mom announced.

Once she left, the boy looked at me. "First things first. Your name is Oreo, mine is Anthony," he said. "Come," Anthony patted the side of his leg and started walking, so I followed.

We stopped at one of the many rooms. "Never *ever* go in here," he said sternly. I started walking in to explore. "No!" Anthony pulled me back hard. "No Oreo! Let's move on."

He led me to a room with a big bed and a nice closet. I could also see a bathroom at the far end.

"Okay," Anthony picked up some slippers. I leaped at them.

"No! You don't do that, Oreo! Bad dog!" he sounded annoyed.

Fine, jeez! I thought.

He began to teach me what not to do.

Like, for example, chew cables, eat socks, snap at insects etc. And whenever we passed the office, he said, "Do NOT go in there!"

After that, we went back to his room and he showed me my new bed and toys. Anthony had a nice bed, a closet, and a corner desk with a laptop. The rest of the room was covered with posters of what looked like a family with big suits and helmets on. There were words written in big letters on each one. From what I could see, all of them said **Tennessee Titans**. It was amazing! I grabbed a pig with weird, misshapen limbs that I was allowed to chew on, and a spiky chest. I threw it across the room.

Anthony laughed. "Silly."

Mom (Anthony's mom, not mine. Though that would be wonderful) came back home later that night. I thought long and hard about my dog family, and what was probably my new family. I sighed in a mixture of satisfaction and nostalgia.

Chapter 3

······················

A Specialist at Getting up to Mischief

In the morning, I found Anthony reading on his bed. _Legends of Football_ I think it was called.

I jumped onto his bed and started chewing his covers.

"Oreo!" exclaimed Anthony, though he was smiling. I got off the bed, the covers still in my mouth. I ran around the house like my life depended on it. Anthony chased after me. I ran into the kitchen with the breakfast table and came to a halt.

Hey, Mom, I thought awkwardly. She was eating breakfast.

"ANTHONY!" she yelled. He came running. "What is it doing with your _covers_?!" she asked, still yelling.

Um, I do have a name, I thought. Anthony seemed to understand.

"Okay, first of all, he's a boy, not an it. Seco--"

"Don't you 'first of all' me young man!" Mom interrupted. "Take it outside, NOW! And don't you _dare_ let him back in!"

"But Mo--!" Anthony started.

"No buts!" Mom said. "Out!" she pointed to the back door. Anthony led me out with a mixture of rage, sadness, and anxiety.

The yard was just as big. There was a small garden, a pool, and grass with a shed in the corner. Strangely, there was a basketball hoop. Strewn across the grass were footballs, small flags, a random assortment of exercise equipment and a helmet or two.

Anthony knelt down to look at me. "Okay boy, this is how it's going to work; you stay here, and maybe even sleep here," he grumbled, "while I try to convince Mom to give you a second chance. Got it?"

I barked in approval, even though I had absolutely no idea what he was talking about.

Once Anthony went inside, I began to explore. The equipment was really… well, random. For example, a ladder was laid out across the floor. The basketball net confused me, since I was pretty sure Anthony played the game called football.

The shed, when I peeked in, was filled with even more "football-y" things, gardening tools, and, oddly, a trumpet.

At one point I came to a door that was a smidge open. I looked through the gap. *The office,* I thought. What was it Anthony had said about this place? Eh, whatever. I trotted inside.

The first things I saw were two desks facing each other. One looked freshly polished, almost gleaming, with a laptop on top. The other one looked like it had been abandoned for at least a year.

There was also a keyboard, as in a *musical* keyboard, which seemed strange, seeing as I was in an office.

Behind it was an armchair that I jumped on top of. Next to the bathroom was a storage closet. I wandered inside and the door accidentally closed behind me.

I smelled Mom come in, she reeked of anger.

The chair at the desk was pulled out and then back in. I scratched at the door.

"What the heck?" she said. I yipped. I could smell her getting angrier by the second. She opened the door.

"ANTHONY!!!" she hollered.

"What's wrong?" Anthony came in, already smelling worried.

"GET THIS THING OUT OF HERE, *NOW!*"

Anthony looked at me, disappointment written all over his face. He attached a leash and collar to my neck and led me outside for a walk.

Why doesn't she call me him, or Oreo? I thought to myself. Or so I thought.

Anthony stopped walking. "Who said that?" he looked around. I did too.

You must be tired, I looked at him in concern.

"Stop messing with me," Anthony said to empty space. "I'm not tired."

My eyes widened. *You can hear me?*

"Yes. Now show yourself!"

I barked. *Down here!*

Anthony looked at me. His jaw dropped. "No way."

I chased my tail and barked again. *Cool! You can hear my thoughts!*

Anthony chuckled like he was crazy. "Maybe I am tired."

Hmph, well, that's mean, I looked away.

"Oh!" Anthony exclaimed. "I-I'm sorry, bud. I really didn't mean that," he patted my head.

We walked over to a big dog park. I sniffed the air. Then I saw a beautiful husky.

Anthony started smelling nervous. His palms were sweaty. I whimpered, worried. Anthony took a deep breath and we walked over to the husky and her owner. She had blonde hair highlighted blue at the tips and blue eyes.

"Hi," Anthony said, much too awkwardly.

"Um, hi," the girl said.

I was too focused on the husky to pay attention to the rest. *She is beautiful,* I thought. The husky jumped into the pond. But I couldn't swim. She barked, which embarrassed me.

I bravely forced myself to get closer and closer to the edge. I was planning to lie down there, but before I could, I slipped and fell into the pond. I barked and yipped, trying to get back up, but I couldn't. I felt somebody grab my collar and pull me to shore.

I shook myself and hid behind Anthony. The husky had saved me.

"You okay, boy?" Anthony crouched next to me and checked for any obvious injuries.

"There's a vet across the street," the girl suggested.

"Thanks," Anthony looked at the husky. "Both of you."

Chapter 4

. . . .

I Hate Cones

Anthony and I walked across the street with the girls. This was obviously what the girl had called the "vet."

We went in. I sniffed the air and was immediately terrified. It smelled like a doctor, sickness, and… depression.

Uh, maybe we could just go back to the park? I thought.

"Relax, it'll only be a check-up," Anthony said out loud before realizing his mistake.

"What?" the girl turned to look at him.

"Um, nothing," Anthony said, trying to change the subject. "It's just, I, uh, never asked what your name was."

"Kate," Kate said. "And yours?"

"Anthony."

We sat down.

"What's his name?" Kate pointed at me.

Oreo, I answered.

"Oreo," Anthony said at the same time. "What about yours?"

"Clover," Kate replied.

I looked at the husky. *Hi,* I said to her.

Hello, Clover thought back. *So, what's your story?*

Well… I started. But I wasn't able to finish. Instead, I started feeling this burning, stinging pain in my side. I yelped, trying to alert Anthony. Before he could even react, I passed out.

I woke up in a room with lots of scary-looking tools.

"Oreo, go back to sleep," Anthony said beside me.

Wait, why… I groaned and fell asleep again.

Thankfully, the next time I stirred myself awake the tools were gone and I was in Anthony's room. I had a terrible itch in my side, so, like any normal dog does, I sat down to scratch it.

What the heck? I thought. Instead of the usual feeling of relief, I heard a thump. It was a… CONE?! A CONE?! No. No, no, no, no, NO! Cone means sick dog! And a sick dog is NOWHERE near good!

I howled in sadness. Anthony shushed me from his bed.

"ANTHONY!!!" hollered Mom.

"Um, OWWW!" Anthony yelled.

"What did you hurt now?" Mom asked, barging in. By then, Anthony had shoved me into his closet.

"I… stubbed my toe!" Anthony pretended.

"Stop overreacting, you'll be fine!" Mom said.

"You are absolutely right, goodbye!" Anthony blurted, rushing her out and closing the door behind her. He opened the closet door.

"Okay Oreo, here's the deal," Anthony told me, "you cannot, I repeat, *can-not* make *any* noise while you're inside the house," he ordered. "Also, you can't scratch yourself. The doctor said preferably not to run," Anthony explained.

But I love running! I protested.

"Doctor's orders," Anthony said sternly. "Another thing, what do you want for your birthday?"

Time for my first ever BIRTHDAY PARTY!

After Anthony had explained what a birthday was, I told him I didn't really know what I wanted.

"What about a toy?" Anthony had suggested.

That'll work! I answered excitedly.

So, we snuck out and walked to the pet store a few blocks away.

Once inside, I took in all of the smells and was immediately in love. I barked in excitement.

"Okay! Okay!" Anthony exclaimed, holding on tight to my leash. "Let's at least get to the toy section first."

As we walked to the toy section, I got even happier.

Food, cat food, toys, more food, I mumbled.

"Okay, pick your favorite," Anthony stopped at the entrance to an aisle.

How do I pick? I said as I searched for the perfect match.

"If Mom was okay with you, I would buy you the whole aisle, but she's not," Anthony replied sadly.

This one! I pawed at the toy I had chosen.

"The football? Are you sure?" Anthony asked.

Don't know what that is, but yeah, I'm sure! I said.

Anthony picked it up and when he squeezed it, something strange happened.

Squeeee! The football went.

What was that?! I yelped in fright, looking around.

Anthony burst out laughing. "It squeaks, silly!"

Right, definitely knew that, I said, pretending to calm down.

"Uh-huh, sure," Anthony said sarcastically.

"Aww, aren't you a cutie!" the cashier said, kneeling down. "Happy birthday," she added, giving me a treat.

Best day ever, I mumbled, chewing as we walked back home.

Chapter 5

Reunited! You're Welcome

Kate and Clover came around to pick me up and she and Anthony talked before we walked to her house. I felt weak, embarrassed, and uncomfortable with the cone.

Anthony had a football game, so I had to stay with them.

On the way to Kate's house, we passed a tall boy with dirty blond hair and greenish-blue eyes. He had a Pitbull with him, another lady.

Kate walked by without a word. I tried to sniff the Pitbull's butt, but Kate was quick to pull me away. The boy was obviously looking back at us.

What was that about? I thought. Too bad Kate couldn't hear me.

We arrived at Kate's house, which was average sized, and a woman greeted us at the door.

"Hi! What a cute dog!" she said.

Thanks, I thought. I licked her legs to show my gratitude.

They let Clover roam free, and she darted upstairs. When she came back down, she had a rope with rubber ends in her mouth. Ooh, I know this game! Um… give me a second… yeah! Tug-Of-War!

Clover growled.

Challenge accepted, I thought.

We played Tug-Of-War for a while. Surprisingly, I won a lot. Then we realized that we were getting bored, so she ran upstairs and came back with a sock. It was probably Kate's, who knows?

Clover and I tore it up in a flash. Kate (to my surprise) just laughed.

Afterwards, we had dinner and went outside to do our business. And, let me tell you, their food was *delicious*! While we were eating, I found out that the woman was Kate's mom.

This is fun! I thought when we went outside.

Kate's mom, bless her heart, took my cone off.

Yay! I thought. Strangely, Clover looked worried.

Then, I started itching a lot. I scratched and scratched, but that only made it hurt.

I went back inside and rolled around on the carpet, but I couldn't get rid of the itch. I howled.

Kate came down from upstairs. "MOM!" she yelled.

"Yes?" Kate's mom asked innocently.

"W-why is Oreo's cone off?!" Kate stuttered.

"Oh! It looked like it was bothering him, so I took it off," her mom said, confused.

Kate grabbed my cone and quickly put it back on.

I shook myself and scowled at Kate's mom. *That would've never happened with Anthony,* I thought.

In the morning, we ate breakfast. Once again, it was amazing. I gulped it down in record time.

Once we were done, Kate let us out for a bathroom break.

We saw the Pitbull and boy again, but Kate pulled me back as I tried to say hi.

Oh, come on! I yanked on the leash, and Kate let go.

I ran over to them and introduced myself: sniffing some Pitbull butt and licking even more human face.

"Ugh, Oreo!" Kate exclaimed, clearly annoyed. She dragged me back inside.

"Wait, Ka-" I heard the boy begin. Kate shut the door. A persistent character, the boy knocked. I glanced at Kate, but she ignored him.

You'll thank me later, I thought as I ran through the doggy door.

"Oreo!" Kate said from inside the house. "Come back!" she opened the door and once again, dragged me back inside

"Kate!" the boy said.

"What?!" Kate turned around angrily.

"I-I just wanted to say… sorry," he said.

"Hm, sorry for what?" Even though the boy had apologized, Kate still sounded angry.

The boy took a deep breath before saying, "I'm sorry for saying that your mom is out of whack."

Oof, I even winced at the insult.

Kate crossed her arms, eyebrows raised.

"And for being offensive… *very* offensive," the boy corrected himself, "to Clover."

Clover growled.

The Pitbull looked confused. The boy had obviously never told her about this.

"You're not forgiven," Kate started to close the door.

"Wait!" The boy held the door open. "Please forgive me, I really do feel bad."

Yeah! What's wrong with you? How stubborn can you possibly be? I barked at Kate.

She rolled her eyes, "Fine." Then she let him come in.

"Um, so, who's the Bernese?" he asked.

"Anthony's dog, Oreo," Kate replied.

"Oh, he's cute," the boy said.

Thank you.

"How's Lucky?" Kate asked sarcastically.

"Good. But who's Anthony?"

"One of my home-schooled neighbors," Kate said.

Lucky finally got a chance to say hello.

Hi, she said.

Hello, I returned.

"Oh… cool," the boy said. "Do you really forgive me?" he asked.

"Yes Jackson, I forgive you," Kate said, this time with a grin on her face.

Jackson, huh? Cool name dude.

So, how did you and Anthony meet? Lucky asked.

Actually, he found me in a pound, I said sadly. *In fact, he rescued me from it.*

I'm a rescue too, Lucky said.

Oh… I wasn't sure what to say. *I'm sorry.*

It's fine, Lucky reassured me. *Anyway, my life is practically perfect now.*

I licked Jackson's face, because I felt like it. He started laughing.

"I like him," he said, still laughing.

"Yeah, he's friendly," Kate said.

"So, you wanna meet at the dog park later?" Jackson asked.

Kate smiled. "Sure."

Clover probably wasn't happy about this, but that didn't concern me. I'd made some new friends!

When the time finally came, after eating lunch, we went to the dog park.

I was extremely excited. I loved the park, and we were going to play with Lucky and Jackson!

They were waiting outside of the wrought-iron gates that led into the park. We walked around for a while, and once we did our business, they let us off our leashes.

"So, why does Oreo have a cone?" Jackson asked.

"Oreo! No running," Kate told me. "He was bitten by a snake at the pond, and he can't scratch or lick the wound."

"Oh. Poor Oreo," Jackson said sympathetically.

"Yeah, I guess."

I ran... no, jogged, over to Lucky, who had brought her monkey toy. Its arms and legs were limp, which meant they stretched out easily. I tugged an arm. Lucky held on to the other. I growled. She growled back.

TUG OF WAR!!! I declared.

Clover hesitated, but eventually joined in, grabbing a leg.

Jackson and Kate sat down on a bench. They laughed at our extremely vigorous game.

I tugged extra hard and won. The girls fell onto the grass.

"Wow! Oreo's strong!" Jackson exclaimed.

"Yeah, well, Bernese Mountains are known for their strength… and friendliness," Kate added. She was obviously trying to protect Clover's reputation because Clover looked annoyed, and she scowled at me.

Okay, I'm stronger than you. Get over it, I told her.

The only reason you won is because I… came in late, Clover said, desperately reaching for an excuse.

Sure, I smiled, proud of myself.

We went back to Kate's house and said goodbye to Jackson and Lucky.

I had a great time, but after we ate dinner and went to bed, I felt something that I had felt a million times before. I missed Anthony.

I sighed. *When can I go back home?*

Chapter 6

· · · · · · · · · · · · · · · · · · · ·

Football

A few days later, I was finally able to go back home to Anthony. Kate had dropped Clover off somewhere after our playdate. I hadn't seen her since then. But I definitely didn't mind. Why? After the Tug of War thing, she had been ignoring me and throwing dirty looks in my direction. I didn't think she would hold a grudge, but apparently, she was just as stubborn as her owner.

Speaking of Kate, Anthony and I were eating breakfast once Mom had left when she rang the doorbell.

"Coming!" Anthony called.

"Hey," Kate said. "Jackson asked if you wanted to walk the dogs, and maybe pay Clover a visit?"

Um, actually, I'm good, I thought, backing away.

What's wrong with you? Anthony thought. "Sure," he answered.

"Okay, then, let's go."

Anthony clipped on my leash. *I don't know what's up but behave yourself.*

He was lucky I loved him.

Jackson and Lucky were waiting for us in our huge yard.

"Hey," Jackson said.

"Hey."

How are you? I asked Lucky as we walked to the park to play.

Pretty good, Lucky paused. *Is Clover still mad at you?*

Last I knew, yes, I said.

I don't understand. Can't she just accept that she can't always be the strongest or whatever? Lucky had read my mind.

I know, right? I said skeptically.

"So, how's Clover?" Jackson asked.

Yeah, is she still stubborn? I added. Lucky giggled. Anthony glared at me, sternly. *Just saying,* I muttered.

Kate tossed my frisbee. "Great, she seems to be enjoying it."

"Good," Anthony said.

We left after playing with the frisbee. Lucky and I spotted a squirrel on the street.

It took everything I had, but I knew not to go. Lucky, however yanked on the leash, and in case you didn't know, Pitbulls are strong too.

"LUCKY!" the humans screamed.

I immediately saw why they were so worried. A truck was heading straight for both the squirrel and Lucky. Of course, the squirrel just scurried away.

Before I even knew it, I was running towards her and had pushed her out of the way, onto the sidewalk.

But Lucky's name definitely doesn't apply to me! The truck hit me and the pain flooded in from all sides, smothering me. I couldn't stay awake.

I woke up still under the truck. I could hear Anthony frantically calling my name.

I groaned. I definitely couldn't move, for various reasons. I also smelled a familiar and strangely calming scent. *Clover,* she didn't smell angry but worried. I could hear her barking, Lucky, too.

I tried my best to crawl at least, but it was useless.

I yelped and squirmed.

The truck finally backed up.

"Oreo!" Anthony was as close as he could get. Police were gathered around the truck and I could hear police sirens wailing all around me.

Thankfully, Lucky was back with Jackson. Jackson was trying to keep Lucky from running over to me. Clover was with the police for some reason, and Kate was with her. As I lost consciousness, I saw Lucky slip from Jackson's grasp and sprint toward me.

I woke up in an animal hospital with Anthony and a vet.

"Oreo," Anthony said, relieved. He petted me gently.

I whimpered. He got the message and leaned in to hug me.

"He's going to need surgery on his leg," the vet said.

"Do I have to pay?" Anthony sounded worried.

"Your parents do. Where are they?" the vet asked.

Mom chose that moment to storm in.

"Who do you think you are, hiding that-that *thing* from me?!" she said.

"But Mo-!"

"No buts!" Mom interrupted. "Give him the surgery."

One of the policemen came in, and Clover was with him.

"Excuse me, ma'am?" he asked.

"Yes?" Mom calmly turned towards him.

"That dog is yours, he's hurt. You are obliged to keep him until further notice, and he *must* be kept inside," he said.

Mom gasped and her face grew even more angry. "Fine."

"Okay, now, if you don't mind, Oreo urgently needs surgery," the vet obviously wanted everyone out.

My leg hurt, but not just hurt, it like, HURT.

I whimpered. *Please don't go,* I pleaded to Anthony.

I'm sorry, boy, Anthony furrowed his eyebrows with concern. *I have to. But I promise, you'll be fine, and I will find a way to convince Mom to let you stay.*

The vet ushered everybody out of the room.

"Okay boy, just relax, you won't even remember this," the vet said in a soothing voice.

I tried my best to follow his instructions, and soon enough, I was asleep.

When I woke up, I was still in the room, but I couldn't feel my leg. I glanced at it.

What. Is. THAT, I stared at the… thing.

Clover appeared in the doorway. I whimpered. We silently made up.

Anthony took me home. But he didn't play with me. Not that I cared, because I usually just slept, wondering about the metal thing attached to my body. Sometimes, we would walk around the house together. I would trip, but Anthony helped me back up.

When we passed by Mom, she would glare at us until we had disappeared around a corner.

I soon got used to walking, just walking, on my new leg. A week had passed, and I hadn't been outside. I did my business on doggy pads that Anthony set down for me.

On my eighth day of being stuck inside, Lucky and Jackson came knocking at our door.

I was lying on the couch, when Anthony ran to get the door.

"Oreo! It's for you!" he called.

I walked slowly to the door. I felt so happy to see friendly faces again that I barked.

Oreo, Lucky said, pawing to show affection. *Thank you.*

Jackson crouched. "That was a really nice thing you did for Lucky," he said. "Thank you." He scratched me behind the ears.

Anything for… friends, I glanced at Lucky.

The next day, while Anthony and I were walking around, the doorbell rang. Mom answered it. The door opened to reveal Clover and the policeman from the hospital.

"Have you been taking care of this dog?" he gestured to me.

"Ugh, yes," Mom replied.

"This is legal notification," the policeman had papers in his hand. "You have to fill these out and return them to the police station," he paused. "It's to show you've actually been taking care of this dog. If you haven't, we'll have to take him in," he finished. He handed Mom the papers.

Woah, woah, woah, hold up, I said, backing into the house. *'Take me in' where?*

Anthony instinctively grabbed my collar. They left, and he started begging Mom to fill them out.

"Please! He won't bother you ever again," Anthony pleaded.

"Well, you might as well call the man so he can take him in," Mom replied.

I whimpered and walked as fast as I could to Anthony's room.

"Okay, just… let me say goodbye," Anthony said from the depths of the house.

Wait, what? I looked around for a place to hide. *The closet,* I nosed it open and crawled inside. I was NOT going back to the pound.

THE ADVENTURES OF OREO

"Okay… but make it quick!" I heard Mom say.

Anthony entered the room. "Oreo?" he said, confused.

"Oh." *Don't worry, boy. I won't give up and I won't let you go back to the pound,* he reassured me. *I have a plan… I think.*

Promise? I asked.

Promise.

I pushed my way out of the closet.

Anthony took me outside. "Come on, boy, run," he urged. "This is what we've been practicing for."

I found that I could run. We ran until we reached a big field of grass with white on it.

A man was there, with a bunch of boys about Anthony's age.

"Anthony! Finally, you're here!" the man said.

"Hey, coach," Anthony said. "Can Oreo watch us practice"

"Uh, sure, "Coach said. "But if he runs away, it's on you."

"Of course," Anthony reassured him. *Please don't run away,* he told me.

I'm surprised you're even asking that, I said, lying down.

"Okay, just stay right there, boy," Anthony said, for Coach's sake.

I jumped up. *AGH! My leg!*

Stretch it out underneath you! Anthony advised.

I followed his advice, and it worked.

"Okay, boys," Coach was saying, "we need to get ready for tomorrow. Time for a scrimmage."

All of the boys, including Anthony, put on a belt small, thin flags attached to it, like the ones at home.

Coach chose two boys, Anthony and one with curly brown hair and glasses.

Each of them took turns choosing the rest of their team until there was nobody left.

After that, they scattered around the field.

A boy had a ball in his hand and was looking between his legs at Anthony. Suddenly, he threw it to Anthony.

Everybody went to a different place. Anthony saw a boy standing apart from the others and threw him the ball. The boy caught it and ran all the way to the end of the field. Anthony's team cheered.

Coach blew his whistle.

After a few minutes, I kind of understood. If somebody did that, they went back to the other end and tried to do it again. If they get to the end, they'd get... three more tries, I think. Once, Anthony did it, and he seemed really happy, so I barked. He turned and grinned at me. I wagged my tail, and he grinned even more.

Anthony's thrower teammate threw the ball way off on their next turn, and it was close to me. I decided that I wanted to join in. I caught the ball in mid-air and ran all the way to the far end of the field. When I got there, I dropped the ball, just like Anthony had.

Speaking of Anthony, he had been chasing after me and calling my name. The team was staring at me.

What? I scored! I said, confused.

"How did you...?" Anthony was staring at me too.

"Have you practiced with him?" Coach asked, running over.

"Never," Anthony said.

Coach thought for a long moment. "Matt! Take a break!" he said.

One of the boys who had scored for Anthony's team sat down on the bench.

Coach crouched down. "Oreo, is it?" I wagged my tail. "Come here." He stood up and walked to Matt's position, and I followed him. Coach pulled a belt-flag out of a bag and wrapped it around my waist.

Ooh, I get to play! Excellent! I exclaimed.

I went along with the game. The other team had the ball, and when they threw it, one of their team members caught it.

Oh, no, buddy boy, you are not getting past me, I sprinted to him and managed to pull his flag off.

Coach blew his whistle. The team cheered and petted me to congratulate me. The other team did, too.

I liked it. In fact, I loved it.

'It' is called football, Anthony told me.

Okay, then I love football, I said.

"Son," somebody called. It was a man who looked remarkably like Anthony. He walked over to us.

"Um, good work, boys," Coach said. "Take five," he winked at Anthony.

No way, I stared at the man as he knelt down to pet me. *You're Anthony's Dad!*

Anthony talked about this man, a lot. Apparently, he and Mom had fought, and it… didn't end well. He smelled like instruments, probably because Anthony had said he was a musician.

"Dad," Anthony gasped.

"Um, I saw you on the news." Dad stood up and smiled at me. "You picked the perfect dog."

Why, thank you, I said.

"Oreo, right?" Dad said. I wagged my tail.

"Yeah," Anthony replied.

"It was nice of your mom to let you have him." Dad's voice cracked at the end.

"About that," Anthony said. "I kinda, maybe… ran away."

Dad chuckled. "No surprise there."

"It's just, he's turned into the little brother I never had," Anthony looked down at me.

Aww, I feel the same about you, I replied.

"Well, good luck winning her over," Dad said.

"Yeah, I'll need it," Anthony frowned.

"I wish I could help, but, well, yeah," Dad frowned too.

"It's OK," Anthony was obviously lying.

"Come here," Dad opened his arms, and they hugged.

The car Dad had come in honked its horn.

"I should go," Dad gestured at it. "'Bye, son."

"'Bye," Anthony said as Dad walked back to the car.

"Okay, boys, let's wrap it up!" Coach called once the car had rounded a corner.

We played for a while, then "huddled," and everybody left.

I wasn't surprised when we walked to the park instead of home. While we played, I wondered if Mom would ever forgive me.

Chapter 7

· ·

More Police

We were still playing when I heard a familiar voice say, "Grab," and next thing I know, Clover is grabbing my collar. I didn't struggle.

Brad, the policeman, ran over. "Your mother needs to sign those papers by noon," he said. Clover dragged me over to him. "Drop," she let go. "She also wanted me to take you home."

Um, sorry, but that can't happen, I glanced at Anthony, and we exchanged a worried look.

Clover and Brad got in the car.

"But, she won't..." Anthony began.

"Get in the car," Brad ordered.

We reluctantly obeyed. But we were worried.

"What's going to happen to Oreo?" Anthony clutched my collar.

"He'll live at the police station with us," Brad answered.

Well, at least it's not the pound, I said, trying to be positive.

"Will I be able to see him?" Anthony asked.

"Absolutely," Brad said. Anthony and I breathed a mental sigh of relief.

Brad pulled up in our driveway. We all got out of the car. Anthony took a deep breath before knocking. Mom appeared.

"Mom, please, *please*, sign the papers," he said.

"Nope," Mom had no hesitation.

Please, Mom! I begged, even though I knew she couldn't hear me.

"Take it," Mom said. "Take the dog."

"Yes, ma'am," Brad took my leash from Anthony.

"Mom, NO!" Anthony screamed.

"Say your goodbyes now," Mom said.

Anthony looked at me sadly. *I promise I'll get you back.*

NO! Please, keep me! I can't go to a police station; I have to go with you! I pleaded and whined. I tried to get into the house, but it was useless.

Anthony hugged me. *You will be with me, I promise,* silent tears rolled down his cheeks.

I sniffled. *Don't take long.*

I won't, Anthony got back up and ran into the house.

I barked at Mom. *I'll be back.*

"Oh, be quiet!" Mom said.

I barked again. *I don't take orders from cruel people.*

"Take it already!" Mom shut the door.

"Yes, ma'am," Brad muttered.

We got in the car. I didn't struggle, but I whimpered at Brad.

I lay down. I didn't know what else to do.

I sighed. *You'd better keep your promise, Anthony, because I don't think I'll survive in a police station for long.*

We came to the police station.

Somebody, probably her trainer, came to collect Clover, and I went with them. Her trainer was a girl but I didn't know her name yet. We went outside to what was probably a training area.

I whimpered. *I'm already trained.*

The trainer told Clover to jump over a stand. She obeyed.

Um, yeah, I have a prosthetic leg… I thought.

"Stop, drop, roll, pick up!" the trainer commanded as she threw a collar into the air.

I sighed. *I can't jump, either.*

"Sniff and find!" the trainer ordered. Clover sniffed the collar. She nosed around and eventually found a toy.

Cool! I exclaimed.

"Alright, chew," the trainer said. Clover chewed the toy.

I barked. *Finally, something interesting!*

Clover dropped the toy at the trainer's feet. I ran over and grabbed it, thinking it was playtime.

"Bad dog!" the trainer screamed.

I dropped it, surprised. *Weren't we playing?* I tilted my head at her.

"Take a break," the trainer told Clover.

She… bowed and walked over to Brad. He said something, and they went inside.

Once they left, we began to train.

"Shake."

Huh?

"Shake, Oreo!"

What do you mean? I thought. *Oh, whatever.* I wandered off, but my trainer stopped me.

"Bad dog, Oreo!"

Okay, okay! Jeez, Luis!

"Shake," my trainer lifted my paw onto her open hand. "Good boy," she gave me a treat.

Oh, okay, I understood now.

"Shake," my trainer held her hand open again. I obeyed. "Good boy, Oreo!" she gave me a treat. "You're the fastest learner I've ever met! Do you know how to sit? Sit, Oreo."

Anthony had taught me this one. *Ouch!* I had forgotten about my leg. I yelped.

"Hmm, it looks like you're going to need some extra help," my trainer thought for a second, then she called, "Roy!"

A man jogged to us. "What's wrong, Anna?" Roy asked.

"This dog, Oreo, is going to need some help," Anna said. "Can you train him?"

"Sure," Roy replied.

"Thank you," Anna went back into the building.

"Okay, Oreo, sit," Roy said.

I didn't do it right away. Instead, I tried to find a way to obey him while not squishing my leg. Roy helped me by stretching it out to the side.

"Good dog," he gave me a treat.

Clover and Anna came back outside. "Free time!" Anna yelled. She freed Clover from her leash. Roy left, and Clover came over to me and wagged her tail.

She nudged me, *Aren't we going to play?*

Aw, yeah! I replied.

Clover took off, running wildly around the yard. She started playing Tug-Of-War with a big German Shepherd. I trotted over.

I barked at them, and they both froze. I tried to join in, but they let go of the rope.

I sighed as they walked away. *Yeah, it's not like I've been through a lot already,* I thought sadly. I looked around. There was an equally sad-looking German Shepherd lying in the grass. She looked… tired.

I skipped towards her. *Hello.*

She didn't look up, probably because she was staring at my prosthetic.

I nudged her gently. *Wanna play?* I bowed. Rump up, front paws down, tongue lolling, and tail wagging. I barked, but quietly. She stood up, looking happier by the second. I pounced on a rope and brought it over to her. She grabbed the other end of it. We played until a man ran outside.

"Line up!" he screamed.

I followed my new friend into the line formed by the dogs. Then a group of people rushed over, including Anna and Roy. Roy clipped a leash onto me. He led me to Brad, who was with Clover. He took us into a building filled with… ok, no thank you. Brad opened one of the evil kennel's doors.

I whimpered. *Nope, not happening.*

"Don't worry, Oreo. Clover will be here too," Brad said. And in spite of my reluctance he got us both into a kennel, right next to each other, and closed the doors. Then he left.

I paced around in the kennel, occasionally clawing at the cage. Clover fell asleep quickly, but I couldn't. I tried, though. I lay down, thinking happy thoughts, but all that did was make me sadder and more worried. My body helped by forcing me to close my eyes and drift off into nightmares.

The next day, Brad took Clover and me out of our kennels (thank goodness) and into the yard. He let Clover roam free, but not me. Instead, he handed me over to Roy, who took me over to a line of people.

"Choose your owner," Roy urged.

No! I immediately exclaimed, tugging and growling.

"Oreo, stop," Roy said. But he said it sincerely.

Don't try to soften me up, a growl formed in my throat, but before I could release it, my friend padded over.

It's okay, she said. *I know how you feel, but this is necessary. And if you don't make a choice, they'll choose for you.*

I glared at the people, then sighed in defeat. *Fine.* I tugged gently at my leash, toward the people this time. Roy clipped off my leash, and I started examining my options.

There was a girl with curly, black hair, but she didn't seem right. A boy with a man bun, which was way too embarrassing, a girl who smelled of honey, and a man who smelled exactly what I think NASTY smells like. As I passed each one, they stood to the side. I stopped at a young lady. She had long, dark brown slightly curly hair, a wonderful smile, and beautiful hazel eyes.

I put my muzzle on her knee and stared at her in wonder. She giggled. *This one,* I thought.

"Fabi! Good to see you here!" Roy called.

"Hey, Roy. He's *so* cute," Fabi scratched behind my ear, and I unconsciously stuck my tongue out.

"Yeah? Well, his name is-"

"Oreo, yeah, I know," Fabi stared sadly at my leg. "You're his trainer, I presume?" she asked Roy.

He nodded. "Yep."

I licked Fabi's chin and barked at her, feeling both happy and sad. She smiled, but there was a hint of sadness in her expression

THE ADVENTURES OF OREO

too. "I hope you don't mind small dogs, 'cause you'll be living with Cookie and me."

Wait, living *with you?!* I backed away from her and howled.

Fabi put a finger to my mouth. "Shh, it's okay. I know you miss Anthony."

Hold up, how do you know who Anthony is? I shook off her finger.

"He's my cousin," Fabi said as if she'd read my mind.

Oh, cool… an idea formed in my head.

"I have a feeling we're thinking the same thing," Fabi grinned at me. "Wanna go for a walk?"

I barked. *Heck, yeah!*

So, we walked. I strained against the leash a lot, urging Fabi to go faster.

Then, we were finally there. It was so wonderful to see him.

I looked at Fabi for permission to tackle him.

"Go ahead," she dropped my leash, "say hi."

I leaped onto Anthony, who hadn't noticed me. He looked, smelled, and tasted exactly the same. Even though we hadn't been apart that long, I had been afraid that I would never see him again.

Anthony laughed. "Okay, if you could let me stand up now, that would be great."

I crawled off him.

"Who brought you here…?" his voice trailed off as Fabi walked up to us.

"Before you say anything," Fabi said as Anthony's mouth opened to talk, "yes, it's me."

Anthony embraced her in a very loving hug. They stayed in that position for about twenty seconds before Anthony stepped away.

"H-how are you?"

"Doing police work somewhere a little more peaceful," Fabi interrupted. "I got tired of New York City."

"Understandable," Anthony agreed. "Are you his owner now?"

"Yep."

Anthony smiled the widest smile I had seen in weeks.

"I can also take him to some of your games if you want," said Fabi.

"That would be great."

Back at my new home, I met Cookie, a Shih Tzu-Bichon Frise mix also known as Teddy Bears, or Zuchons. She hobbled over, her tail wagging, as we came in. I knew to respect my elders, so I politely asked for permission before sniffing her butt.

"Cook, this is Oreo," Fabi explained.

Cookie barked at me. I barked back.

"It's your yearly check-up, sis," Fabi picked up Cookie, and Cookie licked her chin. "Oreo, be a good boy, okay?" she told me as she clipped on Cookie's leash.

I rubbed my face against her leg. *I promise, for once, not to make any trouble.*

Fabi closed the garage door behind her.

I decided to spend my time usefully and unpacked my stuff. I figured my bed would go next to Cookie's, and my toys in a doggy toy chest. Fabi's house was pretty nice, especially her couch. I flung my football toy around on it. I raised my head as a whirring sound came from the kitchen. I sprinted to it, and the weirdest thing was happening.

What the heck are you? I sniffed as a strange robot put food in two bowls, on separate mats. One said Cookie, the other Oreo. The food looked delicious. White twigs (which I would soon learn was rice), Black ovals (beans), and vegetables all mixed together. There was also raw meat.

Once the robot disappeared into a box that automatically closed its door behind it, I set about getting the delicious mixture into my belly.

The girls came back about an hour later. Cookie ate her food, and we all went to sleep.

Now, I already loved Fabi and Cookie, but I still wondered whether Anthony would be able to keep his promise to take me back to live with him. We could do so much together…

Is it possible? I asked myself. *Anthony would have to persuade the police station, Fabi, and hardest of all, Mom.*

I fell asleep feeling very sad… Oh, Anthony, why did you make that promise?

Chapter 8

· · · · · · · · · · · · · · · · · · · ·

You Can Play a Sad Song Now...

In the morning, we ate breakfast. I was surprised to see Fabi pack up all of our things. Once we had finished eating, we drove to the police station. When we pulled up, I saw Clover with a young lady.

Fabi opened the door and helped Cookie out. I just jumped out. We ran up to Clover.

Hi! I said in a friendly greeting.

Hello, Clover told me. And then to Cookie, *Ma'am.*

"Wanna follow me, or should I give you the address?" asked the young lady.

"I'll follow you."

We got back into our car after a quick bathroom break and started following Clover's car. A few minutes later, we pulled up a driveway. Fabi opened the door.

"Are they trained?" the young lady asked.

"Yes, Maddie, they're trained," Fabi snapped.

"How old are they?" said Maddie.

"Oreo's one, and Cookie's ten," Fabi replied.

Clover wagged her tail for some reason.

"Let's go inside," Maddie suggested.

So, we did. Both Cookie and I were startled by the creatures we found hiding inside.

Cats?! I thought skeptically.

Clover disappeared into a room. A few seconds later, she came back out. We all went to the kitchen, but, thankfully, without the cats.

"Do you want to see the horses?" asked Maddie.

Fabi hesitated but eventually agreed.

Outside, I saw an enormous, hairy dog, no, *two* of them. I soon realized that these were the "horses" that Maddie had mentioned. One was grey and the other white with brown spots.

Clover ran over to the grey one's stall. And funnily enough, Cookie went to the one that looked like her. I stayed behind. These animals were new and scary.

"You wanna go for a ride?" Maddie asked. "I'll take Smokey, you can take Rascal."

Rascal? I said. *Yeah, sorry, but that name doesn't appeal to me, horse girl.*

"Um, I guess so," Fabi answered.

Wait, what?!

"Wait, are we bringing the dogs?"

Bless this amazing woman.

"Of course! Why wouldn't we?" said Maddie.

Again, the horse's name is Rascal.

"Because they could get hurt?" Fabi replied.

Get logical, horse girl.

"Nonsense! Let's go!" exclaimed Maddie.

I groaned. *Horse lovers,* I grumbled.

Maddie mounted Smokey. She took Cookie with her.

I guess that makes sense since the horse's name is Rascal, I said grumpily.

"Come on. Wait, you know how to ride, right?" asked Maddie.

"Of course!" Fabi mounted Rascal and clipped my leash onto his reins as Maddie had done with Clover.

Couldn't you have said no? I thought at Fabi.

"Yah!" Maddie, Clover, and Cookie ran off.

Fabi followed, but we went slower. Even so, I had trouble keeping my leg on track.

"Okay, Oreo, take it easy," Fabi said.

Once I finally got the hang of it, we caught up to the others, they were at the top of a mountain.

I was catching my breath when my bad luck caught up to us too. Cookie had just pooped, and she was cleaning her paws while Fabi picked it up. I think everybody knows how we do this, but in case you don't, we kick the ground. It's a pretty simple process, but we were on a mountain, and the rocks weren't exactly very sturdy. So, Cookie slipped. Thankfully, Clover was close by and grabbed Cookie's collar. I knew she couldn't hang on for long, so I helped by grabbing hers. We still weren't strong enough, and we all fell into a cave-like indent in the mountain. And yes, it was a long way down.

My bad luck is like dominoes. My leg couldn't stand the fall. I howled.

The girls were peering down at us.

"Oh, *no, Oreo!*" Fabi screamed.

Maddie threw a rope down, but as much as I struggled to stay awake, I passed out.

I woke up in the animal hospital… again. A vet was checking me over. I made the mistake of looking at my leg; it was a horror show. I howled.

The vet came over to me. "Oh, boy, relax, okay? Your owner's going to decide what to do."

The door opened. Fabi and Anthony ran to my bedside (well, tableside, but same difference).

"Oh, Oreo, I'm so, so sorry," said Fabi.

It's okay. I blame horse girl, I told her.

Anthony snorted.

"What?" Fabi asked.

"Um, I just think he blames… Maddie," Anthony realized.

"It *is* partly her fault…"

You'll be okay. We've been through worse, Anthony said to me, and he was right.

I nuzzled him. *I trust you.*

The vet and Fabi talked seriously.

On second thought, I turned back to Anthony, worried this time, *are you sure?*

"Of course," Anthony whispered. *I hope,* he thought.

Did you forget I can read your mind? I shook Anthony out of his thoughts.

Anthony's eyes widened. *No! I was just… kidding?*

I raised my eyebrows.

Okay, yes, confessed Anthony. *I just… I made you a promise…* he looked away.

Hey, I licked his cheek, *it's fine. So long as I can visit you.*

Anthony smiled.

I started getting dizzy. Fabi was on the phone. She sounded worried. Something about Cookie, and how somebody was panting a lot… and… how something was bad… but I was too dizzy to make any sense of it. I fainted.

When I woke up, the vet was picking out a prosthetic leg from a box. She saw that I was awake and said, "I need you to relax, okay? I would say that this isn't going to hurt, but I'm not going to lie to you."

I squeezed my eyes and looked away. I yelped as she did something to me.

"Okay, plan B," she grabbed a little bottle and squeezed some of its contents into my mouth. I immediately felt… funny.

I giggled as silly thoughts flooded into my head. Wow, this vet was good! I didn't even notice my leg was back on until a few minutes later.

Soon enough, a young lady Fabi's age came to pick me up. She had brown eyes, straight, dark brown hair with streaks of navy blue at the tips. She also had a bag containing something delicious smelling.

"Hey, I'm here to pick up Oreo?" she sounded bored.

"Right here. Jaylee, right?" the vet asked.

"Uh-huh. Does he like, need anything, or whatever?" said Jaylee.

"No," the vet answered.

Jaylee clipped a leash on me, and we went out of the hospital to a car that smelled a lot like the bag. Inside was a small screen playing anime. She watched it for about five minutes before starting to drive.

We pulled up at the house. It had a sad aura about it.

Oh, no, I thought as we hopped out.

We went inside. Fabi was… crying on the couch? Clover was on the couch with her.

An orange cat meowed at Clover as Jaylee and I sat down.

It took me a few moments to realize that, besides Maddie, Cookie was the only one missing. I bolted to where Cookie's bed was, and then absolutely *everywhere*.

No. No, no, NO! I howled in despair.

Clover was peeking out the window. There was a rustle of keys at the door, and Maddie and Kate came in. They had dyed their hair; Maddie pink and Kate blue. To my surprise, Clover greeted them instead of showing Cookie due respect and mourning her death.

I, being the respectful dog I am, continued to mourn her and licked Fabi's tears.

Maddie and Clover rudely went outside.

Can we go home? As in, home *home?* I looked at Fabi expectantly.

"Oh, Oreo," she sniffled. "How 'bout this… you want to go see Anthony?"

I whimpered. *Yes.*

Fabi packed up our stuff *again*. I helped out by bringing her my toys. She told me to put them in a basket, so I did. She got my food and bowls, and I got my bed. Soon, Fabi had two suitcases ready. One was smaller with my stuff in it (Well, besides my squeaky football. I wanted it for the road). The larger one belonged to Fabi.

Maddie came into the living room and we said goodbye.

Finally, we left the house and got into the car. As we drove away, Kate and Maddie waved at us.

"Okay, Oreo," said Fabi. "I'm going to need you to cooperate because," her voice broke. "Well, you know why."

Absolutely.

We pulled up Anthony's driveway. He was waiting for us in the front yard.

I sprinted toward him as soon as Fabi opened the door.

"Hey, Oreo," Anthony sounded sad too. I dropped my football at his feet. I loved it when he threw it. Because when he did, it went *far*.

He did throw it, which was a great distraction for me.

After we played fetch for a while, we went inside. Mom wasn't there. Anthony consoled Fabi for a while, then we left.

Years passed during which nothing much of interest happened. Except for the spa days. I was now four years old, and Anthony fifteen. According to Fabi, I was very close to becoming an "official police dog." She also said that it had only taken this long because of my leg… and my breed.

One pleasant Friday afternoon, after morning training, we went to Anthony's football practice—it was becoming mine too. He was in high school now, but still being home-schooled. He had another nice coach.

"Here we are," Fabi parked in front of the field.

"Oreo!" Anthony exclaimed.

"Nice to see you, Fabi!" Coach called.

"You, too!" Fabi called back.

I ran to the flag bag after licking Anthony's face.

Coach chuckled. "Same old, same old." He put one around my hips.

The team practiced tackle, but as a dog with a prosthetic leg, I needed a flag.

"You can fill in for Johan," Coach told me.

Johan was a wide receiver, so I was pretty happy about this. I trotted over to my place. The boys got ready around me. Anthony was on the other team, which was fine with me. It was his ball.

"Hike!" he said.

"Oreo, defense D!" Coach ordered.

On it! I ran a ways in front of Anthony and started chasing my tail. *Aw, dang it! Almost caught it!* I yelled at him. It didn't stop him, though. The ball flew toward Kaleb, their wide receiver. I frantically barked at Joseph to stop him. He heard me and made the tackle. Kaleb had gotten close, too close for my comfort.

On the second down, I intercepted the ball, giving us possession.

"Set! Hike!" Jason said.

I barked, signaling for him to pass it to me. In just a few seconds, the ball was in my mouth and I was running across the field. Against all odds, Michael tackled me. We had made good progress, though.

Second down. I called for the ball again, and it came soaring through the air. Kevin was there to stop me. I frantically looked for a way out of my situation.

Lord help me, I said. I continued running toward him, picking up speed. At the last second, I ducked/crawled when he jumped to tackle me, giving me a very good chance to score.

I ran as fast as I could. I could hear Anthony behind me, but I was too quick.

Coach blew his whistle. "Touchdown!"

"Yeah!" Joseph ran over. "Good boy, Oreo!"

"Yes, Oreo, good boy!" even Anthony congratulated me. Then his face turned sad. "If only you could play."

"If only," Fabi had walked over. "But you know the rules."

"I'm sure we could figure *something* out," Coach said for the millionth time.

"Coach, I think Fabi's told you this before," Kaleb crossed his arms.

Fabi scoffed. "Exactly. Anyways, Oreo, how in the world did you do that?!" she looked down at me. "It took Clover *years* to master that, and I haven't even shown it to you!"

I don't know, I confessed. *It just… happened.*

We left after a tied game. Anthony came with us, and we stopped at his house.

"Why can't he be part of the team?" Anthony asked in the front yard. "It's not like he'll ever be an official police dog."

"Um, yeah, he will," Fabi corrected.

"What about his leg?" Anthony asked angrily.

"Who told you he couldn't become one because of his leg?" Fabi said, avoiding the question.

"Brad," Anthony crossed his arms.

"Is Brad his owner?" Fabi had turned the tables. Anthony was about to say something but decided against it. "That's what I thought. We should leave," Fabi said.

We walked out to the car. Anthony followed us. I wasn't sure I wanted to go, though. I stopped.

"Oreo, heel," Fabi tugged gently at my leash. But I sat and stayed.

"No offense, but I don't think he wants to be a police dog!" Anthony called.

"Of course he does!" Fabi protested. "I've told him all about it!"

I whimpered. *But you never asked me if I wanted to.*

"Also, his leg! Neither of us wants him getting hurt *again*!" Anthony argued.

"He'll, um, do the easy stuff," said Fabi. But she didn't sound very sure of herself.

"Please Fabi, don't make him do something he doesn't want to do," Anthony begged.

He was right. I was still whimpering.

There was a silence as Fabi gazed down at me.

"Fine," she decided. "Oreo," she crouched down to my level, "you are officially retired."

"Yes!" But then Anthony's face fell. "Wait... now what?"

"I guess I'll just have to give him back to the station..." Fabi said.

I think I was the only one that knew that she was joking because Anthony said, "You know what? I think he should become a police-"

"I'm just kidding!" Fabi grinned. "I'll keep him, of course!"

Just then, the football team burst out of the bushes and started to celebrat.

By now, I had learned to always be on alert. So, I let out a series of yelps, barks, and growls.

Everybody laughed.

I shook myself and growled softly. *Y'all should know better.*

"Anthony, ya thinking what I'm thinking?" Coach asked after everyone calmed down.

Anthony smiled down at me. "Let's make Oreo a star."

Chapter 9

· ·

Dang Airlines

We went back to the field so the team could teach me everything about football.

"Okay, boys!" Coach cracked his knuckles. "Let's teach Oreo how to be a star."

So, my training began. They taught me fumbles, reviewed touchdowns (was that really necessary?), interceptions (just a refresher), three and two point field goals, and turnovers. I'm not going to lie, it was a lot to take in.

The tackling was especially hard for me. Until now, I had relied on my team to do them for me. But, now that I had an actual chance at playing, I had to learn how to do them for myself.

Eventually, I got it right… or close enough. Finally, they taught me how to get past other players a little more simply than I'd chosen to do in the past.

Coach had been on the phone. Finally, he hung up. "Good news; he can play!"

The team cheered.

"And they even said he's allowed to wear a flag!" Coach continued.

The team patted me so hard it was like they were tackling me.

"And I can take care of him for you," Fabi walked over from the bench. "I'll take him to all the games you want."

Anthony smiled at her. "Thanks, Fabi."

"Don't mention it," Fabi hugged the less sweaty side of him.

After more hard work, we went home. Fabi gave me a quick bath before preparing dinner for both of us. Or, more accurately, before she ordered the robot to give me dinner, and then cooked herself some chicken and rice. While we ate, Fabi talked to a woman on the phone.

"I just can't believe it," she said, silent tears rolling down her cheeks.

I could hear the woman crying on the other end of the line.

There was a pause, and then Fabi said, "*Ya te dije*, she died peacefully. I did all I could." She was Mexican.

Another pause. I munched on my food and found myself staring at Cookie's empty bowls. I whimpered as silently as I could.

"Okay. Love you too… 'Bye," Fabi hung up.

I walked over to her, lay down under her chair, and licked her hand, which was hanging limply from the side. Fabi started to cry. I might have shed a few tears myself.

We went to bed, but I couldn't seem to fall asleep. I kept thinking about Cookie. We had given her the funeral she deserved. During the time I had lived with Fabi, all three of us had grown really close. We understood each other, like a triangle. All three sides work together to make the perfect shape. But now that Cookie was gone, our shape had shattered. Fabi and I were missing a side. I could sense that Fabi was awake, too.

I lay in the darkness for a while, until I got restless and looked up to see ifI was right about Fabi being awake. She was staring up at the ceiling.

I jumped onto her bed and licked her fingers. I leaned on her side. *I miss her. Can I sleep here?*

"Could you stay here? I miss her..." Fabi put a hand on my fur.

You've read my mind, I closed my eyes and fell asleep.

The next week, we ate breakfast, packed our stuff, and picked up Anthony on our way to... somewhere new.

We're going to the airport, Anthony explained in response to my thought.

I rode in the front seat on Anthony's lap and stuck my head out the window with my tongue sticking out. I looked behind us and saw...

Mom, I growled softly.

When she saw me, she scowled in disgust. I barked at her. Anthony snorted.

After about an hour, we arrived at a huge, no *humongous,* white building. A lot of people were dragging suitcases behind them. Most of them seemed in a hurry.

Fabi parked at the equally big parking lot. The humans took our suitcases from the trunk.

When we got to the airport building, the team was already there. Coach was ordering them to stay together.

Anthony and his best friend, Joseph, did their handshake routine.

"Okay boys, remember, stick with your partner," Coach said.

"Yes, Coach," the team answered. I barked: dogs' tongues aren't made for speech. The team walked into the airport. I started following them, but Fabi held me back.

She took out a… crate. Only this one didn't tilt when you dragged it across the floor by the handle.

I backed away. *Um, is this really necessary?*

"I'm so sorry, but it's the only way they'll let you on," Fabi said, sounding very sorry.

I struggled as she put me in, but she was too strong. I whimpered as she zipped the door up.

Fabi peeked in. "It's okay, I'm still here."

I tried to focus on Fabi as we caught up to the team. I panicked when I couldn't find Anthony in the crowd.

I'm here, he thought. *Sorry, but Mom's holding me up.*

I sighed in relief. *Thank you.*

Finally, I saw him. And, to my displeasure, he was right. Mom was there.

When she saw me, she scoffed maliciously. "That's where you belong," she said in a matter-of-fact voice.

"Can you at least *try* to like him?" said Anthony angrily.

We stopped at a line. They finally called us, and we went up to a very high desk. There was a man behind it with a goatee and black, messy hair.

His eyes grew wide when he saw all of us. "How many suitcases?" he asked in a high-pitched tone.

"Not one for each person," Coach said. The man looked relieved. "Just seven," Coach finished.

Coach asked Mom and Fabi for a booklet called a "passport," and handed them over along with his. Then he put the suitcases on a scale one by one.

We were just turning to go when the guy said, "Ooh, sorry, but he's going to have to go in the hold." He pointed at me.

I looked at Anthony. *That isn't good, is it?*

He didn't seem to hear me. "Please, can't he go with us? He's very well behaved as long as he's with Fabi or me."

"Sorry, but he's too big."

"He's trained," Fabi added. "As a police dog."

The man still shook his head. "I'm sorry," he took out another crate, without the handle, and opened the door.

I whimpered as Coach, Anthony, and Fabi transferred me from one crate to the other. Once my tail was tucked in, the man closed the door to my prison.

Suddenly, the floor began to move under me. I was being pulled away from my team.

I scratched at the door and whimpered.

It's okay Oreo, it's just a two-hour flight, Anthony didn't sound very encouraging, though. He seemed just as worried as I was. I passed through a curtain of black flags and they disappeared from view.

Now I was somewhere *full to the brim* with suitcases and moving floors.

I had begun to chew on the bars of my prison's door when I saw a familiar face in a carrier like mine.

Lucky! I barked to get her attention, but I didn't need to. She barked back, and we were both bouncing with joy.

Oreo! I'm so glad to have a… well, a cellmate, Lucky said.

Me too! I exclaimed.

We talked for a long time, catching each other up on what was happening in our families. Suddenly, I couldn't hear Lucky any more. I had entered an enclosed room.

I stood up as a man came toward my crate. I saw out of the corner of my eye that Lucky had come out of another room, and a man was putting her back on the moving floor. She seemed… not right. I tried calling out to her but didn't get an answer.

Suddenly, anger stirred inside me, and I growled.

"It's okay boy," the stranger lifted me off of the moving floor, and I watched helplessly as he carried me into another room.

He put me down on a metal table. To my relief, he opened the door. The man was strangely kind and let me pee on a doggy pad.

I was starting to like him until he carried me back to the table. He opened a bag and pulled out something that smelled like chicken. I started to reach out with my tongue, but no, this guy was a stranger, he couldn't be trusted.

I growled.

"Well, I guess you leave me no choice," the man said.

I growled again. *What did you do to Lucky?*

Before I got a chance to snap at him, I was pricked by something sharp, and the world turned fuzzy. I felt tired and weak, I couldn't move. And whenever I tried to lift my head, I got a terrible headache.

The man put me back in the carrier and then onto the moving floor. I tried to lift my head again but ended up passed out.

I woke up feeling dizzy as heck but at least now I was able to lift my head. I was still in my carrier, but not on the moving floor and in a dark room. I could hear suitcases moving all around me.

I didn't like this place, so I whimpered and scratched at the door so somebody would hear me and come to my rescue (fun fact: No one did).

I tried to make sense of what had happened. The stranger had pricked me with something, and I'd immediately felt weak. Probably some kind of drug to make you weak.

I started chewing at the door of my cage when I heard a familiar whine.

Lucky? I asked in no particular direction.

I heard her bark. *Oreo!*

Thank goodness you're alright! Don't worry, I'll get us out of here! I reassured her.

I could barely see, but I decided to find a faster way to get out of my carrier. I studied the door I was dealing with. I closed my eyes and thought back to when the man had opened and closed it. He hadn't put on a lock. Instead, he'd twisted a little knob and pushed the door up at the same time.

I started copying what I'd seen the man do (WARNING: What follows is a guide to opening these kinds of doors). I pawed at the knob, slowly making progress. Finally, it turned all the way, and I tried to pull my paw out, but it got stuck. I started to panic. Then I remembered what Fabi had told me one day at training. She was teaching me how to get out of a deep hole: *Now remember, in these situations, never panic. Keep calm and find a way around the problem.* After she gave me this advice, I had slowly but surely, dug myself a dirt staircase and got myself out.

I took a deep breath and thought of a way to free my paw. I twisted it and slid my paw out.

Now came the harder part. I pushed my muzzle against the door. To my disappointment, only my nose poked out. I started pushing up, but a suitcase knocked it back down, and I yelped as it scratched my muzzle.

Oreo? What's wrong, are you okay? asked Lucky.

I-I'm fine, I stuttered. *Just a little scratch, is all.*

I shook off the pain and tried again. After several minutes, a good push was all I needed. I pushed with all my strength and *bam!* I was free!

I stumbled out and sniffed for Lucky, then I carefully picked out my way toward her. Finally, I was at the door of her crate. Thankfully, it was exactly like mine.

I fumbled with the knob for a minute and got her free.

We have to find Jackson and Anthony, Lucky said.

Agreed, I nodded toward a speck of light. *Come on.*

Suddenly, just as we'd started walking, a suitcase fell on Lucky's leg. In my excitement, I'd gone on ahead, so I started running back to her. That was a mistake. I tripped and another suitcase fell on my prosthetic. At least it didn't have any feeling.

I heard Lucky howl. She was probably in agony. I struggled. Just as I was about to escape, a sharp piece of something cut half of my replacement leg clean off.

Darn it! I thought. I limped toward Lucky, but *another gosh darn* sharp thing lopped (WARNING: Bone-chilling scene coming) my leg cleanoff, what was left of the real one too.

I winced but kept on hobbling toward Lucky. I could tell she'd already passed out from the pain.

I pushed the suitcase off of her and examined her leg.

It did not look good. If she was lucky (no pun intended) it would just be a fracture.

Then, I realized I was helpless. There was absolutely no way I could get Lucky to the speck of light in my condition. So, I spotted a loose blanket nearby and limped back with it to cover Lucky's leg. I curled around her, so as to protect her from any more falling suitcases.

I whimpered and pushed Lucky's face gently. Then I licked her, for comfort.

I watched over her, wondering if someone, *anyone,* would save us. Lucky needed help. Well, me too, but I was only thinking of Lucky. I looked at my leg. It was bleeding out, and I started to feel weak.

I let out one last yelp, and then I blacked out too.

Chapter 10

. . . .

Chicago

I stirred awake as a huge door opened. A woman with light brown hair was there.

When she saw us, her jaw dropped. "Oh gosh, what happened here?!"

I whimpered. Lucky hadn't woken up yet, she seemed to be in a coma.

"Pat! I need help!" the woman called. She walked over to us, and I growled.

"It's okay, boy. I'm Grace. And I'm going to help you. But I need you to cooperate," Grace knelt down beside me.

There was a man coming. *Fine,* I thought.

The man, who I assumed was Pat, looked at us and immediately yelled, "Bring me some stretchers!" He approached us. I let him do what he had to do, mainly because I had no choice.

A group of people was pushing two stretchers our way.

"Let's see whose you are," Pat checked my tag, then Lucky's. "I need Fabiana Salgado and Jackson here, immediately," Pat said into a walkie-talkie.

"Relax, boy," Grace told me. She and Pat lifted Lucky and me onto a stretcher.

"Hang in there," one of the stretcher people ran a hand through my fur.

I was still on alert since these people were strangers.

But then, I saw Fabi, Anthony, and Jackson sprinting towards us, and I let myself pass out.

I cracked an eye open. *Hey, this kind of place is familiar... yay...* Do I even have to tell you? I was at the animal hospital... AGAIN. It wasn't the usual one, but an animal hospital is an animal hospital.

I lifted my head from the bed I was lying on. Fabi was on the phone, and Anthony was at my side.

How're you feeling, boy? he asked.

I licked his chin. *Just fine.*

"Okay, we just need to pop it back on," the vet said.

"Will he be able to play?" Anthony asked.

"Huh?" the vet's face scrunched up in confusion.

"Oh, sorry. He plays on my football team," Anthony explained.

"Oh. Well, in that case, yes, he'll be able to play," the vet replied.

Anthony sighed. "Thank you."

"This is probably going to hurt..." the vet sounded like he pitied me.

I sighed. *You don't have to finish that sentence.*

I squeezed into Anthony, and he held me close.

"Three... two... one," the vet counted down.

I yelped, and then started howling.

"Chill," Anthony held me tight.

I whimpered a little.

You're okay, Anthony told me.

I relaxed into him.

"You're all set," the vet said.

Fabi had been staring into space, but now she noticed me. "Oreo! Thank goodness you're alright!" she hugged my non-prosthetic side.

"Thank you," Anthony told the doctor. "Come on, Oreo," he stood up.

I stretched my leg and followed Fabi and Anthony out of the room.

On our way out of the animal hospital, I smelled a very familiar scent.

I gasped. *Could it be?* I sniffed the air. *Yes!* I yanked so suddenly on my leash, Fabi dropped it.

I ran after Lucky's scent while Anthony and Fabi chased me, calling my name.

I burst into room 24. Jackson, a boy, and a woman were standing by… by Lucky's bed.

I walked slowly up to her bed and jumped onto it. Everybody jumped, but I didn't notice. My eyes were for Lucky, and Lucky alone.

Lucky? I said in despair.

Her leg was a mass of bandages, and she appeared to be in a… a coma…

"Oreo?" Jackson stared at me, shocked. "What are you doing here?"

Anthony and Fabi came running inside.

"Oreo!" Fabi exclaimed angrily. "We're so sorry. He got…" her voice trailed away as she took in the scene before her. "Is that…?"

"Lucky," the woman finished.

"Is she okay? As in, *alive* okay?" Anthony asked.

"No, she's in a coma," Jackson said sadly.

I whimpered. For once in my life, I didn't want to be right.

"Well, we'll be praying for her," said Anthony. "Come Oreo."

I started to follow them but stopped myself. *Why do I listen? I want to be with Lucky,* I jumped back onto her bed.

"Oreo, come on," this time, Anthony sounded stern.

Why? I whined at him. I curled up with Lucky, nose to nose.

After that, the room fell silent.

"Oreo," Jackson said softly, "she'll be okay. Go."

I whimpered one last time, licked Lucky, and followed Fabi and Anthony outside, where the team was waiting.

"How is he?" Coach bounced up from the bench he was sitting on.

"He can play," Anthony answered.

The team cheered. Then they fell silent, probably because Fabi was on the phone again. She whispered something into the phone.

I sighed and lied on the ground.

"Are we sure he's okay?" Joseph glanced at me.

Anthony whispered something into Coach's ear.

"Aw, darn it," Coach sounded very sympathetic. He crouched next to me and put his hand on my head. "I know how you're feeling, pal. But, trust me, it'll get better."

I lifted my head. *Really?*

"Yeah, she'll be okay," Anthony said.

"Of course! That would be amazing!" Fabi exclaimed quite suddenly. She hung up.

"Hey Oreo," Fabi told me. I turned towards her. "Clover's coming to see you play!"

I groaned/growled. *That's... great,* I lied on my back.

Anthony shot daggers at Fabi. "Why did you say 'yes?!'"

"Honestly, I just didn't want to break any hearts," Fabi admitted.

I barked angrily.

"What? You should know by now that Mexicans are *much* more polite than Americans!" Fabi retorted.

"True," Kevin agreed. He was a part of our team.

"Seriously, how many dogs do you need on the team?" Mom said.

Now, sure, this was extremely rude, but, for once, she was asking a good question. Wait, before we continue, let me explain. Remember when we fell off that cliff? Yeah, that was obviously Maddie's fault. And Maddie was friends with Kate, but that meant she was associated with how Cookie's lungs failed. But Maddie obviously didn't tell Kate about that.

"Clover, thankfully, is just coming to patrol," Fabi said.

"Thank goodness," Mom mumbled.

"For once, we agree on something," Anthony muttered.

Hallelujah, sister! I said at the same time. Anthony and I exchanged a look. He snorted off a laugh. Because only Anthony could hear me, I laughed as hard as I could.

"Well, since we've already dropped off our stuff at the hotel, wanna take a tour of the Windy City?" Coach asked.

Everybody cheered. Except for Mom, for some strange reason. This "Windy City," sounded pretty exciting.

"Windy City" is a nickname for Chicago, which is where we are, Anthony explained.

I looked around. *Holy cow…*

The surrounding area was… wow. I-I was speechless. I could also see why Chicago's nickname was Windy City since it was very windy.

We all got into different cars. Anthony with Mom and a few boys. Coach with our other two coaches (for offense and defense). Joseph's mom drove with more of the team, and Fabi and I with the rest of the boys.

"Why does *Oreo* get to sit in the front?" Jamal complained.

"Yeah! He can sit on the floor!" Ethan added.

The others agreed.

I barked. *If you don't stop being so persuasive, I'll pee on your laps!* I growled back at them. That silenced them.

Fabi chuckled. "You should probably leave him be."

I stuck my head out the window, enjoying all the new, amazing smells (besides the pollution).

River, breeze, chocolate, popcorn, subway, pizza… I mumbled.

"I can't believe Anthony's mom got us a game at *Soldier* Field!" Liam was saying.

"Me neither! We're gonna be playing on professional turf!" Zack exclaimed.

"Is it really so amazing?" Calvin asked skeptically. "Dude, they're rich."

"Calvin has a point," Jamal said.

We finally parked next to a huge park. We all got out of the car.

"Sit, Oreo," Fabi ordered.

I listened, but, as Fabi pulled my vest out, I regretted it.

Oh, whatever, I said. I stood still as she slid it on.

Then Fabi got on the phone. "Hey… We're at the Bean…" she waved at…

I growled softly. *Clover.*

Why are you mad? Clover looked puzzled.

Oh, you know why… Ugh, whatever. I'll put it aside… for now. I kept a close eye on Maddie.

Now, Clover had absolutely *nothing* to be mad about, but for some reason, she lunged forward, teeth bared. I stood my ground. She was on a leash anyways.

I sighed. *Clover, let's not do this.*

Why were you looking at Maddie like that, huh? Planning to attack? Clover sounded hysterical.

What? No! I exclaimed. *I would never do that!*

Oh yes, you would, Clover pulled hard on her leash, and Maddie let go.

I knew what she was going to do, so I simply rolled out of the way. *Clover, please.*

She growled. Thankfully, Maddie restrained her.

"What is *wrong* with you?!" Maddie shouted at Clover.

I relaxed, thinking it was over. But I was wrong, Clover batted me with her free paw, and I lunged back, nose bleeding.

I sneezed. It didn't hurt, but still... Clover just made me bleed...

Fabi and Maddie gasped.

"I-I am so sorry," Maddie stuttered. "I don't know-"

"Just like her owner," Fabi knelt down to examine my nose.

"Wait, what?" Maddie stood up, holding Clover's leash tight.

"Uncontrollable," Fabi replied.

"Oh, is this about the mountain?" Maddie asked. "That wasn't my fault."

"Yes, it was," tears rolled down Fabi's cheeks. "We're leaving," I followed her into the park.

I licked her hand. Anthony appeared in front of us, along with the others.

"What happened?!" Anthony stared at my nose and knelt down to examine it.

I'm fine. It doesn't even hurt, I assured him.

"Clover scratched Oreo," Fabi answered.

"He says- I mean, looks," Anthony corrected himself, "fine."

Coach let out a sigh of relief. "Good."

"I'll call Kate," Anthony dialed a number. "Hey... thanks, but... Cool... Clover just scratched Oreo...! I don't know... Proof...? Fine, I'll send you a picture..." Anthony hung up and scoffed. "She says she wants proof." he took a picture of my nose and sent it to Kate.

"Now that that's dealt with, let's move on," Fabi said.

We started walking and stopped at a big, silver... bean? Wow, Chicago's weird.

We went up to it and everybody started taking pictures under the Bean.

I was bored, so I lay down on my back. I barked. I barked again. All the dogs were copying me!

Fabi looked up from her photo. "What's wrong, Oreo?"

I barked. *Why are they copying me?!*

"Oh, silly, that's just your reflection!" Fabi chuckled.

Reflection? I looked around. Anybody who was close to the Bean appeared on it! *Cool.*

After some more pictures, we walked in the park awhile and then started heading back to the car. On our way there, we heard music playing. We walked over.

Hold up, is that...? Yup, my nose never leads me astray! Dad! He was playing the trumpet.

Anthony heard me and was instantly overjoyed. Mom's reaction, however, was quite different. She walked towards a cafe and disappeared inside.

They finished playing, and we cheered. Dad ran over to us and wrapped Anthony up in a big hug.

"Hey, Oreo," Dad ruffled my fur.

"You were amazing!" Anthony said.

"Oh, that? That was nothing," Dad stared at Anthony.

"What?" Anthony asked.

"It's just that... you're so big... and I haven't seen you in so long," Dad hugged Anthony again.

"Hey, Mr. Cane!" Joseph shook his hand.

"Nice to see you, Joe!" Dad exclaimed. "And the others, too!"

Dad was right, though. Anthony was turning sixteen in December (it was November). And I'm pretty sure they hadn't seen each other since flag football.

"Well…" Dad cleared his throat. "What's he doing here?" he pointed at me.

"He's a football player now," Anthony said casually.

"Huh," Dad didn't ask any questions (to my extreme surprise).

"Josh!" a man called out to Dad.

"I'd better go," Dad smiled. "See you later, son," he ran over to his band.

Mom came out of the cafe, the timing was definitely not a coincidence, and said, "Traitor."

Anthony scoffed and we continued walking.

What does she mean by… I cleared my throat. *"Traitor,"* I mocked Mom.

Anthony laughed in his head. *When Dad told Mom that he wanted to start a band, Mom said he should continue working with her. But Dad said music was his passion, so Mom got mad and told him to do whatever he wanted. Then came the divorce,* Anthony finished sadly.

Oof, I exclaimed quietly.

We entered the parking lot. I immediately smelled trouble, but I couldn't put my paw on it. I growled.

"What's wrong, Oreo?" Fabi was now on alert. She could probably feel it, too.

Then the trouble revealed itself. "It" was a man hiding in the shadows. He was fast, very fast. The man grabbed Mom's purse from the car hood and ran for the exit.

I was the first to react. Despite my leg, I sprinted after him.

"Stop in the name of the law!" Fabi barked. She was close behind.

The man muttered a very cruel word. He was fast, and my leg did not like the sprinting. But I kept going.

I barked at the man. All I had to do was knock him down, and Fabi would have her handcuffs ready.

I forced myself to run faster. Once I was close enough, I realized the man had a gun on his belt. Unfortunately, before my brain could fully acknowledge this, I leaped on him, successfully knocking him over.

Bang! The gun went off. Luckily, I had rolled to the side, but the next bullet would be headed for the person right behind me.

Not on my watch, I carefully tackled her from below.

Crash! The bullet hit a pillar.

I jumped on the man, forcing him to drop the gun.

Fabi got back up and handcuffed the thief.

"Good boy," she praised me. "Very, very good boy."

Everybody ran towards us.

"My purse!" Mom quickly grabbed her purse and gave me a shocked look.

I groaned and lied on the floor. My leg was definitely not okay.

"Anthony, quick, hand me my bag," Fabi told him.

Somebody had called the police, and they led the thief into a cruiser.

Anthony tossed Fabi her bag. She pulled out my medicine.

You know, it's really not that bad, I chuckled awkwardly and scooted away. My medicine tastes like Chinese herbs. I don't recommend it!

"Come on, Oreo. It'll help," Fabi said.

The only thing it'll "help" with is ruining my taste buds, I retorted.

Take it or I won't let you play in the game, Anthony said.

I opened my mouth. Fabi dripped the liquid into my mouth. I quickly swallowed it. Then I started to gag. I got up, still gagging, and was treated to a surprise.

"Um…" Mom cleared her throat and sat down next to me. "Maybe I was wrong about you. Thank you, Oreo," she patted my head gingerly.

Anthony grinned. "Is he obedient now?"

Mom looked at him. "Can we still sign those documents?"

We all hugged.

Chapter 11

· · · · · · · · · · · · · · · · · · ·

Girls Are Annoying.

The next day, we went to Soldier Field. And, wow, was it beautiful! I didn't have long to admire it, though. It was almost time for our game.

We were up against McGavock High, also known as the Raiders. We were John Overton High, also known as the Bobcats. Our mascot was obviously superior (not so sure about our school name).

Before the game started, Coach gave us an inspirational speech. Since we were hosting, it was their ball (dang sportsmanship).

If you don't know football, this is how the start of the game works: There's a person alone at the opposite side of the field. In this case, this person is on the opponent's team. The rest of us are on the other side of the field. Over here, there's another person on the Raiders that kicks the ball. The lonely person catches it and sprints toward us. This determines where they start on first down.

So, anyways, this is basically what happened. Luckily, Zack (who's very fast) caught him at their thirty-yard line.

First down. We huddled. Oh, by the way, Anthony is the team captain.

"Okay, guys, let's do this just like Coach said. And no improvising," Anthony said. Everybody stared at me.

I growled. *I can be obedient!*

"Anyways, hands in," Anthony put out his hand. We all put our hands (and paw) in.

"One, two, three, Bobcats!" the team cheered. I jumped into the air and let out a short howl. The crowd roared.

I was cornerback, so my job was to watch the wide receiver.

The Raiders were running the Fake Handoff play. Luckily, we knew exactly what that was. The quarterback threw it after running alongside his friends. Thank goodness he threw it at the wide receiver, because Kaleb was my fellow cornerback, and also our star-catcher. And of course, he caught it.

The team ran over and congratulated him once the referee blew his whistle. I licked his chin.

It was our ball now. I was a wide receiver, so it was my job to... basically to do what I do best.

Kaleb, obviously, was also a wide receiver. And we had a very good plan. Whoever Anthony chooses to throw it to (we were doing the Wide Receiver play) has to run and trust that his fellow W.R. trails behind him, guarding him from tackles. The rest of the team is supposed to follow on and form a shield around the W.R. with the ball.

And that, ladies and gentlemen, was exactly what happened. One of them eventually got through to tackle Kaleb. But we had made it to their twenty-yard line! Twenty!

First down. We had agreed to the Leap Day play, which is basically where the tackles, guards, and center clear the way for the quarterback to leap to the end line.

This time… it didn't go so well. The Raiders had a big guy. And by big, I mean muscular. Anthony leaped into him and was tackled.

"Oof," the crowd went.

Well, that didn't go well, I thought, running over to Anthony.

The breath just got knocked out of my lungs, Anthony said.

Come on, get up, I said. Joseph reached out a hand to help. I pushed from behind.

We huddled.

"Okay, change of plans, we need another play…" Anthony said.

What about the Not-So-Real-Handoff play? I suggested.

"Oreo, that's too risky. It's exactly what they did," Anthony said aloud before he realized what he was doing.

"Are you… talking to him?" Johan asked.

Anthony sighed. "Fine, yes, I'm talking to him. I can hear him, and he can hear me telepathically. More on that later. Anyways, about the plays…"

I cleared my throat in my head.

"Well, what did Oreo suggest?" Mike asked.

"The Not-So-Real-Handoff," Anthony replied.

"Boys, hurry it up over there!" the referee called.

"Let's do that," Jamal said.

"Yeah, okay, fine," Anthony agreed.

"One, two, three, Bobcats!"

The crowd cheered.

"N.S.R.H, N.S.R.H!" Anthony screamed. "Hike!"

Now, the reason this play is risky is because, as Anthony said, they had just run it.

Calvin, our running back, brushed up against Anthony, but Anthony kept the ball.

Okay, that didn't work, I thought. I looked around and saw an open space in the defense, and at the end line, too. I sprinted towards it and hollered at Anthony's head. *PASS IT!!!*

The ball came flying to me. I carefully calculated where it was going to land. Out of the corner of my eye, I saw the big guy running to intercept it. I quickly jumped into the air and caught it right then and there.

The crowd roared. My team came over to pat and praise me.

Good news: we got the extra point! In a flash, it was half-time. The score was 17-9.

"Okay, boys, you're doing good, but they could easily take the lead," Coach explained. "So, we need to tweak our defense. Coach Beck has been studying how they play offense, and we've got an idea."

So, we tweaked it. I'm not going to explain how, but it definitely worked. By the time the third quarter was over, they had only made a field goal, and we had made a touchdown and the extra point. The score was now 24-12.

That's when bad luck caught up to us. With five minutes of the game left, something went very wrong.

It was our ball, and we were at the twenty-yard line. We were running the Wide Receiver play. Anthony threw it to Kaleb, and Kaleb sprinted to the end line. I thought he was going to make it when suddenly the big guy tackled him from the front. They went rolling across the field and finally stopped. I saw their player stand up, but Kaleb didn't.

I bounded over to him and winced when I saw his ankle. He groaned. I licked him and whimpered. I barked. Coach ran over.

"Somebody get us a stretcher!" he said. I whined.

"My ankle," Kaleb groaned.

"I know, just hold on," said Coach. "Can you move it at least?"

"No," Kaleb answered.

I lied down next to him and whimpered. *Please don't say that.*

He put his hand on me as the stretcher came over. "I'll be fine, Oreo. Go to Anthony."

"Yes, Oreo, go to Anthony," Coach gave me a stern look.

I stood up and realized that the team had gone to the bench. I walked over to them with my head down.

Anthony covered his face with his hands and sat down. "Don't tell me."

We have substitutes though! Right…? I tried to cheer everybody up.

Don't worry, we still won. The final score was 27-12. But Coach had told us that Kaleb was out for the season… The whole frickin' season!

But, there's always a bright side to life. In this case, it was that Fabi agreed to give me back to Anthony.

So, we got onto the plane (I was allowed to sit with Anthony) and flew home.

Best. No, worst, I corrected. *No, but… wait, what? Hmmm…* I thought for a minute as I raced across the yard. *Best… Best worst day ever,* I decided.

After I got settled in, Anthony took me for a walk.

I was having a wonderful time when I saw… Kate… And Clover, too. Kate was being dragged by Clover and a golden retriever in our direction.

"Nope," Anthony muttered. We turned back the way we came and walked as fast as we could.

"Aren't you going to help me?!" Kate screeched from the floor: she'd fallen down.

Anthony Stella Cane, don't you dare… I was interrupted by Anthony dragging me over to Kate. He helped her up.

Kate brushed herself off. "Thank you."

I tried my best to not look Clover in the eye.

"So…" Kate said. "Remind me, why do you blame Maddie for what happened?"

And this is why we don't help cousins of enemies up, I wanted to go back home, but Anthony had me on a leash.

"Nice to see you, too," Anthony retorted. "We should go," he went off in the direction I was pulling.

"Anthony, answer my question!" Kate demanded.

"I already told you!" Anthony looked over his shoulder. "And I'd rather you leave me alone," Anthony's voice cracked a little.

Anthony had loved Cookie too.

"Anthony, she was old," Kate said.

That hit me hard. Anthony, too.

What did you say? I slowly turned around.

She said the dog was old, and she was, Clover repeated.

That's it, I lunged at Clover and pulling Anthony off-balance so I could get free. I didn't leap on her, though. I just got the advantage. I'm not a monster, like her.

If you're going to insult Cookie, then you'd better keep your mouths shut, I growled at both of them.

To my surprise, Clover gave in. *Fine. Just back off.*

I went back to Anthony.

"I'm sorry, Anthony. I-I really didn't mean for it to come out like that," Kate apologized.

"Have a nice life," Anthony didn't even bother picking up my leash, he knew I would follow him home.

Anthony sat beside me on the couch.

She was old, Kate's words echoed in my head.

Hey, don't think about her, Anthony said. *There's something wrong with her.*

I stayed silent. She was old? How could she say that? Cookie was perfectly healthy.

"Well, Jackson texted me and asked if you would like to see Lucky," Anthony looked me in the eyes.

Yes, please, I stood up.

"How can I help you?" the receptionist asked as we entered the animal hospital.

I quickly caught Lucky's scent and followed it to her room.

"Just visiting…" Anthony stared after me. "But I think we'll be fine, thanks."

I entered a room. Jackson was sitting beside Lucky's bed. Anthony closed the door behind us.

"Hey, man," he said.

"Hey."

Don't ask, I advised Anthony. I walked up to Lucky's bed and jumped onto it to curl up beside her.

I sighed. *Lucky? It's me, Oreo. You probably can't hear me, but we won our first game. Bad news is, Kaleb can't play anymore. It really sucks. And… And Kate said Cookie only died because she was old,* I scoffed. *You would probably agree that this is preposterous…* I paused. *Lucky,* please *wake up. I can't lose somebody else.*

Anthony looked at me sadly. "Um, where's Aiden and your parents?" he asked Jackson.

"My dad's at work, and my mom is taking Aiden to summer camp," Jackson answered.

"How're Ian and Paige?"

"They're happy."

I could feel the boys looking at me discreetly.

"Do you think…?" Jackson's voice trailed off.

"They definitely fancy each other," Anthony whispered.

Fun fact: Dogs can hear four times better than humans, I told him.

Right, he said awkwardly.

We lay in silence for a couple of minutes.

"We should probably go eat dinner," Anthony looked at his watch. "Blessings."

"Thank you," Jackson said.

Anthony gestured at me to follow him.

We walked home. Mom had made dinner, and the robot had prepared dinner for me.

Thank you, Sally, I thought as the robot left.

Our next game was local and in three days, and that was about it for the week… *Sigh.* More time to think about it…

Chapter 12

· · · · · · · · · · · · · · · · · · · ·

Well, Kids, When a Human
Likes Another Human...

So, we won our second game, and there was a day left before the two other games. And, no, Lucky had not woken up yet.

I was... well, not right. It had been a tough game. I only made an extra point, and the score was 14-12. Everybody knew why I wasn't on my game, so nobody said anything.

I gloomily brought the ball back to Anthony. We were practicing passes and catches with a partner. Basically, it was like fetch, but with a football. This was usually my favorite drill, but I was distracted.

"Come on, Oreo, cheer up," Anthony urged. "We can't let tomorrow's game get as tight as yesterday," he picked up the ball.

I silently walked back to my position.

"Coach, shouldn't we have a water break?" Anthony asked Coach mysteriously after a few more throws.

"What? But we've only..." Coach paused. I was staring at the grass. "You're... absolutely right! Boys, water break!"

I lay down on the grass, I couldn't be bothered to hydrate.

"Yo, you have to do something," Joseph told Anthony. I knew they were looking at me, I was just focused on the thing. "We can't..."

"Yeah, I know, bro," Anthony interrupted. "Trust me, I know."

"Well then, fix him," said Liam.

"It's just… The only cure is, well, you know," Anthony whispered something directly into Joseph and Liam's ears.

"Yeah…" Joseph said.

"Um, Anthony, a word," Coach pulled Anthony aside. Anthony's eyes widened and a smile spread across his face after Coach told him something.

"Oreo, follow me," Anthony ordered.

I stared at the floor as we walked along. When I looked up, we were at the animal hospital.

Ugh, therapy? You guys are really getting desperate, I protested.

Jackson came out of Lucky's room, looking strangely happy. "Come on!"

We rushed into the room and… Holy smokes, Lucky was awake!

Lucky, Lucky, Lucky! I jumped onto her bed and licked her.

Oreo! She licked me back.

I looked around. Jaylee, her chinchilla Moldy, Mrs. and Mr. Jacobs, and Aiden were all there.

"Aww," everybody said.

Be quiet. Humans do it, too, I protested.

Moldy joined in our celebration.

"Careful with Moldy!" said Jaylee.

Lucky and I sniffed Moldy. He smelled like… well, like a chinchilla.

"We got to go!" Anthony probably meant for that to sound stern, but he was laughing. In fact, everybody was.

Anthony, Mom, Jackson, Jackson's parents, Aiden, Lucky, Jaylee, Moldy, and I rode in our large but not too showy car. Meanwhile our butler guy, Marth, drove our extra-large car with all the luggage. We also picked up Fabi on our way to the airport. I was wrong, Mom got us another game in a cool stadium in Georgia.

"Hey guys!" Fabi climbed into the car.

"Hello cousin," Anthony said.

The ride was wonderful. We sang "Celebrate Good Times" (the newest version) the whole car ride. Lucky and I howled and barked to it, while Moldy did his best to yap along.

We parked at the usual lot, and Marth helped us with the luggage.

Lucky, Moldy and I got to ride with the humans. And, thanks to Mom, we also got to go in our private jet. It was fun. The personal flight attendants spoiled us the whole way to Athens, Georgia. We animals got to watch The Story of a Golden Retriever. My favorite is the main character, Buddy.

It was a short flight. We didn't even finish the movie. The team met us in the parking lot.

Marth had come with us, so he drove us to our hotel. The team went with a chauffeur in a limo.

Everybody was split into a lot of rooms. I stayed with Anthony, Mom, and Fabi.

I slept like a log that night. The dog bed was *so* comfortable.

In the morning, the whole team got dressed, ate breakfast, and headed to the stadium. The others would come at game time.

It was surprisingly cold. Still, we practiced. We were playing against the Otters.

Anthony looked nervous for some reason. I didn't know why. He was sitting on the bench, so I trotted over to him. I put my face on his leg, looked up at him, and pulled out my signature move, the head tilt.

Anthony chuckled. "Fine, you caught me. I'll stop being nervous." He stood up and we went back to practice.

After a few minutes of my favorite drill, Coach pulled us to the side.

"Um, I need to tell you guys something," he said.

"Yes?" Anthony and I said at the same time.

"I might've, kind of, invited Clover and her, um, people to the game," Coach stuttered.

"What?!" Anthony stepped back. "Why?!"

"They asked me, and I'm just too polite, darn it!" It was a good answer.

Those people are always playing tricks on us, I grumbled.

"Now, get back to practice," Coach commanded.

"Yes, sir," Anthony muttered.

I caught the ball. *You know, maybe this time we could just ignore them,* I suggested, my voice muffled by the ball.

You're right. That's what we'll do, agreed Anthony, throwing the ball once I got in position.

At fifteen minutes before the game, the Otters arrived, along with the crowd. I could see our family among them.

Coach called us in two minutes before kick off. "Okay boys, just like we practiced."

Mattias was Kaleb's substitute. Thankfully, he had practiced extra hard.

"Hands in," Coach said. "And paw," he added glancing at me. "Bobcats on three, Bobcats on three!"

"One, two, three, Bobcats!" we finished. Our fans cheered.

Long story short, everything went well. The final score was 23-13. In our favor, of course.

After Coach's speech, something very weird happened. Anthony was staring at the cheerleaders. No... *a* cheerleader.

She had her back to us, so all I could see was her light brown hair in a ponytail. I was pleased to see she was a Bobcat.

Why are you staring at her? I asked Anthony. No answer. *Anthony? Earth to Anthony!* He didn't seem to hear me.

Joseph saw him. "Hm, somebody has a crush," he said in a teasing voice.

Oh, like me and Lucky? But with humans? I thought about it for a minute. *Ew!*

"Go get her!" Joseph said.

"Are you crazy?!" Anthony turned around. "She's a cheerleader!"

"Dude, just go!" Joseph pushed Anthony as hard as he could a few times, eventually Anthony bumped into the girl. I followed him.

"Oh, sorry. Hi," Anthony's palms were getting sweaty.

"Hullo," the girl had a thick British accent. She started to sweat too.

Anthony held out his hand. "I'm Anthony."

"Amy," the girl said. They shook hands.

I like you; you smell like fresh biscuits.

Suddenly, I saw Clover creeping up behind me.

Anthony, code Monster! I thought frantically.

Anthony spun around. "Clover, back off!"

"What's wrong?" Amy asked.

"Long story short, her owner caused a beloved dog's death," Anthony answered.

Amy gasped. "That's horrible! Shoo!" Amy batted Clover with her pom-pom. Clover yelped and ran away.

Anthony and I froze for a minute, but then I turned back around. *Okay, now I love you.*

Anthony slowed down his breathing. "Thanks," he looked back at Amy.

"No worries," Amy said. "Um, I should probably go. Cheerio," she walked away.

Say hi to your mum for us! I said in an imitation British accent.

"You sound ridiculous."

Oh, pish, posh! I turned off my accent. *You should've asked for her number.*

Anthony sighed. "I know. Maybe… Maybe another time."

I kinda felt bad for him. *Come on.*

As we were walking back to our team, the monsters came back. Kate and Clover stepped in front of us.

"Anthony, can I talk to you?" the rude girl asked (Actually, they're both rude, but I'm talking about Kate).

Anthony silently stepped around her and kept walking. Kate and Clover trailed behind us.

"Are you ignoring me?" Kate asked in amazement.

We just kept walking.

"Hey!" Kate grabbed Anthony's arm.

Anthony batted her hand away. "Did you not get the picture?!"

"Wait, listen to me!"

"Why should I listen to you after what you said?!" Anthony stared at her with fierce eyes.

"I…" Kate went speechless for a minute. "You're right. You have no reason to listen to me. I just wanted to apologize."

Anthony sighed. "Fine, I forgive you."

"No, you don't. You're just saying that."

"No, Kate, I mean it."

"Really?" Kate asked.

"I basically have no choice, since you always find a way to get into my business," Anthony turned back around.

"Close enough," Kate murmured. "Oh, and, will you tell Fabi that Maddie is really, *really* sorry?"

Anthony stopped walking. "She's not going to forgive her."

"And you think that's right?"

"Absolutely not. Fabi and Maddie have been friends since they were babies," Anthony said.

Kate sighed. "I know."

"But I'll try," Anthony smiled.

"Thank you."

"Anthony, what's the hold up?" Joseph called. He ran over to us. Joseph sucked his breath in when he saw Kate. "I thought we were..."

"I've forgiven her," Anthony said quickly.

"Oh, cool. Hey, Kate."

"Hi," Kate said. "Anyways, I saw you staring at a cheerleader. What's the lucky girl's name?" Kate asked in a wheedling voice.

Anthony groaned. "Amy."

"Uh-huh, okay," Kate walked over to Amy.

So, we're just going to forgive her? I asked Anthony in surprise.

We have to, Anthony replied, and he sounded like he meant it.

Ugh, fine.

"What do you think she's doing?" said Joseph.

"I don't know. I hope it isn't anything embarrassing," Anthony sounded nervous now.

"Boys, don't just stand there, come and help!" Coach called.

We were about to finish packing up when Kate came back to Joseph, Anthony, and me. She gave Anthony a piece of paper.

"It's... her number," Anthony looked up at Kate. "Thanks."

"No problem," Kate smiled.

"Amy's coming over," Joseph said out of the corner of his mouth. Anthony started sweating again.

"By the way, do I know you from somewhere?" Amy asked Kate.

"Uh, school, I think," Kate replied.

"Oh, that's right. How old are you?" Amy said.

"Sixteen. You?" Kate questioned.

"Same. Oh, um, hi again," Amy said to Anthony. Amy started getting sweaty a second time.

"Um, hi. I, uh, I…" Anthony went speechless. "I'm starting real school," he blurted.

Woah! Hold up! Why wasn't I included in this decision?! I hollered at Anthony.

Kate almost fell over in shock. "You're what?"

"Yep, in two weeks," Anthony said.

"Well, it's always good to have goals," Kate said.

"What do you mean?" Anthony seemed confused.

"Well, making friends in high school isn't exactly a walk in a jolly old park," Amy explained.

Great, now you're going to talk about high school. Bye-bye, I left them talking and trotted off to help the team.

"Hey, Oreo," Tami said as I walked by. I barked in response.

Some time passed, and I was helping to pick up the cones, when I noticed Amy. She was sitting on the bleachers.

I walked over to her.

"Oh, hi, Oreo," said Amy.

Silence followed. Amy opened the locket on her necklace and looked at the picture inside. I peered over her shoulder. It was a picture of a man and a woman, probably her parents. But then… Why wasn't she there?

Something clicked in my mind. *Oh… you're an orphan.*

Okay, before we continue, I just wanted to let you know that she's adopted… Probably… Hopefully.

I tried to comfort her by cuddling with her.

She sniffled and closed the locket. "The wonky part is that I can't seem to remember even a smidgen of my time with them."

Aw, dang it, now I felt really bad. *I need to cheer you up.* I jumped onto the field and started to chase my tail and roll around. Sure, it was humiliating, but it worked for Amy.

Soon enough, to my delight, she was laughing.

My job's done, I licked her cheek and went looking for my own crush. *Where is she?* I sniffed the air. *There,* Lucky and Jackson were helping Coach finish up with the packing.

Hi, Lucky, we licked each other. *Jackson,* I wagged my tail at him.

"Hi, Oreo," said Jackson.

"Oreo, come on! The pilot can't wait for long!" Anthony called.

Coming! I licked Lucky one last time (she licked me back) and followed Anthony to the parking lot. Mom and Marth were waiting in the car.

"Ready?" she asked.

"Yup."

"Johan told me you have a girlfriend," Mom said as Marth began driving. "Is she nice?" That was the third time… Wait, no, or maybe the fourth? Ha! I lost track of how many times Anthony was teased that day!

"Mom!" Anthony complained.

Marth and Mom laughed.

"You haven't answered my question!" Mom persisted.

"Yes, she's very nice."

"What's her name?" Mom asked.

"Amy," said Anthony. Just saying her name brought a smile to his face.

Chapter 13

· · · · · · · · · · · · · · · · · · · ·

School?! Oh, Come On!

At the airport, we were treated to a lovely surprise.

Amy! I gently leaped onto her and licked her chin.

"Oh!" Amy exclaimed. "Hullo there, Oreo!"

"Sorry about that," Anthony pulled me away. *Don't embarrass me!* he thought at me.

"It's alright," Amy said.

"Hullo," Amy's mother said. She sounded British too.

"Hi," said Mom.

"Anthony, I need to tell you something," Amy sounded very anxious and nervous.

"What is it?" Anthony urged.

"I-I'm adopted," Amy stammered.

"Oh, right..." Anthony glared at me. I'd already told him. "I... also have something to confess."

"Go on."

"Um... Oreo and I... can... Well, we have a telepathic connection," Anthony looked at his feet. "So, I already knew."

"Sick," Amy replied casually.

Anthony and I both breathed out a sigh of relief.

"But… I'm sorry," Anthony said, hugging Amy. We all enjoyed a nice group hug.

"We should go," Amy's dad broke the silence.

"Lovely meeting you," Amy's mom said.

"You, too," Mom shook their hands.

We parted.

"She *is* nice!" Mom exclaimed.

"Mom, stop it!" Anthony nudged her gently.

We went back to our private jet. It was fun, but I found myself thinking about how Amy's actual parents had died. Car crash? No, Amy would be terrified of cars. Same with planes… Drowning? No… Murdered? Wow, that got dark fast.

The flight attendant passed by. "Does Oreo want a snack?" she asked.

I wagged my tail. *Yes, please!*

Anthony stifled a laugh. "Probably."

While I ate my chicken, I noticed Anthony muttering to himself.

"Friday, five o'clock. Or is it four o'clock?" he glanced at his phone "No, five," Anthony sighed. "Wait, is today Friday?!"

Um, yeah, I answered.

"Attention passengers, we will be landing in a moment," the pilot announced.

Anthony's eyes widened. "Uh, Mom, what time is it?" he said in a small voice.

"Three-thirty."

Anthony took a deep breath. "Good."

I munched on my chicken. When we landed, our luggage was already there.

"Marth, could you get the car and meet us here?" Mom asked.

"Of course, milady," Marth jogged away.

We were soon home.

"Mom, I have to go," Anthony checked his watch.

"Okay. Enjoy your first date!" Mom called as Anthony and I ran off.

Anthony groaned. "A little privacy, please!" he called back.

We rounded a corner and stopped at a Starbucks. Anthony and I often come here after his lessons. Amy seemed to have just arrived.

"Hey," Anthony said.

"Hi. Come on," Amy went inside. We followed her.

As usual, Anthony got a Cookie Crumble Frappuccino, and a Puppuccino for me. Amy got Iced Tea with Lemonade.

We sat outside.

I lapped at my drink. *Say something, you idiot,* I told Anthony.

"So…" thankfully, Amy started the conversation. "Are you sure you want to go to school?"

"Positive," Anthony answered.

"Blimey, you really don't know anything, do you?" Amy covered her face with her hands. "You're starting late, it's high school, and you've been home-schooled all your life."

"I know what you mean, but I have more than enough friends at school," Anthony said. "Plus, everybody just knows me as 'Oreo's Owner'."

"Point taken. But…"

"Amy," Anthony interrupted. "I'll be fine. Besides, I have you," they held hands.

Amy smiled.

"We're officially a couple, right?" Anthony asked.

"Absobloodylutely," Amy replied.

What does that mean? Anthony asked.

Absolutely, or yes, indeed, I said helpfully.

Two weeks passed, and on Monday, something weird happened. Usually this is how our Monday mornings go: Anthony stays in his pajamas, eats breakfast, and Mom leaves to go to work. Then, Anthony gets on his computer in his room to do his lessons. He tells me he's way ahead of the game. This morning, except for Mom leaving for work, was very different.

Anthony changed. We did eat breakfast, but he was strangely hurried. Then, he grabbed his… backpack? And he left with Mom!

See you later, bud, he told me.

I think you're confused, I thought frantically.

"Anthony, come on! You're going to be late!" Mom called from the garage.

"'Bye, Oreo," Anthony left.

I paced around the house. *No Anthony, no Anthony, no Anthony…* I murmured. *Robot!* I thought as it whirred by. *Sally, do you know where he went?* I carefully stepped in front of her.

"Oreo, please move out of the way," Sally's mechanical voice said. "I suggest you go play outside."

I backed away. *Maybe I will,* I thought after a minute. I ran out to the backyard. *Hmm,* I thought. *Football!* I pounced on my squeaky football. *Squeak!* it went. *That's the stuff. But I can't play with it by myself,* I thought, feeling very disappointed.

I scanned the backyard for something, *anything*, to keep me entertained. *There,* I stared at the football tackle dummy. I leaped on it and jumped back to the floor. And, guess what? It bounced back!

I growled and repeatedly tackled the dummy, but it kept coming back.

I did this for a long time, sometimes I went crazy and sprinted around the back yard. But I always went back to the dummy.

After a very long time, at about noon, I did my business and went inside for a drink and a nap.

When I woke up, Anthony was home! I licked his chin.

"Hey, Oreo," Anthony sounded strangely gloomy. "Let's go for a walk," he clipped on my leash.

Outside we saw Clover and Kate. We went up to them.

"I'm going to the dog park," Kate said.

Can we go? I asked Anthony.

"Oh, I just need to take Oreo out for a second. I have something to do," Anthony said.

"Ok, 'bye," Kate mumbled.

"'Bye."

We trotted away.

"That was weird," Anthony whispered.

Ya think? Also, what do you have to do?

We rounded a corner.

A date, Anthony replied. And then, "Hey, Amy."

Amy! I licked her face.

She giggled. "Hullo you," she booped my nose. "Hey," Amy reached out for Anthony's hand, and he took it.

We were at the pet place.

Anthony kissed her cheek. "Come on."

Third wheel, here I come, I thought to myself.

Thankfully, the pet place wasn't like the pound.

"Hi," Amy said to the person behind the counter. "Do you have any Australian Shepherds?"

"Yep, just follow me," the woman came out from behind the counter and gestured for us to follow her.

We entered a room full of Australian Shepherds.

"This is one of our rescues, Sky. She's a Blue Merle Tricolor," the woman explained as she stopped at a kennel.

Inside was a pup huddled in a corner. She had a nasty scar across her back.

I put my nose to the bars of the kennel. *Hello Sky.*

I didn't get an answer.

"We found her in the sewers, poor thing," the woman lowered her voice.

Amy knelt down next to me. "Hullo, Sky."

Sky growled.

"We think she was traumatized by somebody, so she won't let us near her," the woman said.

"Sky?" said Amy. "I won't hurt you; I promise."

Sky stood up. She slowly made her way toward us. She sniffed my nose. I stood as still as a statue.

Amy put her fingers around the bar, and Sky licked them after sniffing them first. Anthony slowly crouched down and let Sky do the same to him.

"She seems to like you guys," the woman remarked, sounding surprised.

"I'll take her," Amy stood up. Anthony followed.

The woman unlocked the kennel and let Amy pick up Sky.

"You're a good girl, aren't you?" Amy said as Sky licked her cheeks.

"Here," the woman handed Amy a leash and collar for Sky.

I barked at Sky. She yipped back and squirmed for freedom.

"There you go," Amy put her down.

Sky stared at me intently and got in the play position.

I like you, I decided.

Sky tried to tackle me, but just ended up trying to climb me since I was way bigger than her.

Everybody laughed. I gently shook Sky off.

"Come on, let's go home," Anthony said, still chuckling.

Amy clipped on Sky's collar and leash.

"'Bye!" the very nice woman called as we left.

"Thank you!" Amy called back.

We were almost home when Anthony halted to a stop.

"Oh no, I'm so stupid! Today's Kate's birthday!"

Amy gasped. "I'm such a plonker!"

We speed-walked to Kate's house. Once we arrived, Anthony knocked on the door. Kate answered it.

"Hi Kate," Anthony said. "Happy birthday."

Kate hesitated before saying, "Thanks."

"Seventeen, right?" Amy asked.

"Yeah," Kate replied.

"Sorry for not congratulating you earlier," Anthony apologized.

"It's fine. Who's the new dog?" Kate said.

"Sky. Who's the kitten?" Amy gestured at a new kitten.

"Oh, that's Trixie," Kate answered.

Silence.

"So..." said Anthony.

"Um..." Kate said.

Amy looked at her feet.

"Kate, I need to tell you something," Anthony slowly started.

Oh, Lord help us, I thought.

"What?" Kate urged.

"We're a couple," Amy blurted.

Kate looked like she was going to faint. "Great," she said with a fake smile.

I only noticed Clover when Sky tackled her playfully. Clover rudely backed away.

What's her problem? Sky murmured to me.

Just ignore her, I advised.

"I have to go…" Kate said. "Thanks for stopping by," she shut the door.

Anthony sighed. "Yep. Of course, she didn't take it very well."

"Honestly, what were you expecting?" Amy asked sardonically.

"You're right," Anthony looked angry now.

"Now what?" Amy said after an uncomfortable silence.

Anthony sighed. "Now we go home."

We parted ways at our house. When Anthony and I went inside, Mom was cooking.

"How'd it go?" she asked.

"Fine. Amy got an Australian Shepherd rescue named Sky," Anthony told her. Then he stared into space for a while.

Mom noticed. "What else?"

Anthony hesitated before letting it all spill out.

"But it's so stupid!" Anthony exclaimed angrily. "Shouldn't she be happy for us?!"

Dude, we both know that Kate is stubborn as heck.

"Well, she'll get over it eventually," Mom said.

"Sure," Anthony growled. He grabbed his backpack and went to his room to sulk. I followed him.

Anthony sat down at his desk and unzipped his backpack.

What are you doing? I asked. *It's way past our playtime!*

"Sorry, Oreo," Anthony looked at me with an expression of regret on his face. "I got homework."

Oh… ok, I went back to the kitchen, where Mom was still cooking.

She glanced at me. "He's got homework, huh?"

I sighed and lied down. *Yes.*

"Well, you could go outside and practice," Mom suggested. "Remember, you have a game next week."

I sighed again. *Okay,* I slowly made my way outside to the backyard. I looked around, once again, for entertainment.

What's this? I trotted to a contraption with a cannon thing and button.

Mom walked outside. "Oh, that's for catching," she explained, coming over to me. Mom pressed the button, and a football went flying out of the cannon.

Out of pure instinct, I chased after it and caught it in mid-air.

Mom laughed with delight. "There you go!" she went back inside.

I practiced catching for a while and then practiced tackling the dummy. I tackled it again, and again.

I was panting. *I… give… up.*

I strolled back inside.

"Anthony!" Mom called. "Time for dinner!" No response. Mom clucked her tongue. Then saw me come in. "Oreo, would you get Anthony for me?" she asked.

I barked. *Sure.*

When I arrived in his room, he was on the computer, with the headphones on.

I jumped on Anthony's lap and barked. *Mom says to come eat.*

Okay, he said.

The dinner was nice and very delicious. But Anthony was strangely quiet. Usually, he would be telling Mom some crazy story, but not this time.

Ring! Mom's phone went. She picked it up.

"Sure, when?" Mom said after a few seconds. "Okay… 'Bye," she hung up and smiled. "Mrs. Shearer has invited us to Kate's horse race." (Shearer is Kate's last name.)

Anthony sighed. "And you said yes?"

"Of course!" Mom exclaimed.

Anthony stared at his food.

Mom frowned. "Honey, I only said yes because I hoped that it would help you to make up."

"Mom, you know very well that Kate doesn't forgive easily," I could sense the anger bubbling up inside of Anthony.

"She… does when she wants to," Mom said.

"Okay," Anthony strode off to his room.

I looked at Mom and whimpered.

She sighed. "I hope this works, bud," she told me.

Chapter 14

• • • • • • • • • • • • • • • • • • •

Humans Are Jerks 90% of the Time.

On Saturday morning, we got ready for the race.

Soon enough, Marth was opening the doors of our Tesla SUV.

"Are you excited?" Mom asked Anthony as Marth pulled out of the driveway.

"Are you really asking?" Anthony grumbled.

No, I confirmed.

Yes, Anthony still didn't want to go. It was understandable though. If you haven't got it yet, Kate is either stubborn or rude 90% of the time.

"Here we are, ma'am," Marth said after about twenty minutes of silence. The car stopped, and Marth opened the doors.

"Thank you, Marth," Mom said once she stepped out. "Would you like to watch the race with us?" she asked him.

"Yes, ma'am," Marth answered, sounding surprisingly eager.

"Anthony!" Amy waved at us. Sky yipped in her arms.

You're the best! I thanked Anthony as we ran over.

Thank you, Anthony said.

Amy put down Sky so we could say hi. She tried tackling me again. I just sniffed her.

"I invited the Jacobs," Amy gestured behind her.

And you're even better! I exclaimed, sprinting to my beloved (It's not icky. You humans are way worse).

Jackson, Jackson's younger brother Aiden, Mrs. Jacobs, and Lucky were all there. It was truly a miracle.

Hugs, pats, handshakes, and licks all round.

Anthony clipped on my leash, and we headed to the bleachers.

"We'll get a good view from here," Mom sat down. We all spread out around her.

Anthony sat in between Jackson and Amy, so I lay down with Lucky.

"So, you guys are, like, officially boyfriend and girlfriend?" Jackson glanced at the happy couple.

"Yes," Amy replied.

"It's starting!" Aiden exclaimed (he hadn't met Kate).

A gunshot went off, and the race started.

The moms cheered. Blah, blah, blah. Anthony, Jackson, and Amy just chatted. I assume Kate won because the moms whooped and the children clapped.

"Come on, let's go say hello," Mrs. Jacobs insisted, standing up.

"Why?" Jackson said gloomily.

"If you don't come, we'll tell everyone your middle names," Mom stood up and crossed her arms.

"Mine is Stella," Anthony announced.

"Well, Jackson's is..."

"You know what? Let's go!" Jackson bolted down the bleachers.

I snorted as we followed him. *Anthony Stella Cane.*

Oh, shut up. I already told you, Anthony said.

Yeah, but it's really funny, I chuckled.

Kate and Mrs. Shearer were in the stables.

"Hi!" Mrs. Shearer said.

Kate looked away.

Jackson cleared his throat. "Hi."

Kate scanned the room. "Mom, I'm gonna go see Amber and her horse, Star," she paused. "Come on, Clover."

They walked away.

Mrs. Shearer sighed. "Sorry about her."

"It's OK," Amy replied.

"We'll just go," said Anthony.

We began to walk off, but the moms, Marth and Aiden stayed. I peered over my shoulder, and the moms exchanged a look.

"Nuh-uh," they all said.

"What do you mean, 'nuh-uh?'" Jackson spun around.

"We're not leaving until we fix your friendship with Kate," Mom explained.

"Mom, she's too stubborn," Anthony protested.

That's a fact right there, I quipped.

Definitely a fact, Lucky agreed with me.

"Yes, she is *very* stubborn," Mrs. Shearer admitted. "But she can also be… reasonable."

Suddenly, Kate and Clover came back. And this time, Kate was on a horse.

Kate sighed. "Mom, I have to get River back home."

"Not yet. Anthony has something to say to you," said Mrs. Shearer.

I could sense Anthony's stomach clenching.

Kate rolled her eyes. "What?"

"Um," Anthony took a deep breath. "I'm sorry I…" *Okay, why should I be sorry?* he thought.

Don't ask me, I retreated.

"Uh-huh, yeah. Let's go," Kate adjusted her grip on the reins.

"I'm sorry too, for forgetting your birthday," Amy blurted. "And for, you know," her fingers twitched onto Anthony's.

Kate trotted to their van. Clover followed. Mrs. Shearer waved and followed.

That was painful to watch, Sky said.

Tell me about it, said Lucky.

Anthony ran over to them, and I followed. They turned around.

"Kate, I'm really sorry, believe me," Anthony insisted.

"I know," Kate said. "I forgive you," she loaded up the horse, and they drove away.

"Now what?" Amy tilted her head. "Why do I feel like we keep repeating ourselves?"

"Because my life is a mess," Anthony sat down on the street.

My goodness, you're a little right, I trotted over to him. *But your life is not a mess. You're a teenage boy with a very pretty girlfriend, you go to normal school, play football, and you're from a rich family,* I raised my eyebrows at him. *And none of that sounds like a messed-up life to me. Also, you have a very loyal dog by your side, even if I say so myself,* I sat down with my chin up for a moment, and then I stood back up and barked. *Now, get up!* I pushed Anthony.

"Fine, I'm getting up," he said.

Jackson held out a hand. "Oreo's right. You're amazing, and I think Kate meant it this time," he added.

"You think so?" Anthony said.

"We know so," Amy held Anthony's hand.

"And sir, please stop sitting down on the street," Marth said, wincing when he saw Anthony's clothes.

Everybody laughed, including Marth.

"Now, let's go home," Mom said once the laughter had died down.

Before we got in the car, Jackson asked us a favor.

"We're visiting North Carolina..."

"Nice," Anthony commented.

"Thanks, but I don't think Lucky wants to go on the plane because…" Jackson hesitated.

"Mmhm, go on," Anthony said.

"So, I was wondering if you could keep her until we get back?" Jackson asked.

Oh, you better say yes, boy. 'Cause if you don't, I'll…

"Sure," Anthony said. "When should I pick her up?"

"We'll just drop her off on our way to the airport tomorrow," Jackson answered.

"Okay. See you then," said Anthony.

Jackson nodded, and we went home.

The next morning, Anthony was getting ready for school.

No, please don't go! I tugged Anthony's shirt and whined.

"Mom is going to take you to pick me up, so relax," Anthony nudged me off. "Besides, you're going to see your girlfriend," he teased.

Oh, so are you! I said in a sing-song voice.

Anthony smirked and headed to the garage door.

No! I blocked his way.

"Dog bed, Oreo," Anthony ordered. I knew that that meant to go to my bed, but I didn't want him to leave. I stayed put.

"I don't have time for this, Oreo," Anthony said sternly.

I did not budge.

"Oreo, move," he didn't wait this time. Anthony shoved me out of the way.

Wait! I ran after him. He was almost at the door. *I promise I'll behave just please don't...* Anthony shut the garage door. *Leave,* I finished in defeat. I scratched at the door and sighed. *It's no use.*

I walked to the living room (the one I'm allowed in) and jumped onto the couch.

Well, since we've got to a place in the story where I'm bored, I'll briefly explain our house: It's four stories, but I can only be on the first one because of my leg. We have… eleven guest rooms according to Anthony. Only one on my floor. It has twenty-eight bathrooms, five living rooms, seven kitchens, a lounge, a games room, the office, and an indoor and outdoor pool. Oh, and I think we also have, like, three vacation houses. That's about it.

I was just waking up from a nap when I noticed Mom was home. And that meant…

The doorbell rang. *Joy!* I sprang up from the couch, ran to the front door, and barked.

"Coming!" Mom called. She opened the door.

Oreo! Lucky exclaimed, her tail wagging.

Lucky! I said at the same time. We tackled each other.

"Thanks for doing this," Jackson said to Mom, handing her Lucky's leash.

"No problem," Mom smiled.

"'Bye!" Jackson said from his car.

Mom waved and we went back inside.

"Okay, you two," Mom peered at us and put her hands on her hips. "I need to go to work. Marth will be here to supervise you, so you'd better behave."

I barked at Mom. *Sure.*

Once Mom left, I led Lucky to the couch. We snuggled there and eventually fell asleep.

When we woke up, we felt like playing, so we went outside. I searched the shed and found my Tug-Of-War rope.

Lucky growled playfully and said, *Challenge accepted,* she grabbed the other end of it and walked backward.

TUG-OF-WAR! we yelled.

I was very glad Lucky was a pit bull because it meant she was very strong. And a strong opponent in Tug-Of-War makes for a great match.

Suddenly, Lucky tugged extra hard, and I almost tripped. But I replied with an even stronger pull and she just slipped a little, nothing else. We played like that for a while longer until we tugged our strongest at the exact same time, and fell into each other.

Let's call it a tie, I grunted as I stood up.

Good idea, Lucky looked at me and grinned. I wagged my tailback.

We sauntered back inside for a drink. Marth had set up Lucky's bowls right next to mine.

I lapped up some water.

Refreshing, Lucky licked her snout.

Yep, I brushed my muzzle against her. She did the same.

After our drinks, we silently agreed to spend some quality time on the couch. We watched some National Geographic while resting on top of each other. Lucky fell asleep at some point.

I snapped my head up at the sound of the alarm. That meant Mom was home, which meant we were going to pick up Anthony!

"Slow down!" Mom said as I dragged her and Lucky to the car. Marth was standing by.

He opened the door for Mom, and then for me and Lucky.

"Ore..." Marth started.

I leaped into the car. *Thank you!*

Marth looked startled. Mom tittered.

I poked my head out the window with Lucky as we pulled up to the school.

"Do you mind waiting here?" Mom asked Marth.

"Not at all," Marth assured her.

Lucky, Mom and I got out of the car.

I can't believe Anthony wasn't nervous. I stared up at the school. *This place is enormous.*

We rounded a corner, and I saw my favorite human.

Anthony!!! Mom dropped my leash, and I tackled him before licking him effusively.

Anthony howled on the floor. "Hey, bud," he shouldered me off, hugged Mom, and scratched Lucky in her favorite spot.

"See you Monday," Joseph said behind Anthony. They did their handshake. "'Bye Mrs. M." he waved at Mom.

"'Bye Joe," she said. "I'm going to go talk to Mrs. Todd," Mom told Anthony.

"Don't embarrass me," Anthony begged.

"No promises," Mom beamed and walked away, leaving Anthony, Lucky and I alone.

"Your mommy babying you, Cane?" a voice said behind us.

Three boys appeared from behind a pillar. The one in the middle had *way* too much hair gel on his black hair. To his left was a boy dressed like a homeless person. And the other one had strange, gray eyes.

"Tom," Anthony scowled.

"Do you like smoochies from your mommy?" Tom taunted.

"Looks like your mommy overdid it with the hair gel," Anthony retorted.

"Well, while you were being home-schooled, I'll bet she tucked you into bed every night," the boy with gray eyes mocked.

The one dressed in rags cracked up. "You are *so* right, Jay!"

"Shut up, Mike," Anthony snapped at him.

"Why should I listen to you, dork?" Mike said.

I growled. *At least he's smarter than you.*

And stronger, Lucky added, growling too.

"Aw, his dogs are protecting him!" Tom chortled, and the others joined in.

You've messed with the wrong dog, I pounced on Tom and bit into his shoulder.

Tom yelped in alarm. Jay and Mike tried to knock me off but were surprisingly weak. Anthony stood frozen in place.

Lucky barked. *That's enough!*

I got off of Tom, still growling for good measure. He cursed.

Before anybody could say anything else, Mom turned around and started walking our way.

"This isn't over, Cane," Tom sneered. He, Jay, and Mike ran away, Tom's shoulder bleeding.

"Is his shoulder bleeding?" Mom pointed at Tom.

"Nah, it's just his shirt," Anthony lied.

"Oh," Mom squinted. "I guess you're right."

As we walked to the car, Anthony gave me a mischievous grin, ruffled my hair, and said, "Good boy."

Chapter 15

• •

Seven

Clover's family invited us to dinner a few weeks later. Lucky was still with us. They had a new, bigger house. Not bigger than ours, but still pretty big.

We got out of the car and Anthony rang the doorbell.

I didn't get to explore the house completely so unfortunately, I can't describe it.

Mrs. Shearer answered the door. "Welcome! Maddie will be here soon. Kate's upstairs."

I could see Clover, Trixie, and a Border Collie.

"Thank you for inviting us," Mom said as we came in.

The Border Collie looked puzzled for some reason.

"Clover, go get Kate please," Mrs. Shearer told her.

Clover disappeared upstairs.

"Who's the Border Collie?" Anthony asked, pointing.

"Oh, that's Storm. She showed up on our doorstep in the middle of a thunderstorm," Mrs. Shearer explained.

Lucky and I were greeting Storm when Kate came downstairs with Clover.

"Hi," Kate said. "Lucky's here?" she asked.

"Um, yeah. Jackson went to North Carolina," Anthony replied.

"So, what's for dinner?" Kate said.

"It'll be a while. Why don't you two go for a ride?" Mrs. Shearer suggested. "Maddie will be here when you get back."

"Uh, I guess," Kate grabbed Storm and Clover's leashes. She walked out the back. "Come on," Kate told Anthony.

Anthony and I exchanged a glance before following the girls. Lucky came with us.

Kate went to a stall and got two saddles.

"You know how to tack up a horse? And ride?" Kate added.

"Yep," Anthony replied to my surprise.

"Here," Kate gave him the saddle.

"Ready?" Kate asked after Anthony got ready.

"Let's go," Anthony paused. "Why aren't we wearing helmets?"

"Oh, here," Kate tossed him one, but didn't put one on herself.

I looked at Anthony. *Are you sure about this…?* My voice might've been trembling a little.

Anthony gave me a sincere look. *Do you trust me?*

Yes, I said right away.

Then believe me when I say that we'll be fine, Anthony said.

"Up, Clover," I heard Kate say. Clover jumped onto River.

Please don't, I immediately said.

"Just follow," my amazing owner commanded. *"Don't wander off."*

Yes, sir! I stood up, soldier-like.

"Come on, Ash," Anthony squeezed the horse's sides a little bit, and Ash started trotting. I followed them.

Ash is kind of… slow, I said, being cautious with my words.

"She's a bit of a slow one," Kate said. "If you want to switch, I can put the saddle on River."

I hadn't realized that Kate didn't have a saddle.

"And I'll ride Ash," she finished.

That's a good idea, I grinned at Anthony, hoping he would accept the request.

"It's fine," Anthony shot daggers at me.

Oh, come on! I exclaimed in frustration.

I'm trying not to go back to being enemies, Anthony said.

Fine, Mr Sensitive, I said, chuckling at my joke.

"Let's go to the arena," Kate suggested. She started galloping away. I did not catch the rest of that sentence, but, knowing Kate, it probably went something like: *Because I'm an expert, and I'll leave you in the dust!* *Ahem* Jeez, she has a high-pitched voice.

Before we continue, a word of warning so you horse lovers don't hunt me down. I… Okay, I do not hate horses, but I don't like them either since the… incident happened. I tried to focus on something besides the idea of the horses going rogue and squashing me… and maybe Anthony too. So, I didn't really pay attention to anything.

We got to the arena. It wasn't really an arena; it was a race track.

"Wanna race, Anthony?" Kate said. "I usually race with Ash, so we'll have to switch. You know, so she doesn't buck."

I rolled my eyes. *More like; "So I can win."* Then, my stomach clenched as I saw the pock-marked surface of the track.

Anthony's voice wavered a little as he accepted the challenge.

Relax, bud. We'll be fine. I promise, Anthony said in a gentle voice.

I took a deep breath. *Yeah, okay.*

"Oh, Clover races, too," said Kate casually.

"So I guess Oreo can, too," Anthony gave me a pleading look.

"Oh, he can run?" Kate asked, rather stupidly.

Cough Football. *Cough*

"He plays football, Kate," Anthony snapped.

"Two laps," Kate said. "And… go!"

We started. I didn't want to run, so I jogged. Somehow, Anthony still ended up in last place. Clover's expression was so serious she looked like she thought this was a national championship. Kate too.

I sat down to wait for Anthony and started jogging with him once he caught up.

Anthony fumbled with the reins, trying to make the horse go faster.

Having some trouble there? I asked, chuckling.

"Oh, shut up," Anthony scoffed at me. "You can't even get second place."

Because I don't want *to,* I yawned. *I'd rather be helping you with your homework.*

Anthony yelped as River almost bucked. "At least you're not on a horse."

I immediately ran as far away as I could from the horse, and I won third place.

"Nice riding," Kate lied. "Dinner's probably ready; let's go."

As we traveled back, I noticed Anthony trying to hide a limp.

I sighed. *This is why I don't trust horses.* I discreetly helped Anthony walk by slipping under his arm.

I'm fine, Anthony thought when we could finally see Kate's house. I walked ahead, pining for my beloved. We put the horses back in the stables and went inside.

Lucky! I licked her.

Are you ok?! She asked frantically, checking me for injuries.

Surprisingly, yes, I assured her.

Lucky showered me with affection. Maddie was at the house now, so Clover jumped over the couch and tackled her. I suddenly felt a longing for Amy and Sky.

Maddie laughed. "Same old top-dog," she said.

Lucky tackled me playfully.

I am so glad I met you! I exclaimed, escaping from her grip. This is how our game of You-Can't-Pin-Me-But-I-Can-Pin-You started. It's kind of like wrestling, but with less blood.

I pounced on her and counted, *One Mississippi, two Mississippi, three Mississippi! I* barked. *Victory is mine!* Then I crawled off Lucky.

She got up and looked at the stairs. *Mm, it smells like socks up there,* she frowned at me, *I wish you could climb.*

I glanced at my leg. *Yeah… Go,* I said after thinking for a minute.

Lucky tilted her head. *Nah, we can play down here,* but I saw her staring longingly up the stairs.

It's fine. Go, I sat down and nodded at Lucky.

Are you sure?

Yes, I answered.

Lucky ran upstairs, with Storm and Trixie behind her. I could smell Clover up there, too.

I lay down on the floor and sighed. I snapped my head back up as Lucky, Trixie, Storm, and Clover came back down.

Is there turkey for dinner? I sniffed the air. Then, I got startled as they all got a grip of my collar and pushed me to the stairs.

Are you sure about this? I said, worried.

We're not leaving you down here, Lucky said. She meant it.

I grunted and lifted my legs as they hauled me to the second floor. I didn't know cats were strong, but they are. We stopped for a break halfway and then continued.

Finally, we arrived at the second floor.

"Oreo!" I heard as I got up and shook myself. "It's time to go!" Anthony called.

I groaned. *Oh, come on!*

"Oreo? Where are you?" said Anthony.

Over here! I barked.

"How are you upstairs?!" Anthony stared up at us. He came up and carried me back down. "Come on, Lucky."

Aww, but I just got up here! I complained.

Clover whimpered and grabbed hold of Anthony's shirt.

Yeah, can we play? I pleaded.

We have to go.

Then, we left.

Stupid human schedule, I mumbled as Anthony put me in the car.

"Don't blame me, Amy's dad wants to get to know me." Anthony explained.

After a short nap, we stopped in front of Amy's house and Anthony got out of the car.

"See you guys later," he said to Lucky, Mom, and me.

"'Bye sweetie!" called Mom.

'Bye, I yawned. *Jeez, I'm tired.*

Marth drove us home. We went inside, and Mom told us she had to go to work.

"I won't be long," Mom shut the garage door.

I yawned again. Lucky yawned too. *Ah, you're contagious,* she said sleepily.

Come on, let's go take a nap, I suggested.

We stumbled onto the couch and fell asleep.

I blinked my eyes open. *Lucky, you awake?* I uncurled myself from around her. She was, but something seemed (smelled) different. Eh, probably just that squirrel.

I think I smell a squirrel outside, I bounded excitedly to the back door. I looked back and was surprised that Lucky hadn't followed me.

What's wrong? I ran back to the couch.

I feel... fragile, Lucky tilted her head.

Fragile? I shook myself. *What does that even mean?*

Oh, it means to feel...

No, I mean, what do you mean you feel "fragile"? I interrupted.

I don't know, but I just feel like I shouldn't... I feel like I should be careful, Lucky said, still not making things clear for me.

Welcome to my life, I quipped, getting nervous and worried. I started chasing my tail.

Honey, relax. I'm sure it's nothing, said Lucky.

The alarm sounded as somebody arrived.

"Oreo!" Anthony's voice called. "I'm home!"

I saw Amy and Sky with him. I barked, and they came over to us.

"Hey, lad. Everything okay?" Amy patted my head. Sky jumped onto the couch and climbed me.

Anthony, Lucky says she feels fragile and like she needs to be careful, I explained frantically.

"What do you mean 'fragile?'" Anthony said.

That's what I said!

"What's wrong?" Amy asked.

"Nothing, but just in case, we should take Lucky to the vet," Anthony grabbed our leashes and clipped them on.

The doctor saw Lucky pretty quickly, much to my relief.

The vet looked up from his computer. "Well, I've got amazing news," he grinned. "She's pregnant."

We all stood frozen for a minute. Except for Sky, who was chasing an ant.

Holy moly, I whispered.

My gosh, Lucky said.

"Blimey," Amy mumbled.

"Bless my heart," Anthony muttered.

Sky spit out the poor ant. *What're we talking about?*

I unfroze myself and jumped onto the bed, bouncing with joy. *I'm going to be a father!* I licked Lucky.

Anthony called the Jacobs' and told them the news. A lot of screaming came from the other end. Once he hung up, he smiled at me and said, "Congrats, bud."

Turns out Lucky had been pregnant for a day.

About a month passed, but the Jacobs' still had not come back.

Weren't they supposed to be back last week? I asked Anthony as we walked to the new nursery with more water for Lucky. Sadly, it had to be upstairs because we didn't have a spare room on my level, so Anthony had to carry me.

"Yeah, I'm going to call them," he said as he put me down on the second floor. Anthony dialed a number. "Amy," he whispered with the phone to his ear. She came out of the nursery and took the water bowl from him. I went into the nursery while Anthony stayed in the hall, talking to the Jacobs'. Amy followed me.

She set down the bowl of water by Lucky's bed, "I do hope they're alright."

"Yeah, me too," Mom petted Lucky's head.

I nuzzled her.

Anthony came in, "Their aunt is sick, so they'll be staying to help out," he explained.

Another week passed… I was getting really excited-nervous. I mean, tackling the dummy twenty times a day, nervous, chasing my tail for twenty minutes excited, and rolling around on the football field at practice… excited-nervous.

The doorbell rang. Sky and I ran to the front door and started barking. Well, I barked down the stairs.

"Coming!" Anthony called, helping me down.

Amy's parents came in. I ran around their legs, Sky behind me.

Amy's dad chuckled, "Well, hullo there, pups."

We went back up to the nursery.

"Lovely day, isn't it?" Amy's mom told Mom.

"Yes," Mom and her hugged.

"Congrats, doggos," Amy's dad said to Lucky and I.

Why, thank you, ol' chap! I said in my best version of his accent.

"Thanks for coming," Anthony told Amy's parents.

"Oh, pish-posh, your place is simply lovely!" Amy's mom said. "Fit for a toff!"

Mom said something in sign language to Anthony. He got a thoughtful look on his face for a minute, and then asked me, *What's a toff?*

Um… I was stumped.

"Where did you get the chandelier?" Amy's mom asked, thankfully changing the subject.

"Uh, Homely Goods," Mom answered.

Upper-class person! I exclaimed quite suddenly. *"Toff" means a rich or upper-class person!*

Anthony translated in sign language.

"Well, I'm glad you think it's classy," Mom said.

"Oh, it's just a fact," said Amy's mom kindly.

I'll ask how you know these kinds of things later, Anthony glanced at me.

"Yes, I love how you decorated," Amy's dad said.

"Why don't you two take Lucky for a walk?" Mom suggested to Amy and Anthony.

"Splendid idea," Amy said, grabbing Lucky's leash. "Sky, Oreo, would you like to come?"

Yeah! Sky shook off a dust bunny and ran to Amy.

Sure, I agreed.

"What happened when my mother said 'toff?'" asked Amy on the walk.

"Um, my mom and I didn't really know what that meant, so my mom asked me in sign language, then I asked Oreo, he knew for some reason, and I translated into sign language for my mom's case," Anthony explained. "Which reminds me," he turned his head toward me, "how *did* you know that?"

No reason, I looked at my paws.

Didn't you tell me you watch the Great British Baking Show? Sky giggled. *You know, that dumb cake-making stuff with British people?*

Do not insult my show! I said sternly. *Also, it's the Great British Baking Show 3.0. The original was ages ago.*

Anthony laughed. "You watch the Great British Baking Show 3.0?" he said, still laughing.

I blushed. *I've been lonely recently.*

Oh, sweetie, it's nothing to be ashamed of, Lucky nose-kissed me.

Amy chortled. "Really?"

I glared at Sky.

When we got back, Amy's parents said it was time to go. After they left, I walked back up to the nursery, with some help from Anthony. I found Lucky asleep. I carefully curled up beside her and followed in her footsteps.

When I woke up, I could hear Anthony and Mom having a heated argument downstairs. I peeked down from the stairs.

"Would you relax?! What's your problem with him?!" Anthony yelled.

"NO! HE CANNOT MOVE TO NASHVILLE!" Mom hollered back.

Oh, no, I thought. *This is about dad.*

"Just stop! He's moving; get over it!" Anthony said furiously.

"CALL HIM RIGHT NOW AND TELL THE TRAITOR TO STAY IN CHICAGO!" Mom screamed.

"He's not a traitor, and you can't force him!" Anthony shouted.

"Well, if he doesn't, tell him that we're moving!" Mom's voice was hoarse.

I stared at her. *What?*

Anthony was at a loss for words. "Fine," he marched off to his room.

Mom saw me staring at her. "Why are you looking at me like that, you filthy animal!" she said, and stomped off to her own room.

I checked whether Lucky was still asleep. Yep. I let out a little yelp. Anthony came back and helped me down. We went to his room, and he sat down at his desk, Anthony was very frustrated. He rested his head on the desk.

Silence.

Well, we both know that she'll do anything to get away from Dad… I spotted Anthony's phone charging on his chest of drawers, *So you should probably tell him,* I handed it to Anthony, trying my best not to slobber all over it.

He silently dialed Dad. I gave him some privacy and went out to the backyard. I had planned to play on the way there, but I ended up sighing, lying down, and staring up at the sky.

The following evening, Lucky and I had just gotten back from a walk. I went out to play.

As I flung my football around the backyard, I imagined police sirens in the background.

Huh? I focused on those sirens. *Wait, that's not my...*

BAM! A gun went off.

I jumped. *Holy smokes!*

I ran inside and barked.

"Oreo, quiet! Get over here!" Anthony was in the safe room with the girls. It was by the front door, for obvious reasons.

I peeked out the super-strong window. *Oh, no, no, no, no, no, no,* I muttered.

Caring, brown eyes, wavy dark brown hair, and the stern face I knew so well. Why did it have to be Fabi?

I strained my ears and heard her say, "Put your hands up!"

The criminal kept his gun up.

"Put your hands up, NOW!" Fabi repeated.

"Well, I kind of like what I stole," the man said in a harsh, scratchy voice.

"IN THE NAME OF THE LAW, PUT YOUR HANDS UP," Fabi said louder.

"Fine, fine," the criminal put his gun down on the floor and put his hands up.

I sniffed hard but didn't recognize him. Then, my heart stopped as I realized his sleeve was bulging slightly.

A back-up gun.

I looked at Fabi. She didn't know. Neither did the other policemen and women.

I ran out of the safe room.

"Oreo!" Anthony said. "What're you doing?!"

He has a gun in his sleeve! I barged out through the doggy-door.

"On your knees," Fabi commanded. "Khan Roberts, you're under arrest." My eyes widened. *Khan Roberts?!? He's more dangerous than the definition of dangerous! Especially to... Why am I telling myself this? Of course, he's in our neighborhood.*

The criminal got down on his knees, "Now, don't be mean! I was gonna settle down after this," I could see him reaching for his gun. By then, I was very close to them.

In a panic, I barked to distract him. Roberts looked at me, and I immediately sprinted and pounced on him. The gun slipped out of his sleeve. I kicked it away.

"Oreo?" Fabi said, startled. She ran over and handcuffed Roberts.

I climbed off of him, *Hey, Mexigirl,* I had given her that nickname when she told me that she was born in Mexico City. Some officers took Khan Roberts away. I licked Fabi.

"Oreo!" Fabi hugged me, "Good boy, Lieutenant Trouble," she smiled and stood up. That was her nickname for me after we watched this really old movie, "Captain Marvel."

"Fabi!" Anthony ran over and hugged her. Mom was behind him. Lucky had stayed by the door.

"Hey, cuz!" Fabi said, "Aunt Holly!" she hugged Mom.

"How you doin'?" Mom asked.

"Pretty good, actually," Fabi grinned dreamily, "I met this boy Alex, and now I have a boyfriend."

I gagged.

You're gonna be a father, Anthony raised his eyebrows at me.

That is very different! I protested. *Humans aren't discreet about their… relationships.*

Good point, Anthony scrunched up his face.

"Is he 'the one?'" Mom said.

"I think so," Fabi said, though she didn't sound sure.

I licked her hand. *Be confident, Mexigirl.*

She patted my head.

"Officer Fabiana!" a cop called.

"I should probably go," Fabi knelt down and kissed my forehead. "See you guys," she said, jogging toward a police cruiser.

Mom, Anthony, and I went back inside. I made sure she was settled and set off to find Anthony.

I walked into his room and sighed.

"How could she?" he muttered to himself. "She could just *avoid* him."

I was hoping you wouldn't remember.

"Why wouldn't I remember?" Anthony scowled.

Khan Roberts just tried to rob our neighbors, I reminded him.

"Mom *forced* Dad not to move!" Anthony said.

I gave him some time to calm down and then said, *You know, I've been thinking…* I paused. *You could tell Dad that Mom changed her mind, and that he can move.*

Anthony's eyes beamed for a second, but then his shoulders slumped. "She'd find out," he said sadly.

Not if you tell Dad once he moves in that Mom actually didn't *change her mind,* I finished.

"It's not a bad idea, but, like I said, she'd eventually find out," Anthony said.

By that time, she would have to admit that he isn't a troublemaker or whatever, I said.

"She's stubborn," Anthony said.

Do you want Dad back or not?! I was getting really annoyed with Anthony's negativity. I took a deep breath. *She isn't nearly so stubborn as Kate, thankfully, so I think we'll be fine.*

Anthony stared into space for a moment before calling Dad on his phone.

I smiled and went back to the nursery. Lucky saw me come in. *Why are you smiling?* she asked, tilting her head.

Nothing, I lay down next to her, still smiling.

Two months passed and, finally, the time came.

They took Lucky away into a special room. I was very angry when they slammed the door right in my face. I scratched at it.

Excuse me! I'm the father! I thought.

I heard a bark and turned around. Clover was hobbling over. I looked down and saw that her paw was bandaged. I continued scratching the door. Anthony was talking to somebody, probably Kate, but I kept my focus on the door.

I whimpered. *Come on…!* I scratched the door again.

A few minutes later, a vet finally opened the door. "Does the father want to…?"

I didn't let him finish. I barged through the door, startling the vet as I searched for Lucky. She was on a much bigger table this time. It also had cloth draped over it. But where were…

"Over here, pal," the vet said gently, gesturing toward his colleagues. Their backs were to me. Then, I heard whines from in front of them. I walked over.

Hello there, I whispered in awe. On another table were seven puppies, all bundled together. The vets were picking them up one by one, checking them for any defects.

The vet that had opened the door grinned at me. "Your pups are the healthiest batch we've ever seen."

I let out an anxious breath. I had been really confident about their health, because Mom, Anthony, Lucky, and me had been praying to God day and night for it, but, well, I'm a parent. You still get anxious.

The vets carried the pups to Lucky's table. I followed and jumped very carefully onto it. Lucky and I started licking them as gently as possible.

Three were pure Pit bulls, another three were pure Bernese Mountain. There was only one that was a mix. I stared at her. I felt like I knew her very well. And not just because I was her father. They all had their eyes shut tight.

"Mrs. Cane?" the vet called. Mom and Anthony came in.

I didn't pay much attention. I realized that one of the puppies, a pure Bernese Mountain, seemed to be keeping her distance. She was curled into a tight ball.

I licked her reassuringly. *It's OK.*

She slowly uncurled and allowed herself to be placed in the pile of puppies.

I studied the rest. *Four girls, and three boys,* I said to myself.

The third one, a boy, seemed to be studying his surroundings, even though he couldn't see.

Another, a girl, kept yelping for more cleansing licks. One of her sisters was flailing her paws in the air.

I chuckled and licked the energetic one. *Calm down.*

The other two boys were pretty calm, snuggled against each other.

Suddenly, all of the pups started letting out little yelps and whines of hunger.

Lucky looked at me. *Feeding time.*

I nodded in understanding and jumped down.

Mom, Anthony, and the vet were talking about the care the puppies needed.

"They'll drink milk from their mother for about four weeks," the vet was explaining. "They should open their eyes in a couple of weeks. If they don't, bring them over right away," he told us.

"So, we start feeding them in four weeks," Anthony repeated, typing it down on his phone.

"Yep. I'll send y'all a video of the mixture," the vet confirmed.

Mom nodded. "Thank you."

After some more talk, the vet gave a very small kennel with the pups inside to Anthony.

After talking for a little while longer, we finally went home.

A young woman was waiting for us at the door. I assumed this was the nurse Mom and the vet had discussed. She had a white coat, lush, black hair, and seemed pretty friendly.

"Hello, Mrs. Cane," she said.

"Long time no see, Eileen," Mom and Eileen hugged.

"This is my son, Anthony," Mom gestured to Anthony.

"Hi," he said.

Hmm, I sniffed Eileen's hand, checking to see if she was trustworthy. She smelled of biscuits and muffins. *Yeah, you're good,* I smiled and licked her hand.

"I'll assume you're Oreo," Eileen knelt down and shook my paw. "Nice to meet you."

Oh, you're very *good,* I licked her chin.

Hello, Lucky sat in front of Eileen.

"And you must be Lucky," Eileen did the same to her. Lucky nuzzled her in approval. "Congratulations," Eileen said to both of us, standing up.

Thank you, Lucky and I said at the same time.

We all went inside and into the nursery. Lucky settled on the bed, and Anthony and I took the pups out of the kennel, carefully placing them in Lucky's care. As we did this, Eileen examined the pups, moving their limbs gently this-way-and-that and then handing them to Lucky.

After Eileen said that they were absolutely fine, Anthony and I went outside to practice.

When's our next game? I asked, picking up a football.

"Two days from now," Anthony answered, grabbing it from my mouth. "Go long."

I ran backwards as far as I could. He threw it, and I caught it in mid-air.

We practiced for two hours (with breaks, of course).

I decided to check on Lucky and the pups.

They were being supervised by Eileen. She turned around as I came in and gestured for me to be quiet.

I looked over at the puppies. They were sound asleep, as was Lucky.

"You have an amazing litter," Eileen whispered. "Seven perfectly healthy puppies," she stroked my fur.

Yeah, I thought.

When I got to Anthony's room, he was asleep too. I walked to my bed and lay down.

As I drifted into sleep, I thought about how lucky I was to have such a good relationship with God.

Thank you, I prayed, knowing He would hear me.

Chapter 16

· ·

Sweet Nashville

Anthony shook me awake.

As soon as we all ate breakfast and got dressed, we started to pack up. The Jacobs arrived early to pick up the puppies and Lucky. I licked Lucky and the pups goodbye. They left.

At last, we got everything together, and Marth drove us to the airport, where the team was waiting for us. Everybody cheered when they saw us.

"Congrats, Oreo!" Joseph patted me.

The whole team congratulated me.

"Congratulations," said a familiar voice.

Amy and Sky! I exclaimed, pushing past the team. Anthony followed.

"Hey," Anthony said. The couple hugged.

Sky had obviously had a haircut. She tried to tackle me. Sky had grown but, thankfully, I was still stronger.

"Come on, team, let's get a move on," Coach Kim said.

We all waited in the private airplane's waiting room for the cheerleaders to arrive. It was small, so a lot of the team had to sit on the floor.

Once the cheerleaders got there, we took our seats on the plane. I sat with Sky. We watched the Zoology Channel. I glanced over at Anthony (who was on the other side of the aisle) during a commercial break. He was watching a football program, with Amy's head on his shoulder.

After close to a two-hour flight, we came to Miami, Florida. Marth drove us in a rented limo to a hotel near Miami Gardens, which is where the Hard Rock Stadium is. After a few hours and a very nice lunch, we drove to the stadium.

Woah, I thought when we entered.

The team started running around, and I was going to go with them, but Anthony stopped me.

He knelt down, "The vet said that you should get a different leg for football," Anthony said, "'Because you could get hurt."

Uh, okay, I said.

Anthony explained how I could practice for half an hour and then we would go to the local vet, "I'll go tell Coach," he finished.

At the vet, I got to try on a sick sports leg. I even got to customize it with our school colors! I also tried a waterproof one. Both fit perfectly after the fourth try.

We drove to the beach to test out my waterproof leg. And to have some fun, of course. We had brought Amy, Sky, and Mom along.

The water was the absolute perfect temperature. It was Sky's first time swimming in the ocean (Amy has a pool), so Amy had to tell her not to drink the water. I, on the other hand, had once gone for a swim with Fabi and… *gulp* and Cookie.

Sky suddenly shrieked in surprise. *What's on my leg?!*

THE ADVENTURES OF OREO

I peered behind me. A piece of seaweed was clinging onto her leg as she tried to shake it off.

Oh, it's just seaweed, I took it off with my teeth because Amy and Anthony were playing with a beach ball farther into the ocean.

Oh... Sky watched the seaweed drift to the ocean floor. *Cool.*

After we had chased a school of fish, Sky and I agreed to get out. I shook the salt off my fur.

I saw another dog running to the water and immediately recognized Clover. She was kind of far away. I could see that she still had a waterproof bandage wrapped around her paw.

"Oreo! Come on!" Anthony called from the water.

I realized that Kate was there, squinting at me. I barked and ran/swam over to them.

"Oreo!" Kate laughed when I got to them. "Hey buddy," Kate patted me.

I swam back to Anthony, Amy, and Sky.

Kate's here! I told Anthony.

"Nice," Anthony said.

"Huh?" Amy asked.

"Kate's here," Anthony nodded toward them.

We ran over. Kate, Clover, and Storm got out of the water.

"Hey," Kate said.

"Hi," Anthony and Amy said in unison.

Silence. *Awkwaaard,* I thought.

It's not awkward, Anthony hissed back.

"Well, this is awkward..." said Kate.

Told you so.

"Um, who's the Collie?" Amy pointed at Storm.

"Huh? Oh! That's Storm," Kate replied, picking her up.

"So..." Anthony said.

I glanced at Clover. *You wanna get out of here?*

Heck yeah! Clover answered. She nodded at Storm. We sprinted to the water.

"Clover! Get over here!" Kate yelled. Clover stayed in the water. "Oh, whatever."

Yet *another* dog was swimming towards a ball.

Clover flew after it for some reason. She was close, but the dog grabbed it. Clover growled.

I swam over to see what the trouble was. *Isn't it his?* I asked Clover. She didn't seem to hear me. She was staring at the ball.

The dog ignored her and started swimming back to his owner.

As soon as I saw one of Clover's famous looks, one I called "the lockdown look," I knew he had made a mistake. *Oh, no.*

Clover tried her best to intercept him, but her paw was weak.

"Clover, come back!" Kate was serious this time. Storm swam back to her.

"Oreo, stop her!" Anthony said.

I spun around and realized that Clover was already pretty far away for someone with a hurt paw.

Clover, stop! I swam to her as fast as I could. I was almost in front of her, but a massive wave hit me. It must have crashed over Clover and the other dog as well.

I quickly regained my senses, spitting out sea water. I managed to open my eyes a tiny bit under the water. I found out that it was much easier to do this in a pool. I saw Clover gasping in air, but I couldn't spot the stranger.

Hold on, Clover, I swam to her. Once I was close enough, I grabbed her collar and hauled her to shore.

Anthony, Kate, Amy, and Sky were waiting anxiously close by. They all helped me drag Clover onto the sand. I shook myself.

"Clover!" Kate cried out.

I turned around. Clover's injured paw was bleeding. She whimpered.

I frantically looked around and eventually saw some bottles of water. I picked one up and brought it over to Kate.

"Just relax, Clover," Kate reassured her. "You'll be fine," she sprinkled water onto her paw.

Thankfully, the other dog was very strong and was able to swim to shore. His owners were hugging him and looking our way.

Clover let out another whimper.

"Come on, we should get her to the vet," Anthony said.

Kate and Mom quickly greeted each other.

"I can take Oreo and Sky back to the hotel," Kate suggested.

"That would be great," Mom said.

Sky, Kate, Clover, Storm, and I walked to their truck.

"Load up," Kate opened the tailgate.

Storm jumped up, followed very gingerly by Clover. Kate helped her up. Sky also jumped up, but I was stuck on the floor with my leg. Kate lifted me up, and I lay down. All the swimming and football practice beforehand had tired me out.

Soon enough, we got to the hotel. Kate opened the tailgate, and everybody piled out, except me.

"Here boy," Kate lifted me down.

Anthony, Amy, and Mom got out of our car.

"I've got to go to practice. 'Cause, you know, game tomorrow," Anthony said, taking my leash.

"Now that you mention it, so do I," Amy said. She took Sky's leash.

"Okay, we'll be at my friend's ranch. If you need anything, my phone is always on," Kate said.

"Okay, 'bye," Anthony said. We walked away.

We got to the stadium, where the team was still practicing. They'd probably taken a break, though. Anthony replaced my waterproof leg with my sports one.

It was almost three o'clock, not a good time to practice when you're in Miami.

While we were doing my favorite drill, Anthony and I saw Joseph staring at something I couldn't see from my angle.

We jogged over.

"W'sup, bro?" Anthony said.

OREO! A dog screamed at me. I turned around and saw Clover. I spun back to Joseph.

What are you looking at? Clover called.

Love scene with Joseph… I think, I replied.

"Oh, uh, nothing," Joseph told Anthony, still staring.

I looked where he was staring and started laughing. *Anthony, he's looking at the cheerleaders!*

"Are you checking out the cheerleaders?" Tami asked.

"Hypocrite!" Anthony and I said in unison.

"No, I'm not!" Joseph whirred around.

"Joseph likes a cheerleader!" Tami teased.

A few more boys started gathering around us and chuckling.

"Boys!" Coach Kim yelled. "Stop dilly-dallying and start practice!"

Everybody scattered.

"Well, who do you like?" Anthony asked, a grin quickly spreading across his face.

Joseph groaned, "Lily Ramos."

"Hm, solid pick," Anthony said. "Your turn, my friend," he escorted Joseph over to the lucky girl.

Lily had purple glasses, hazel eyes, and wavy, black hair.

Anthony kept his distance but asked me to spy on them.

No problem, I crawled over to them ninja-style.

They had had an awkward exchange of greetings, and now Lily was walking away. I saw no sign of a phone number in Joseph's hand.

Well, guess what? Kate's not here this time! I shoved Joseph into her.

"Are you okay?" Lily asked.

"Um…" Joseph cleared his throat, "Yeah, sorry, my friend's dog pushed me," he mumbled, staring angrily at me.

Lily smiled at Joseph and knelt down to look at me. "Hello there," she scratched me behind my ears. "You're Oreo, right?"

"Yeah," Joseph answered for me.

Lily stood up, and her hand brushed Joseph's. She blushed.

Joseph smiled awkwardly, "Do you maybe, wanna, maybe… hang out sometime?" he spluttered.

"Sure," Lily said. They successfully exchanged numbers.

"Lily!" somebody called again.

Lily and Joseph waved at each other as she went back to practice.

Joseph and I walked back to Anthony.

"How'd it go?" Anthony asked.

"I think we just agreed on a date," Joseph whispered.

Anthony glanced at me for confirmation.

Definitely, I agreed.

"Congra…" Anthony started.

"BOYS! FOR THE LAST TIME, GET TO WORK!" Coach Kim screamed at us.

We continued practicing until five o'clock. We were packing up when Amy ran down from the bleachers and gave Anthony a big hug.

"Woah, everything okay?" Anthony asked.

"Are you only dating me because you know I'm a bloody orphan?" Amy asked in a small voice, letting Anthony go.

"Amelia Mullins," Anthony looked skeptical, "It makes no sense for you to ask that; I fell for you before I even knew that you were adopted!" he hugged her again.

And this boy right here isn't that type of guy, which is probably one of the reasons you fell for him, I said.

Anthony translated.

"Thank you," Amy scratched me behind my ears.

Yeah, yeah, anything for you… I thought in satisfaction.

Anthony smirked and mocked me for Amy's sake before saying, "More like, 'Anything for a good scratch'.'."

Amy giggled.

"Anthony!" Joseph ran over, "Your mom said you have to go. Oh, hey, Amy."

"Hullo," Amy said.

"Be there in a sec," Anthony said. Joseph jogged away. "You do understand I like you, right?" Anthony told Amy.

"Now I do," Amy kissed his cheek.

Anthony blushed.

At that moment, I realized what was about to happen. I had watched plenty of romantic movies with Mom, so as soon as I saw the famous look, I ran over to the car. Thankfully, they were the only people in the parking lot, and the stadium was empty.

I glanced back and smiled, *Congrats, Anthony. You just accomplished your "First Kiss."*

Dinner was delicious.

We were all tired, so we promptly collapsed onto our beds. I was in a room with Mom and Anthony.

The next morning, we woke up, got dressed, and ate breakfast. It was as good as lunch and dinner.

We headed to the stadium. This game was a special one for two reasons:

1. Archbishop McCarthy was the only school in the league that wasn't in Tennessee. Instead, they were in Cooper City.
2. They were also the only private school in the league.

"OK boys, let's warm-up!" Coach Kim called.

I saw the Mavericks (Archbishop) enter the stadium right as he said this.

We stretched and then did the usual pre-game drills.

After a while, the head referee called for the team captains. There were two for each team, and Coach had decided to make me the second.

"Bobcats, heads or tails?" the ref asked in a gruff voice.

I wagged my tail at Anthony. *Tails.*

"Tails," Anthony said.

Luckily, it landed tails.

"Ball or side?" the ref said.

"Ball."

Our starting eleven were Anthony, Joseph, me, Kaleb, Jamal, Kevin, Calvin, Zack, Joshua, Finn, and Matthew.

Kaleb was still taking it a bit easy, so I was up for the starting play. I got in position and stared at the dude way over on the other side of the field. The referee blew his whistle, and the dude kicked the ball.

I caught it and started sprinting. I could hear the thunder of feet as the Mavericks tried to catch me. I got to the forty-yard line before somebody took me down.

"HIKE!" Anthony yelled.

We were doing the Wide Receiver play. I looked around quickly to search for open spots and realized that the Mavericks were focusing on me. I peered over at Kaleb and realized he was in the same situation.

THEY KNOW ABOUT OUR PLAY! I hollered at Anthony.

In a blur, Anthony handed it off to Joseph, and Joseph started running.

Sike! No, he didn't! The Mavericks thought this, though, probably because they realized in a panic that they'd got our play wrong.

I barked at Anthony and started running backward, towards the end line. The Mavericks were already starting to realize what was going on. Anthony passed it to me. The cornerback on my side of the field made the mistake of leaping to tackle me. I only had to duck my head low to dodge the move. From there, I only had one more guy to beat. He looked bulky, though. Make that two. Both of the safeties had their eyes on me. I started looking around for a way out, but I couldn't see any.

"He needs help!" Zack called.

Jamal was the offensive tackle on my side of the field, so he started sprinting to help. But I knew that they were too close by now for him to get there in time.

I dug deep into my memory, looking for advice that might help me. Instead, I found a joke.

"You know, if you ever got cornered by criminals, you wouldn't have any trouble getting past them," Fabi said.

I tilted my head in confusion. What do you mean?

"All you'd have to do is be cute, and that would distract them."

Here, like this, Cookie said. I turned to look at her. She tucked in her ears, beamed at Fabi, and tilted her head.

Fabi stared at her, and Cookie jumped on her. Fabi laughed. "Yup, just like that," she glanced at me, "I'm not saying you should actually do it in a dangerous situation, but you know how it is."

I barked and jumped on her as well. Fabi giggled.

Of course, this all went through my mind very quickly. I knew it was the only way out and set my plan in motion.

I tucked in my ears, beamed at the safeties, and tilted my head.

They didn't stop, but they sure did slow down. I heard the crowd go "Aww!" I had them *all* hypnotized.

I swerved around them and calmly scored the touchdown. The head referee blew his whistle, but it didn't go on the scoreboard. The referees were conferring with one another.

Coach Kim called a quick huddle and fixed his eyes on me once I had arrived. The whole team was looking at me.

What? I improv...

"What did we say about improvising?!" Coach Kim lectured me. "That was *not* necessary! You could've at least *tried* to hold them off until Jamal got there! And if not, we could've just gone to second down!" Coach Kim looked down at me, rage etched all over his face.

I sat down, looked at my paws, and let my tail droop in shame. *Sorry, Coach,* I looked up at him, with an expression that conveyed my sadness and shame.

Coach Kim frowned. "Now, don't give me that face."

I stared at my paws.

Coach knelt down, and I was forced to look at him. "I'm sorry, boy. But you don't always have to do it on first down," he stroked my fur.

Yes, sir.

The referee blew his whistle, and six points appeared on the board under "Away."

Everybody cheered.

Next came the extra point. Finn went up to the ball, which was already positioned. We all got in our own positions and waited for the whistle.

Finn successfully scored the point, and it was their ball. I was cornerback on defense, so I got into position.

"Code Blue! Code Blue! Hike!" their quarterback called.

Everything happened quickly. Our team was always in sync, so it was easy to know where to go.

The quarterback handed it off to the center, and he ran. In no time at all, Jamal had tackled him, and we were calmly helping him up.

That was basically how the whole game went. Coach Kim put the substitutes in, and Coach Beck tweaked our defense to make it even better. Once the subs got tired, Coach Kim put Anthony and me in while putting the guys who usually don't get to play in the game (actually, that's not true. They get to play every game because the OP starters keep the score steady. Our substitutes just aren't the best on the team.)

At half-time, Joseph gestured to an older man with wrinkles on his face, neatly combed black hair and an orange shirt. I saw that it had a "UM" symbol on it.

I could feel Anthony's stomach clenching from my water bowl. I trotted over. *Who's the dude?*

"He's not just a dude," Anthony's voice was trembling in awe. "He's the University of Miami football coach, Manny Dominguez."

My eyes widened and I got a bit nauseous. *Oh...* I gulped. *I see.*

"Now the pressure's really on," Joseph whispered.

Don't say that, you pinhead! I pushed him into the grass. *It'll be fine,* I turned to Anthony. *Just play the way you usually do.*

Anthony kept looking over at Mr. Dominguez.

"Cane, Oreo, Joseph! Get over here!" Coach Conn, our offensive coach, barked. He gestured to us. The team was huddled around him.

We scurried over to him.

It was our ball. The score was 21-9. We were winning. After the first down, we were at the twenty-yard line. I could see Anthony nervously glancing toward Mr. Dominguez.

An apple a day keeps the doctor away, if you hit him with it hard enough, I told him, in an attempt to make him focus.

He chuckled in his head. "Leap Day! Leap Day! Hike!" he grunted aloud.

Leap Day, of course, is the quarterback's time to shine. Kaleb and I pushed the safeties to the sides, and the rest of the team did this with the other players. But, even so, Anthony still had to make the effort of scoring a touchdown.

He spun, feinted, and sprinted to the end line. Finally, he spiked the football, and we'd scored.

Kaleb and I let go of the safeties and cheered. The rest of the team followed suit, patting and congratulating Anthony.

Luke, one of the substitutes, successfully scored the extra point. We won 28-15.

Anthony was tapping his foot nervously after Coach Kim's after-game speech at the bench. He was obviously waiting for Mr. Dominguez to come over. I might've gotten a bit nervous too.

Then, we saw him walk over to Coach Kim.

"Anthony and Joseph, could you come over here?" he called.

We walked over.

"You guys have talent. I would love it if you…" Mr. Dominguez stopped talking as he looked at me. "Who's the dog?"

I fidgeted. Gosh, he doesn't even know who I am.

"Um, that's Oreo," Anthony said. "He plays too."

Mr. Dominguez looked shocked. "I thought I was hallucinating."

I tilted my head. *You weren't.*

"Well, he plays really well," Coach Kim said. "In fact, we could show you some drills. I-if you want," he finished nervously.

"That would be fantastic," Mr. Dominguez said.

I gulped. *Right then.*

Coach Kim nodded. "Joseph and Anthony, you're on the opposite team. Let's do the starting play."

I ran to the left side of the field. Joseph and Anthony ran to the right.

I took a deep breath and found a memory to encourage me.

What are you doing? I asked as Anthony let go of my leash and walked to one of the pillars. I fidgeted with my leg, forced to keep standing because I didn't know how to sit down yet, if I ever learned.

"We've all been a bit down, so I want to show you that anything's possible," *Anthony seemed to be hugging the pillar now.*

All at once, he was shimmying up it. I whimpered quietly and slowly walked around the pillar, startled.

Suddenly, Mom came in. "Anthony!" *she exclaimed, jogging to the pillar.* "Get down from there!" *Mom stared at me.* "Did this stupid animal encourage your ridiculous behavior?!"

I whimpered and scurried away from her, looking down at my paws.

"No, no!" *Anthony practically jumped to the floor.* "I was just… having fun," *he said since Mom would get even madder if he told the truth.*

She made as if to kick me, and then walked to her room.

Anthony knelt down and stroked my fur. "Sorry, boy. The point is, you can do anything with no legs."

I licked him. I understood.

And with that, we went on getting me used to my prosthetic leg. I promised myself that I'd always remember his amazing advice.

I returned to the present. More focused now than ever.

Anthony kicked the ball, and it went flying toward me.

I calculated almost perfectly and caught it. I started sprinting to the end line. Anthony and Joseph were in my way. I looked for a gap, but they basically had everything covered.

I did a spin move to get past Joseph, but I knew he'd be back soon, and Anthony was still in front of me.

I jinked past Anthony, but Joseph was right behind me. I stopped abruptly, knowing he would leap at me. He tripped over me and

I sprinted ahead. I dropped the ball at the end line and glanced behind me. Anthony was helping Joseph up.

We trotted back to the coaches. Mr. Dominguez nodded approvingly, smiling and writing on his clipboard. "Amazing."

I sat down, grinning in my head.

"We'd be happy to take all of you," Mr. Dominguez produced two shirts that read "Miami Hurricanes" from out of nowhere and gave them to Anthony and Joseph. He glanced at me. "We'll have one for you at the start of the season. All of you get a one-year scholarship," he finished.

"Thank you, Mr. Dominguez," being best friends, Joseph and Anthony sometimes said things in unison.

"Hm, call me *Coach* Dominguez," Coach Dominguez shook their hands (and my paw).

When we got to the car, Anthony revealed his shirt and grinned.

Mom squealed; I barked and licked her chin.

"Oh, yeah, and Oreo, too," Anthony said.

We had lunch at Chick-Fil-A. Then we headed back to the hotel, where Anthony and I took a nap.

I woke up in time to see everybody packing up again. In no time, the whole team was back on the jet. We landed and went straight home.

I entered Anthony's room and found him on the phone with somebody.

"Sure… You okay…? Call me if you need anything… Okay… Blessings… Love you too… 'Bye," he hung up. "Mr. Mullins is in the hospital, so we'll be taking care of Sky," Anthony explained.

By now, I had guessed it was Amy. *Okay, but is he okay?*

"Yeah, he's just getting surgery on his back. They should be back home in a month or so," Anthony told me.

'Kay, cool.

We went to pick up Sky while Mom caught up with work. Sky is fun to be around, but she gets up to some crazy stuff. For example: She chews on cables, chases lizards, and barks at butterflies or any other animal that crosses her path (not that I blame her for that).

About an hour or so after we picked her up, Jackson came over with Lucky. After greeting them, Sky stayed in the backyard chasing around after random animals.

"How'd you do?" Jackson asked on the fourth-floor balcony. (Anthony had to carry me up.)

Lucky and I licked each other a lot, and then Lucky started asking me questions about my adventures.

"We won 28-15. And guess what?" Anthony smiled.

"What?" Jackson urged.

"Joseph, Oreo, and I got invited to UM!" Anthony said excitedly.

Jackson's jaw dropped. "Dude! That's awesome!"

"Yeah! And I have an aunt in Miami, so…" Anthony's voice trailed off.

"What's wrong?" Jackson said.

Anthony bit his lip. "Living in Miami…" he sighed. "I just realized that I'll probably never see any of this again," he gazed out from the balcony.

I'd been so busy answering questions that I hadn't looked out at the incredible view in front of us. The balcony overlooked all of North Nashville, a beautiful sight. The horizon made it especially magical.

"Well, your only options in Nashville are to follow in your mom's footsteps or learn agriculture," Jackson pointed out. "And we both know that you don't like the idea of doing what your mom does, and agriculture these days is just telling robots what to do."

I was still taking in what Anthony had said. He didn't just mean the spectacular view, he meant Nashville, and all the amazing people he knew there.

I glanced at Lucky. *What if I don't get to see you and the pups again?*

You'll visit us, Lucky said.

Yeah, but what if I'm so caught up in football that I can't visit? I started panicking a little.

Lucky had no answer. She started licking her nuzzle nervously.

I don't want to leave! I shouted at Anthony, jumping up.

He frowned at me.

"What'd he say?" Jackson asked.

"He doesn't want to move because he thinks he won't be able to make time to visit," Anthony's heart sank.

"Oh."

We all sat in silence for a few minutes.

"Hey, didn't you say you moved here from Miami?" Anthony said.

"South Florida," Jackson corrected.

"Yeah, whatever," Anthony said. "Why did you move?"

Jackson thought back to a very long time ago. "My dad had a great opportunity to preach here for a year, so we all came with him. The original plan was to move back once he was done, but by the time he finished, Aiden and I had already started school, and my mom said we should finish. The next year, my mom also got invited to preach, and we stayed again," Jackson paused. "Huh. Now that I think about it, we should've gone back after that. I guess we all kind of forgot…" he frowned. "I was really looking forward to going back."

"So, you like it better there?" Anthony beamed.

"Yeah…"

"What about your family?"

"Aiden still keeps all his stuff from there, and mom and dad loved the church, so yeah," Jackson said.

"Are you thinking what I'm thinking?" Anthony was practically bouncing up and down with excitement.

"Are you... hungry?" Jackson guessed after a few seconds.

Anthony nodded toward him and raised his eyebrows.

Jackson's face lit up with realization. "Oh! I think I am!"

YES! Lucky and I yelled at the same time.

Jackson managed to get into UM, along with Amy. Later, we found out Kaleb was going, too. The Bobcats won the championship and passed into school legend. Anthony's graduation ceremony was amazing, Amy's dad was perfectly fine, and the aunt in Miami agreed to let us stay with her. Anthony and Amy walked to a Starbucks every once in a while, they were a great couple. And Sky grew big enough to tackle me. (Just to be clear, that's not a hypothetical. We were walking to a Starbucks and she tackled me from out of nowhere.) I soaked up as much of Nashville as I could, knowing I would miss that wonderful place.

Chapter 17

·····················

It's Very, Very Hot in Miami

On our last day in Nashville, I found Anthony dialing Dad's number in his room after I had finished breakfast.

"We're leaving today… Um, I need to tell you something…" Anthony glanced at me. "I lied about Mom not minding… I just really wanted to see you… Yeah, she probably will… Bu..." I assumed that Dad had cut him off. "Okay…" Anthony's shoulders slumped, and for some reason, I sensed anger in him. "Yeah, fine… 'Bye," he hung up.

"Everything okay?" Mom peeked in.

Anthony forced a smile. "Um, yeah. Just… settling some things with…" he hesitated.

Amy, I suggested.

"Amy!" Anthony said a bit too loudly.

"Okay…" Mom walked in and looked around. All the cupboards and shelves were bare, the walls blank.

Anthony wrapped an arm around Mom. I saw silent tears trail down her cheeks.

Anthony sighed and kissed her forehead. "We should get going."

We walked out to Anthony's car. Mom and Marth waved at us as we drove away. I fell asleep on our way to the airport. Mom very kindly let us take the private jet.

"We're gonna stay at Aunt Sonia's until we get used to Miami… and South Florida," Anthony said, probably remembering what Jackson had said on the balcony.

Who's Aunt Sonia? I asked, peeling my eyes from an intense NBA game. Bulls vs. Clippers. They were bitter rivals.

"Fabi's mom. Her stepdad lives there too," Anthony gestured toward the game. "In fact, she's Emil's mother."

My eyes widened in shock. *Number 21?!*

"Yep."

I grinned. *Oh, yes.*

We slept on each other half the way.

We landed at Fort Lauderdale Airport, because it was close to Aunt Sonia's. Anthony called an Uber to pick us up.

Aunt Sonia's house was average-sized, with a tan exterior and a clay-colored roof. The driveway was pretty small, with a basketball hoop on the grass beside it. The garage doors were brown, one big, and one small. There was a walkway to the right that led to the front door. There were several plants lining the walkway and pillars in front of the front door. Aunt Sonia and Eric (Fabi's stepdad) had put up Christmas decorations.

Anthony rang the doorbell. Aunt Sonia opened the door. She looked remarkably like Fabi, just older.

"Anthony!" she hugged him.

"Hey, aunt!" Anthony said.

"Come in, come in," Aunt Sonia moved aside.

Once we were inside, we found the dining room to our left and to our right a table with a pair of lamps and assorted paraphernalia. Stretched out before us was a fancy living room with a piano but no TV and three large windows that looked out onto a backyard. Outside, underneath an awning were a pair of tables with seats and a pool. One of the tables was covered. Beyond that was a lawn and a lake. A mirror hung by the kitchen and behind that was a breakfast table and another living room which did have a TV. I could also see a Christmas tree with lights blinking in the living room. I went on down another hallway to my right where I found two bedrooms and a bathroom were to the side. One bedroom probably belonged to Fabi, the other to Aunt Sonia and Eric.

I ran back to Anthony and Aunt Sonia, who had gone into the kitchen.

"Anthony, this is my husband, Eric," Aunt Sonia introduced a man who was getting up from the couch. Eric was Asian and had incredible eyes.

Anthony and Eric shook hands. He leaned down and ruffled my fur. I put my paw on his hand.

"Follow me," Aunt Sonia said.

She led us to another hallway and opened a door to a bedroom.

"You can stay in Emil's old room," Aunt Sonia nodded at it. Emil, of course, was Mr. Salgado.

A Star Wars bed stood in the middle. There was a desk, a closet with a sliding, glass door, and a couch in the corner by the window.

"We'll have dinner soon, so I'll leave you to get settled," Aunt Sonia said.

"Thanks," Anthony told her.

"Call me if you need anything," and with that, Aunt Sonia left.

I walked into the room and looked at Anthony. *I miss everybody already.*

"Yeah, me too," Anthony said. We both jumped onto the bed.

While Anthony unpacked, I checked out our hallway. There was a restroom with two sinks, a toilet, and a bathtub/shower. A laundry room was to our right, and I assumed it led to the garage. There was also a closet beside that, and in front of the closet was another bedroom with clothes everywhere.

"Boys, dinner!" I heard Aunt Sonia call a few minutes into my explorations.

I sprinted to the kitchen, sliding everywhere. Oh, was I hungry! I could smell the mixture that Fabi used to make us, so she probably got it from Aunt Sonia.

I started wolfing down my food, but I stopped mid-bite.

What is that smell? I thought, sniffing the food tray. *Female... Small... Canine... Bichon,* I gasped and stumbled away from my food, banging into several cupboards behind me.

"Whoa, you okay?" Anthony helped me up.

I stood there, shaking. *Bichon Frise-Shih-Tzu mix...*

Anthony's shoulders slumped. "Oh."

"Are you doing the physic-connection thing?" Eric asked.

"Yeah," Anthony breathed. "Um, *tia?*" he turned to Aunt Sonia. "Did Cookie eat from that tray?"

Aunt Sonia froze and sniffled. "Y-Yes," she stammered.

I looked around and immediately felt guilty. I had made everybody sad, and it was just a stupid tray.

Anthony and Eric gave Aunt Sonia a hug. I ran away, too embarrassed to eat. I jumped onto our bed and scolded myself. Then, I felt sad. Actually, I felt like I was being stabbed in the gut with daggers of sadness.

I sighed and slumped into a memory.

Cookie coughed in the middle of another one of Fabi's "original" movies.

You okay? I asked, worried.

Cookie cleared her throat and smiled. Yes, I'm just fine.

I frowned. Cookie, maybe you should tell Fabi to take you to the vet.

Now, Cookie didn't have a physic-connection, but there were ways for her to make herself understood.

No, really, I'm fine, Cookie argued. Suddenly, she coughed louder, loud enough for Fabi to hear.

"You OK, Cook?" Fabi glanced at Cookie and her eyebrows furrowed with worry.

I don't know, maybe you should...

I'm fine! Cookie interrupted me. She barked and licked Fabi's chin.

I frowned again. Cookie…

Look, Oreo, Cookie turned to me. I don't want to live the rest of my life in the vet's office. I'd rather live life to the fullest and tell her when I'm ready, she said.

But maybe the vet could help! I protested, getting really worried. And what if, by the time you're ready, it's too late?

Cookie smiled. Well, I'll always be with you.

I leaned into her gently. She leaned into my fur. Fabi lay down with us, and we finished watching the movie.

"Hey, bud," Anthony brought me back to the present. He was at the door.

I didn't answer.

"Eric went to get a new tray…" Anthony continued.

Silence.

"Well, I'm going to pick up Amy, if you want to come."

No thank you.

"It'll take your mind off of…" Anthony's voice cracked. "Cookie."

I already said I didn't want to go.

Anthony gave up and left.

I gulped. *I'll always be with you…* the words echoed in my head. I walked to my small suitcase, which was half empty. I pulled out Cookie's favorite toy; a dragon with chewed off pink spine things and a blue body with bumps on it. I had taken it from her bed a few days after… you-know-what.

I chewed its chest. The squeak was slightly more high-pitched then my football. Strangely, it filled me with a sense of joy, joy that I still had a part of Cookie with me.

Eric appeared at the door. "Hm, that was Cookie's," he smiled and came in. "The new tray is out. You must not like the food, so I'll just leave you alone," he looked up at the ceiling.

I licked my muzzle. I was still pretty hungry, and the food was delicious. I walked out of the room and into the kitchen, where a new tray lay with my bowls.

I dug in and finished my bowl. Eric looked up from his phone and grinned. "Attaboy."

The doorbell rang. I barked and ran to it. Aunt Sonia got there first.

Amy, Anthony, and Sky appeared.

"I guess this is the famous Amy?" Aunt Sonia said.

"Yeah," Anthony said.

They greeted one another. I rolled to the side as Sky lunged at me. *Not today,* I stood up and shook myself.

Sky giggled. *Come on, don't be such a buzzkill!* She lunged at me again. I let myself be pounced on. All of us sat at the breakfast table. The humans talked while I frantically tried to get away from Sky.

"So, when do you guys start school?" Eric asked.

I growled at Sky. *Okay, I'm serious now. Stop it.*

Fine, Sky sat down. *Let's play I'm-More-Scary-Than-You,* she towered over me and growled.

"Well, our Senior year was kind of extended because they had to find another teacher, so we're starting late," Amy said.

"Yeah, they said we can start in February," Anthony said.

"Good," Aunt Sonia said.

"How's Emil's team doing?" Anthony questioned.

That was good, but watch this, I bared my teeth and snarled at Sky, looking her directly in the eye.

"Anthony, they're the Bulls," Amy said.

"Smart girl," Eric said.

Everybody laughed.

Sky backed away. *Alright, you win.*

I grinned.

Later in the evening, once Amy and Sky had left, I heard Anthony on the phone.

"Sorry about the thing, I shouldn't have done that… I just… I never get to see you anymore… What…? But didn't you say…? That-That's amazing…! But what if… But you *have* to keep your distance from her… Okay… So, you're telling her…? Okay… Christmas Eve, I guess… Okay…" Anthony put his phone down. A grin spread across his face.

I read his mind (literally). *Oh, yeah! And Aunt Sonia and Eric like him!*

Now, you might be wondering, what the heck is going on? Well, basically, now that Anthony had moved out, Mom couldn't force Dad to stay away from him, so he was going to move to Miami… South Florida to spend more time with us!

After Anthony settled some other stuff with Dad, we went for a walk. The neighborhood was nice and peaceful.

"I can't believe I'm going to college," Anthony said.

Me neither, I agreed. *Also, I can't believe you're eighteen.*

"In one week," Anthony corrected.

Yeah, I said.

We talked about memories from the past. We'd come so far. We'd been together for *six years*. Crazy, right?

How do you feel about your birthday being on a holiday? I asked Anthony.

"Well, it's Christmas, so I like it, mainly because I get double the gifts."

Yep, Anthony's birthday was on Christmas Day.

Chapter 18

· ·

University of Miami

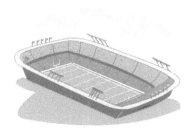

This is why I never told you about Christmas. It was always crazy and sometimes even overwhelming. But, since now we were in Mi... South Florida, I'll tell you about it.

Before we start, though, let's talk about Dad. He was coming the next day. Better yet, he was going to live in the same complex!

The following day, Anthony's phone *dinged!* We were pumped.

"Okay," he looked at me. "We'd better get over there."

On the ride there, I couldn't sit still. Anthony was driving.

I saw someone waving at us as we drove into a driveway.

Bless the Lord Almighty, he's actually here! I thought, jumping out of the car.

A small truck was parked outside of his house. Anthony and I practically tackled Dad, we hugged (and licked) him so hard.

"Woah!" he exclaimed. "You guys got strong!"

I sniffed the air. *Is that a dog I smell?*

"Did I tell you guys about Milo?" Dad said.

We looked at him, confused.

He laughed. "OK, I guess I forgot. Milo!" Dad called.

A scruffy mutt came bounding out of the garage. He had tan-colored fur and triangle-shaped ears.

We barked at each other in greeting.

"This is Milo," Dad said. "I found him on the streets and decided to take him in."

Milo wagged his tail. *Hi there, pal.*

Hello, I said. *I'm Oreo.*

Like the cookie? Milo tilted his head.

Yeah, I said.

We started chasing one another around the driveway. Dad and Anthony continued talking.

"Anthony?" a familiar voice said.

I spun around and gasped at the sight of the person standing on the sidewalk.

Dirty-blonde hair, green-blue eyes… Jackson! And Lucky!!!

We ran to each other, licking hard.

"You live here?" Anthony asked.

"A couple of houses down!" Jackson replied. "Hey, Mr. C," he shook Dad's hand.

"Hello, Jackson," Dad said.

Lucky, this is Milo. Milo, my wife, Lucky, I said to introduce them.

Hello, Lucky sniffed Milo's butt.

Hi, Milo also licked her behind.

"Anyways, should we go inside?" Anthony gestured to the house.

"Probably. Wanna come?" Dad asked Jackson.

"I wish I could, but I better go help with the pups," Jackson answered.

See you, my love, I licked Lucky.

See you, Lucky licked me back.

Dad's house was nice. Like Aunt Sonia's house, the garage door led to the laundry room. To the right, there was a bedroom and pretty steep stairs next to that. The house wasn't very tall, so it must've been an attic or something. Past the stairs was a living room and a sliding, glass door to the left that led to the yard. Dad's front door opened onto it. There was a pool here too. Beyond that were the kitchen and a larger bedroom.

"Nice place," Anthony said, sitting at the kitchen bar.

Yeah, I agreed.

"News flash," Dad said, "it was 30% off."

Anthony chuckled. "Of course, it was."

"I should get settled," Dad said. "I'll see you around."

Anthony hugged him. "See you around."

Before I knew it, Christmas (and Anthony's birthday) were here!

We had done Christmas Eve practically alone, but we had an amazing Christmas party.

Aunt Sonia invited a lot of people. Mom, uncles and aunts, cousins, Fabi's grandparents, Emil Salgado and his wife, Brooke, Eric's daughter Lauren (he had another daughter, Julia, but she couldn't make it) and her husband, Fabi, and her boyfriend, Alex (a very nice guy), and a group of the Salgado's friends they had nicknamed "The Minions." A lot of them came from Mexico.

The doorbell rang.

"*Mi niña,* could you get that?" Aunt Sonia asked Fabi from the kitchen.

I followed Fabi to the door. We had been playing. She opened the door. On the Christmas rug lay a long package.

Fabi picked it up, and her eyes widened. She ran to Anthony, who was talking to Emil. "Sorry, brother dear, but I have to borrow Anthony for a minute."

"That's cool," Emil said, looking at Fabi. "Just never call me 'brother dear' ever again."

Fabi pulled Anthony into our hallway. "It's from your dad," she shoved the package into his hands.

Anthony beamed. "Thanks."

Fabi went back to the party. Anthony and I went to our room.

Anthony stared at the box in his hands.

Well? Open it! I urged.

He did. On top was a card. Anthony picked it up. In Dad's handwriting it read:

> Dear Anthony, Merry Christmas and Happy Birthday. I can't believe you're eighteen! Wish I could be there. I hope you like what I got you.
>
> With love,
> Dad.

Anthony pulled the present out of the box. It was a…

"It's his old bass," Anthony whispered.

Of course! Anthony told me how he always loved to steal Dad's bass guitar to play! And he claimed to be pretty good, too.

It was navy blue, Anthony's favorite color, with white specks all over it.

Anthony plucked a string and played a short tune. It sounded like the start of a really old song called "Another One Bites the Dust," by a group called Queen.

Anthony played most of it. I was awe-struck. He was right: he was good.

"Anthony? You okay?" Mom asked from the hallway.

Hide the box, Anthony told me. "Yeah, I'm fine," he said aloud.

I shoved the huge box behind the desk. Anthony put the card and bass in the closet.

"Then why are you cooped up in here?" Mom came in. "It's Christmas."

"I was just um… making sure Oreo's leg was OK," Anthony said.

I panted. *Yeah, it was getting… stiff.*

I was fibbing.

"Okay then," Mom said. She left.

Anthony and I breathed a sigh of relief.

We sang really cool songs and had a lot of fun. Anthony got a chocolate cake.

New Year's Eve was just as fun.

The next day, January 1st, Jackson told us to come over immediately.

"What's up?" Anthony said as we entered the Jacobs' new/old house.

"One of the pups opened their eyes!" Jackson exclaimed.

Well, why didn't you say that in the text?! I sprinted to the living room. Lucky was on the carpet with the pups. By now, all of the puppies had opened their eyes.

The same pup that had been flailing her paws around was now trying to stand up.

Aunt Sonia and Eric came in behind us.

Chill, I told the pup. *You're only two weeks old.*

She calmed down a little.

"Any suggestions for names?" Mrs. Jacobs said from the kitchen.

"That energetic one," Aiden pointed at the pup I was with, "is it a girl or a boy?"

A Girl, I said.

"Girl," Anthony said.

"What about Go-Go?" Eric suggested.

Go-Go bark-yelped at her new name.

"Sounds good," Mr. Jacobs said.

"What about this one?" Jackson gestured at a boy, who was growling softly at a teddy bear.

It's not going to hurt you, Lucky laughed.

"Hunter sounds good for him," Aunt Sonia said.

"Yep," Anthony chuckled.

"This one looks like…" Eric's voice trailed off.

I turned to look at him. He was holding the mix. I finally realized why she had looked familiar. *Cookie,* I whispered.

The whole room froze.

Am I in trouble? the pup pouted and whimpered.

No, sweetie, I said quickly. *She can be Cookie Junior,* I told Anthony.

"Cookie Jr.," Anthony typed it into his phone.

Lucky picked up a boy who had been nibbling on one of his siblings.

"That one looks like a Max," Aiden said.

"Agreed," Jackson said.

The pup Max had been nibbling on was cleaning herself.

You're a little lady, aren't you? I licked her.

"Lady…" Anthony repeated. "Yeah, Lady!"

The others nodded in agreement.

Lady glared at me. *I just cleaned there,* she grumbled.

I chuckled.

"This one has a spot over his eye," Mr. Jacobs picked a boy up.

He did have a black spot, right over his right eye. He was a pit bull, but his face was white.

"What about Spot?" Aunt Sonia said.

"Why not?" Eric said.

The last one was huddled up to her mother shyly. I picked her up, and she whimpered softly. I realized this one was the one that had been keeping her distance.

It's okay. Daddy's got you, I told her. I set her down next to her siblings.

You look like a Molly, I said.

"Oreo thinks that one looks like a Molly," Anthony translated.

"That sounds good," Mrs. Jacobs came over to the living room.

"So, Go-Go, Hunter, Cookie Jr., Max, Lady, Spot, and Molly," Anthony read from his phone.

Molly had dragged herself back to Lucky.

"Why is she so shy?" Aiden wondered.

"Maybe because there are so many of us," Jackson said.

"Yeah," Anthony said.

I slowly approached Molly. She squirmed deeper into Lucky's fur. *It's OK,* I said gently. *Nobody's going to hurt you, I promise.*

There are too many giants, Molly's eyes darted at the humans, looking panicked.

They're humans, I explained. *They're nice and friendly.*

In fact, some of them saved your dad and me, Lucky added.

Really? Molly said.

Really, I reassured her. I lifted Molly up and brought her to Anthony. *Just let them show you,* I put her down.

Anthony put his hand in front of Molly so she could sniff it. She did, and then she licked it.

"There you go," Anthony gently petted her.

I felt something on my tail. I turned around.

Right… I dragged my tail in front of me. *Hello Spot,* I thought.

Spot had somehow managed to get over to me. It didn't hurt at all, so I let him do his thing. Lady had also dragged herself over to me and started licking (cleaning?) me.

Eh, I lay down.

Suddenly, all the pups except Go-Go (who was still trying to stand up) were on or around me. Max started trying to nibble my ears. Cookie Jr. was helping Lady out. Hunter stared at me curiously. Finally, Molly flopped onto me before climbing onto my back.

Everybody laughed.

"Stop harassing your dad!" Jackson said, still laughing.

Nah, it's fine, I said.

"He says it's fine," Anthony repeated.

"Cookie Jr., not the leg," Aunt Sonia said.

I turned around. Cookie Jr. was sniffing my prosthetic from my back. She looked at me and whimpered.

It's OK. Just leave it alone, I told her.

Cookie Jr. whimpered again. *Why?*

I got into an accident, I said, not wanting to scare them.

Poor papa, Lady stopped licking me.

I'm fine now, I said.

Does it hurt? Spot asked.

Sometimes, I answered.

What's it made of? Hunter said, examining it with laser eyes.

Metal, obviously, Molly said.

No, it's plastic! Max interjected.

It's metal, I said.

Told you so, Molly said.

What does it feel like? Go-Go called from the carpet. She was panting heavily.

Just another limb, I replied as Lucky put her next to me. *I had to get used to it, but once I did, it felt normal,* I explained.

The pups lay down in a row.

Can you please tell us the story? Spot begged.

I looked at Lucky. She nodded. *Okay then,* I said. *It all started in a kennel…*

I told them my whole story. From the kennel to the present day. By the time I finished, they had fallen asleep.

I yawned. Then so did Lucky. Soon, we were all in a pile, asleep.

Four days later, I woke up from a nap. I was surprised to see that Anthony was gone. He had been reading on his bed.

I stretched. How long had I been asleep? I looked outside. It looked like it was evening, so not that long.

I went to the living room. Eric was watching a game of football: Bears vs. Packers.

Where's Anthony? I asked. But of course, he couldn't hear me. I decided to check on Aunt Sonia. She was in her room, looking at her phone in bed.

Where could that boy be? I heard the doorbell. I ran to greet whoever came in. Eric opened the door. *Antho...? Oh,* I said, *hey, Amy. Sky.*

Hi, Sky told me. She didn't look at me, though. From what I saw, she was busy trying to catch a lizard.

"Hey, Oreo," she said. "Have you seen Anthony?"

No. In fact, I was going to ask you *that,* but for Amy's sake, I whimpered.

"He's practicing at the new field, at UM," Aunt Sonia answered, coming out of her room.

Oh, I thought.

"Oh, good. We were about to go there anyways," Amy glanced at Sky as she yanked on her leash in an attempt to catch the lizard. "Sky, leave that poor creature alone!" she pulled her away from it and Sky sat down, still staring at the lizard, who had scurried away.

"Come along, Oreo," Amy said, walking out to her car.

I grabbed my leash from the corner and followed her. She clipped it on.

Amy drove us to the University of Miami, more commonly known as UM. I sat in the front seat, and Sky in the back.

Question! Sky exclaimed suddenly.

Answer, I said.

What's football? Sky asked.

Football is a sport. The main goal is to take the ball to the end of the field and score points to win, I explained.

Oh, Sky scrunched her face up. *That sounds hard with so many people on the team.*

Eh, I said. *Basketball is probably a bit harder.*

Ooh, I know what basketball is! Sky put her chin up. *It's the sport where you put the ball in the basket!*

Yeah, I said.

We found Anthony and Joseph on the field. And, oh, was the campus big and beautiful! Even the field looked clean (is that possible?).

"Hey, Amy," Anthony and her hugged. "Thanks for bringing Oreo."

"No problem," Amy said.

"Hi, Amy," Joseph called from the field.

She waved at him. "I'd better go to cheer practice. Could you watch Sky?"

Sky barked at her name.

"Sure," Anthony replied. *You're watching Sky,* he told me.

Wait, what? I looked at him.

"Thank you," Amy kissed him on the cheek.

Once she had rounded the corner, I turned on Anthony. *She asked* you *to watch Sky, not me.*

"I need to practice," Anthony countered.

I need to practice, too! I argued.

"Coach Dominguez practically thinks you're a pro. You'll be fine," Anthony said, quite truthfully. "Make sure Sky is okay."

I groaned. I wasn't a babysitter! I heard a bark behind me and turned around.

Sky was looking at the... sky. The blue sky. Her paws were waving around in the air.

I considered what Anthony had told me. *Are you okay?* I asked Sky.

Yeah, but I'm bored, she said.

Same here, I lay down.

Sky looked past me. *Can we play with one of those balls?*

I followed her line of sight. She was talking about the footballs.

Sure, knock yourself out, I said.

I got lost in my thoughts. We had visited the pups every day so far, but I'm a father. *Is Go-Go too energetic? Did Hunter really stare at something so hard that he broke it? Has Molly gone back into her shell* (this was the question I asked myself most often)*? And if so, is somebody helping her? Is Spot going to accidentally burn down the house? If so, is Lady stressed about all the ash? Is Max okay? Are the pups okay?!?* I rolled around in the grass, anxious to see them again.

All this while I didn't notice Sky heading into the school.

See you later, Oreo! she said, snapping me out of my thoughts.

What do you mean? I looked at her. Sky had *actually* managed to get in! *Wait!* I was a second too late. She ran inside. Dogs are only allowed in with a special ID. I looked around for mine, but Anthony had no reason to bring it. I followed Sky inside.

I'm sure the building had a nice interior, but I was too busy chasing a puppy to notice.

Sky! Sky! Come back! Please come back! I begged.

"Hey!" I heard someone bark. "Get back here, dog!"

I ran around the corner and halted.

Sky was backed up to the wall, cornered by a big, burly man with a goatee. He was dressed as a janitor and was holding a mop.

I knew exactly what to do. I leaped over to Sky, grabbed her by the collar, and rolled out of the janitor's line of view. My leg scraped my body, and I winced.

"Stop!" the janitor said.

Run, I ordered Sky. She obeyed and I followed her.

After a few more corners, I saw the exit straight ahead. I barreled through it. I skidded around another corner and saw the field.

ANTHONY! HELP! I shouted.

He turned around. He was sitting on a bench, drinking water. "Oreo? Where'd you...?"

Help, you dummy! I screamed.

Anthony's eyes widened. "Woah, woah, woah, I'm sorry. Is there a problem here?" he said to the janitor, coming in-between us and him.

"Are these your dogs?" the janitor growled. Anthony nodded. "Well, keep them *away* from the building! Only pets with special IDs can get into the school."

Anthony glared at me. "I will, I'm so sorry."

The janitor stormed past us.

"Hey, Anthony," Joseph said from behind us. I realized... Clover was with him! "Any idea why Clover is here?" he finished.

"Kate is moving here," Anthony replied casually. "What were you thinking?!" he glared sharply at me.

Woah, hold up. This wasn't my *fault. Also, you never told me Kate and Clover were moving here!* I smiled, trying to change the subject.

"Don't change the subject. You can't go into a *college* without your ID!" Anthony looked mad.

F.Y.I., I was looking after Sky.

"Yeah, sure you were."

Relax, nothing bad happened.

"Except you running around a college!"

"Okay, enough! Both of you, chill!" Joseph stepped in-between us. "I have... no idea what you're saying," he told me, "but, just *chill.*"

Tell him *that,* I turned my head to Anthony.

Anthony opened his mouth to say something but was clever enough to stop himself.

Come on, Sky, I told her.

Once we were out of Anthony's earshot, I asked Sky a second time, *Are you okay?*

Yeah, Sky paused. *Sorry.*

For what? I said.

For getting you in trouble, she looked at her paws.

I stopped walking and turned around to look at her. I hadn't realized I would make her feel guilty. I sighed. *It wasn't your fault.*

The look Sky gave me broke my heart. *Hey, everybody gets curious sometimes.*

But what I did was really bad.

I snorted, almost chuckled. *That wasn't bad. I should know.*

Just then, Clover walked over to us.

Long time, no see, I told her.

Yup, she said.

Clover! Sky tried to jump on her.

Hey, Sky, Clover said.

Who are you with? I asked Clover.

Kate, she replied. *So...*

Which school is Kate going to? I said.

Here, Clover answered.

Oh, I said.

Oreo, are we going to visit the pups after this? Sky asked.

I hope so, I said. And I really, *really* did.

Can I come? Clover said.

Depends on the humans, I told her.

Clover nodded and walked away.

I sighed and lied down. Sky did the same. I saw Anthony walking towards us and turned my back to him.

"Oreo, I'm sorry," he said. "I didn't mean to get mad at you. It's just," Anthony hesitated, "you shouldn't have done that."

I already told you that it wasn't my fault, I looked at Sky, *or anybody's fault.*

"This one yours, too?" somebody said.

I turned around. The janitor was dragging Clover behind him.

Clover growled, and he dropped her.

165

"Is it?" the janitor demanded.

"Not really," Anthony said.

"Then whose is it?" the janitor asked, sounding frustrated.

I AM NOT AN IT! Clover hollered. She turned and snapped at his ankle.

"Aye! Dog, scram!" he shooed her away with his mop.

Clover snarled.

Suddenly, Kate ran over.

"Get away from my dog!" she shouted.

The janitor grunted and stomped away.

"Oh, hey, Kate," Anthony said casually.

Kate looked at him. "Oh, hi."

Hello! Sky jumped onto her knees.

"Hey, Sky," Kate patted her head.

After Anthony and Kate had talked for a while, they left.

"Let's go, the Jacobs are waiting for us," Anthony announced.

I sighed with relief. *Good.*

Yay! Sky said happily

Is Amy coming? I asked as we walked to the car.

"She's gonna meet us there," Anthony replied.

Double yay! Sky bounced with joy.

I chuckled.

Do you forgive me? Anthony asked me tentatively.

I smiled. *Brothers fight,* I shoved him playfully. He grinned and ruffled my fur.

Amy's car was already parked in the Jacobs' driveway when we arrived.

"Hullo, my little angel," Amy said as Sky leaped onto her chest. "Was she good?"

Anthony and I glanced at each other.

"Well?" Amy started to sound worried.

"Yeah… of course," Anthony lied.

"Good girl!" Amy praised Sky.

I ran to the front door, jumped up, and rang the doorbell myself. Aiden opened it. "Hey, Oreo."

I went into the house. The layout was a lot like Dad's house.

Jackson and Mr. and Mrs. Jacobs were huddled around the pups and Lucky.

How are you guys? I immediately asked Lucky.

Amazing. Go-Go was finally able to stand up, she nodded at her.

Go-Go was standing up on shaky legs, trying to walk. She stumbled again and again.

I pushed her gently with my nose. *Maybe in a few days, OK?* I knew that pups are able to walk around with a wobbly gait at about 3 weeks of age, so she would be ready soon.

Dad! She licked me.

Hey, sweetheart, I said, licking her back.

Dad! Hunter said. In a rush, he stood up and tried running over to me but fell back to the ground with a little *thump!*

I rushed over to him, picked him up, and put him on the couch. *You okay, Hunter?* I licked the side he had fallen on. Lucky was right behind me.

Yeah, I think so, he grinned goofily at me and licked my face.

I smiled and brushed my muzzle against his side. The humans brought the rest of the pups over to me and Lucky so they could say hi. One by one, they were able to stand up. Go-Go even took a few steps.

Five days later, we visited again, and now they could all stand steadily. A week or so after that, they'd started running.

I walked onto the carpet and was swarmed by seven furry puppies.

I laughed. *Maybe in a year.*

The first one to run the length of the carpet was Go-Go (no surprise there). Then Spot, Molly, Lady, Max, and, finally, Cookie Jr. We introduced Sky to them. They loved her.

Molly walked underneath me, mimicking my movements.

I played along. *Wait, weren't there seven puppies?* I pretended to gasp. *Where could Molly be?* She giggled under me. *Oh, I'm so sad, I'm going to lie down!* I started to lie down, and Molly came running out, squealing in happiness.

I grinned. *Come here, you!* I slid under Molly, so she was riding me like a horse.

Molly giggled in surprise. *Giddy up!* she said.

I whinnied like a horse. The other pups and Sky started chasing us.

That horsey would make a perfect trophy! Hunter declared.

Wait, what? I said.

Get him! Go-Go shouted.

Run, horsey, run! Molly urged.

We ran around the carpet until Lady got in between us.

Stop! she commanded, sounding like a queen. *I am the president of this horsey, and I say it's mine!*

Sorry, Ms. President, Max said, sitting down.

I lay down, careful not to drop Molly.

Suddenly, somebody joined Molly on my back. I turned around. *Okay, seriously, why do I keep falling for that?*

It's Spot, Lucky told me.

Another pup hopped on, and I heard them giggle.

Hello, Cookie Jr, I guessed.

They shushed each other but kept giggling.

I played along. *This horse is going crazy!* I declared, chasing my tail.

Spot, Lady, and Molly screamed in delight.

Go-Go to the rescue! Go-Go pounced on my paws and nibbled on them.

Horsey going down! I pretended to stumble onto the (soft) carpet.

Pile on Dad! Hunter said. All of the pups jumped onto me. Lucky walked over and curled into my side.

After wrestling with each other for a few minutes, the pups were tired.

Molly yawned as I carried her to their bed. *Good horsey,* she mumbled.

Lucky and I carried the rest of them over to join her.

The humans had were sitting at the dining table, eating.

The doorbell rang.

"Coming!" Jackson called. I followed him; he opened it.

"Hello, Jackson," Aunt Sonia said. Eric was with her.

"Hey, Mrs. Sonia," Jackson said.

They came in and said hi. I couldn't help but look at the pups like I always did when they were asleep.

Max was snoring loudly. Go-Go was mumbling something about a race. Lady and Molly were sleeping on top of each other. Spot was rolling around and laughing ever so softly. And Hunter was pawing at the air.

Cookie Jr. was wide awake for some reason. She looked... confused.

What's wrong? I whispered to her.

Why isn't my name just *"Cookie?"* she asked. *Why am I "Cookie Jr.?"*

I froze. I hadn't expected her to ask that. *Well, there was once a pup who you look remarkably like,* I added.

Oh, right! Do you mean Cookie from your stories? Cookie Jr. looked very happy with herself.

Yes, I said, my gut clenching. I knew exactly what she was going to say next. I hadn't told the pups about her death because it was sad, so I kind of just left them on a cliff-hanger.

So whatever happened to her? And there it was. *You just skipped ahead to the part where you and Anthony finally get back together.*

I gulped and said, *I'll tell you when you're older.*

Cookie Jr. squinted at me. *Why?*

I'll tell you that when you're older, too.

Well, if you don't tell me right now, I'm gonna… I'm gonna howl as loud as I can! Cookie Jr. held her chin up defiantly, getting ready to do just that.

Fine, I'll tell you! I hissed. *Just don't wake up your siblings!*

Cookie Jr. grinned and looked back at me expectantly.

I gulped and took a deep breath. *Well, you know how I said Cookie was older?*

Yeah, Cookie Jr. nodded.

She… I hesitated. *She's gone.*

Cookie Jr. looked confused again, but then she whimpered softly. She nuzzled my fur and leaned against my chest.

I know, princess, I said, nuzzled her back.

We sat there for a while until, eventually, she fell asleep. I picked her up and put her back to bed.

I looked around and realized that Sky and Amy were gone.

Did Sky and Amy leave? I asked Anthony.

Yeah, she had an emergency, Anthony said.

Oh, I said.

What did Cookie Jr. ask you? Lucky said from the couch.

I froze again.

Oreo?

She asked about her name, I said, hoping she would understand.

Her name? What do you…? Oh, Lucky's shoulders slumped.

I lay down under Anthony.

Are you okay, bud? Anthony questioned.

Yeah, I lied.

You're not okay.

Of course, I am, I insisted.

I can read your mind, Anthony said stubbornly.

Just pay attention to your human stuff, I turned away from him. He went quiet.

I miss you, Cookie, I sighed to the sky.

The next few days were filled with football practice and more visits.

On January 21st, Aunt Sonia and Anthony were rushing around, preparing for… something.

What are you guys doing? I asked, extremely curious.

Anthony was carrying two boxes with him to the living room. "Tell you later," was all he told me. "Aunt Sonia! Where do I put these boxes?"

I heard the garage door close. Aunt Sonia came into the room with another box. "Just put them on the floor over there."

Just tell me! I got in his way, assuming the boxes were heavy. *The suspense is killing me!*

"Fine! It's Eric's birthday! Now, *please* get out of the way!" Anthony pleaded.

I moved aside. *How old will he be?* I followed him.

"Now, that's just rude," Anthony said.

Just asking, I smelled Anthony's curiosity and smirked.

In a few hours, balloons, banners, and tables were set up in the backyard. There was a big 72 made entirely out of balloons (courtesy of Aunt Sonia) by the front door.

Seventy-two, huh? I said as Aunt Sonia balanced it. *He's gorgeous.*
Seriously? Anthony told me.
What? I'm just stating a fact.

Anthony scoffed in his head. I followed him back inside to the living room, where Aunt Sonia had set up a mini buffet on the kitchen isle. There was a sign on the breakfast table that read:

Presents

I went out to the backyard. *Wow,* I said, impressed. The table had been uncovered, moved to the left of the pool, and prepared for the party guests. There was a new table for (I thought) the cake. The whole place was lit with soft light from the candles on the tables.

"Yeah," Anthony agreed.

The doorbell rang. Within a few minutes, all of the guests had arrived.

Aunt Sonia glanced at me. "Oh!" she exclaimed and gestured for me to come with her.

I obeyed. She took out a bow-tie-collar and wrapped it around my neck.

"There. Now, you're ready," Aunt Sonia smiled at me.

Nice, I loved my new accessory. My ear twitched as I heard the garage door *whirr* open. I had been told to alert Aunt Sonia if I heard it, so I barked.

Aunt Sonia gasped. "He's here! Places everyone! Places!"

We turned off the lights and stood in the fancy living room.

Nice bow tie, Anthony complimented me.

Thanks, I said.

The alarm *dinged!* as the laundry/garage door opened, and Eric appeared. Somebody turned on the lights.

"Surprise!" we all shouted (besides me, I happily barked).

"Woah! Pat? Beth?" Eric exclaimed. "What's everybody doing here?"

"Take a wild guess," one of the guests gestured to Aunt Sonia.

"Aw, thanks, baby," she and Eric hugged.

The party was fun. Anthony and I were waiters (my police training came in handy). Everybody enjoyed themselves.

We were exhausted by the time all of the guests had left. Anthony and I practically collapsed into bed.

A few days later, Anthony and Amy agreed to meet at a Starbucks nearby.

"So, excited about school tomorrow?" Amy asked as we sat down at a table outside. Sky was getting spayed, so she wasn't there.

Anthony looked up from his cappuccino, "Of course," he answered. "You're studying architecture, right?"

"Right," Amy said. "And you're studying," she hesitated, "bananas, right?"

This deserves an explanation. Mom has people everywhere because of her business, and they're supposed to alert her to any talk about anything related to Dad. So, we have to have a code word and agreed on bananas.

"Yeah," Anthony winked at Amy, and she giggled.

"You do realize she'll find out eventually," Amy whispered.

"It'll be fine."

They chatted for a while. I thought about the pups and Lucky, as usual. I also wondered what would happen when Mom found out what Anthony was studying.

Ding! Amy's phone went. She glanced at it and her eyes widened.

"Emergency," Amy stated.

"Emergency?" Anthony asked at the same time.

Ask her! I quickly said. *She's had* so *many emergencies this week!*

Anthony hesitated, but then said, "What are all these emergencies about?"

Amy looked up. "Um… just a… thing," she said. "Love you!" and with that, she ran off.

I got over the shock before Anthony did. *That's… weird. With you, she's usually straight up about absolutely* everything.

"Yeah…" Anthony frowned. "I hope I haven't done anything wrong…"

No chance. You guys are the sweetest couple I've ever seen, I said.

"Then, what isn't she telling me?" Anthony wondered aloud.

I don't know…

The next day, Anthony and I went to college. The building was absolutely amazing. Trophies gleamed everywhere, and it was full of college kids. Everybody stared at me, knowing I was the only animal on the football team.

I could tell Anthony really enjoyed music. I was happy for him but also sad because I knew what would happen when Mom found out (which she probably would).

A few hours later, Anthony changed into his football clothes. I switched legs, and we headed out to practice.

I'm not going to lie, I was nervous. Why? For two reasons:

1. High school football and college football are completely different.
2. Our team hadn't really changed from middle school to high school because we were in the same school, so I'd never had to get to know a new team before.

There were 43 players in all, so we weren't exactly going to get to know everyone right away. But everybody seemed to like me.

I'll admit that college football was much tougher. Thankfully, Joseph was still with us.

Once practice was over, Anthony was dripping in sweat, and I was panting heavily.

"Good practice," Anthony said as he poured water into my water bowl.

Yeah, I agreed.

"We're going to meet at Jackson's house at five, ok?" Anthony told me.

OK, I meant to sound pumped, but I was tired.

"How was practice?" Aunt Sonia asked as we plopped onto the couch. She was putting the dishes in the dishwasher.

"Great," Anthony replied.

"What are you studying?" Aunt Sonia asked.

Help, Anthony told me.

Uh, oceanology! I said frantically.

"Oceanology?" Anthony said hesitantly.

"Oh… OK," Aunt Sonia said, confused by his tone of voice.

Anthony took a shower. Meanwhile, Aunt Sonia and Eric gave me a quick bath.

Finally, it was time to go, I don't know how I stood the wait.

Daddy! Lady squealed as I came in. All of the pups tried to climb on top of me again.

Hey, love, I licked Lucky. She licked me back.

Mommy says we're going to get to go Outside, Spot said dramatically.

Really? I said.

"Pups!" Mrs. Jacobs called.

They all tumbled towards her. She picked them up, put them in a basket, and we went outside. I knew that they were going to be going outside soon because they were starting to transition from Lucky's milk to solid food.

The Jacobs had made a little fenced area in the grass next to their driveway, so the pups could roam freely without being able to escape.

Lucky and I went inside, and Mrs. Jacobs released them into the fenced area.

Woah… Cookie Jr. looked around in amazement.

This green stuff is great for running! Go-Go said as she sprinted around.

It's called grass, Lucky told her.

I like grass, Hunter rolled around.

I smiled. That was exactly what I had said and done so many years ago.

Max chewed it. *Blargh. It doesn't taste good, though,* he sputtered.

Lady squealed in disgust as Go-Go skidded across the grass and made it go flying everywhere, especially all over her. *It's so messy!* She backed into me.

You'll get used to it, I reassured her.

Molly giggled and rolled over. *It tickles!*

Spot peed.

"Good boy, Spot!" Jackson said happily.

Wait, we get praised for peeing?! Cookie Jr. cried out.

Only if you do it outside, I said quickly.

Yay! Cookie Jr. peed too.

"Good girl!" Aiden said.

The others followed suit, and all received praise. Well, everybody except Lady.

Come on, sis. Just do it! Go-Go urged her.

Absolutely not! Lady ran away from her. *It's preposterous!*

Even dad did it! Molly said.

I halted mid-scratch. *No, I…* Molly glared at me. *I mean, of course I did,* I corrected myself.

Well, if dad did it… Lady said hesitantly.

The other pups waited, expectant.

Fine! Lady decided.

The pups cheered.

But don't look! Lady said.

We turned away, and she peed (I assume).

"Good girl, Lady!" Eric said.

We stayed outside until lunch time. The pups, Lucky, and I were under the table when I had a brilliant idea.

I wish we could get human food, Max was saying.

But they'd never let us, Hunter said in a disappointed voice.

Puppy eyes, I suggested casually, not even ooking at the pups.

Huh? Cookie Jr. said behind me.

Sit next to somebody's feet, stare at them, and whimper, I instructed, still not turning around.

Really? And they'll give us food? Spot said.

Yep, I confirmed.

Unless they're cold-hearted, Lucky added.

Hmm, Go-Go walked over by Aunt Sonia's feet and sat down.

Good choice, I told her.

Go-Go flattened her ears all the way down, looked up at Aunt Sonia, and whimpered softly.

Aunt Sonia peeked down at her. "Sorry, girl, I can't," Aunt Sonia looked back up.

Now what? Go-Go asked.

I turned around. *Keep trying. She'll eventually give in.*

Go-Go tried again, whimpering louder this time.

Aunt Sonia glanced at her and whispered, "Fine, but don't tell anyone," she snuck a chunk of bread under the table.

Molly gasped. *I want some, too!* she said as Go-Go ate her bread.

All the other pups murmured in agreement and walked around, getting pieces of bread and steak from the humans. They wanted to try for a second round, but I told them to let up.

"Remember that really old movie with the dream song?" Jackson said above us.

"Yeah, Cinderella or something," Anthony said.

They continued to talk about old movies.

What's a dream? Max asked.

Well, a dream is… I thought about it and came to a weird conclusion. *A dream is a wish your heart makes… When you're fast asleep,* I finished.

Where'd you get that from, sweetie? Lucky tilted her head at me.

I… don't know, I was mystified by my own statement.

Once the humans finished eating and we put the pups to sleep, we left.

In bed, while Anthony was reading, I thought about what I had said. And then it came to me.

One evening in our kennel…

"I had a really weird dream last night," one of the humans who took care of us said.

What's a dream? one of my sisters asked.

Mind if I sing the answer to you? my mom said.

Sing! we all exclaimed.

Mommy laughed. Okay then, this was my old humans' favorite.

We cuddled close to her, and she started singing.

♪ A dream is a wish your heart makes… When you're fast asleep… In dreams you will lose your heartaches… Whatever you wish for you keep… ♪ mommy nuzzled us and continued. ♪ Have faith in your dreams and someday… your rainbow will come smiling through… No matter how your heart is grieving… if you keep on believing… the dream that you wish will come true… ♪ she finished.

I yawned. All of my siblings had fallen asleep, and I followed suit.

"You okay, bud?" Anthony asked me.

Yeah, I smiled, *I'm great.*

We visited every day for the rest of the week. College got better and better, and Mom visited us on the weekend.

"What are you studying?" Mom asked at the table. We were having dessert.

Anthony froze.

"Oceanology, right, *mi hijo*?" Aunt Sonia glanced at Anthony.

"Um, yeah. Oceanology," he said.

Mom raised an eyebrow. "Really?"

Anthony nodded.

Mom looked at her phone for a few seconds and then said, "It says here that there isn't a course for… oceanology," she finished.

Uh, oh.

"Special… case?" Anthony said uncertainly.

"Don't lie to me," Mom said, giving Anthony a death stare.

Anthony gulped. Mom waited expectantly.

"I'm studying… music," he looked into his lap, expecting the worst punishment ever.

Instead, Mom smiled. "I was going to tell you today."

Anthony looked at her, confused.

I didn't blame him. *I think we've accidentally driven her insane,* I concluded.

"Your dad and I," she said "dad" without a hint of the usual disgust, "have come to an agreement: No more fighting."

Anthony grinned wider than ever.

Chapter 19

· · · · · · · · · · · · · · · · · · ·

Rose

Mom left on Monday on a very happy note.

Anthony and I were walking to Starbucks after practice when I heard a weak yip.

Huh? I halted.

"What's wrong, bud?" Anthony asked.

I turned around. There was an alleyway behind us.

Yip! There it was again! I tugged on my leash, and Anthony let go.

I walked towards the sound. It appeared to be coming from a small, cardboard box.

Yip!

I peeked carefully into the box and gasped. From inside, a tiny yorkie peered up at me. She yelped and fell backwards, knocking the box over.

Anthony ran to me. "What's going on?"

I nodded the box. The puppy stumbled out and bumped into the wall, trembling from head to tail. She was clutching a rose gently and protectively in her mouth.

It's okay, I said softly. *We're not gonna hurt you,* she let me walk over to her.

Anthony started to creep closer, but she stumbled back into a corner, afraid of him. He stopped.

Why are you afraid of him? I tilted my head at the pup.

A lot of humans a-are evil, she hid behind me.

I immediately knew what had happened to her. *Were you abandoned?* I asked her gently.

She sniffled. *Worse. My owners were killed.*

I froze, startled. *Um, well, Anthony won't hurt you, I promise.*

How do you know? she whispered.

He's like my brother. I know him very well. In fact, I've practically spent my whole life with him, I explained. I nodded at Anthony and told him privately. *Try again.*

He slowly crept over to us. The pup stayed hidden behind me but she didn't run away. Anthony slid his hand very slowly toward her. She poked out her nose and sniffed it. Then, she licked it. Finally, the pup came over to Anthony on shaky legs and slumped onto his lap.

Poor thing, Anthony had read my mind earlier, so he knew what had happened to her.

Yeah, I whispered.

"What should we call you?" Anthony asked her.

Too late, she was asleep. She still had the rose hanging from her mouth.

How about "Rose?" I suggested.

Perfect, Anthony replied.

We took Rose to the vet. We didn't know how long she had been abandoned, so Anthony said we should move quickly.

"Where did you find her?" the vet asked Anthony as he checked Rose's breathing.

"In an alley. Actually, Oreo found her," Anthony gestured to me. "From what I know, her owners were killed."

The vet frowned. "Poor thing. If only someone could adopt her…"

Where will she be taken? I asked.

Anthony repeated my question to the vet.

"We have plenty of families who'd be happy to foster her, but I'm afraid that she'll only be comfortable with one of you two around," the vet nodded at us.

A light bulb lit up in my head. *Do you think Aunt Sonia and Eric would adopt her?* I told Anthony.

Anthony's eyes widened. "Excuse me for a minute," he said.

A few minutes later, Rose woke up and stumbled away from the vet.

"Woah, it's okay, I won't hurt you," the vet told her.

I walked over to the table. *He's a good guy, Rose,* I assume that was her name, since she didn't object.

Oh, Rose didn't relax, though. I stayed with her until Aunt Sonia and Eric came into the room. Rose immediately hid behind my head.

After a few attempts, Rose let both of them pet and carry her, but she insisted that either me or Anthony stay with her.

"You wanna come home with us?" a few minutes later, Rose was in Aunt Sonia's arms. By now, she barely even noticed if me or Anthony left the room.

Yes, yes, yes! she licked her chin.

Aunt Sonia and Eric laughed.

Next, we visited the pups, and introduced them to Rose.

Da... Lady skidded to a stop, making all of the pups behind her fall like dominoes. *Who's that?* she asked.

This is Rose, I answered.

Hello, Rose said a little tentatively.

Hi, Rose! Max said enthusiastically.

Wanna play tag? Go-Go asked her.

Rose nodded.

Tag, you're it! Cookie Jr. bumped into Hunter.

Have fun! I called as Hunter started chasing Molly.

We left after the pups got tired and fell asleep.

I glanced at Rose's rose on the ride home. *Where's that from?* I asked her.

Hannah, Rose whispered. She stared at it for a while.

I assumed that Hannah had been her owner.

Rose walked over to me with her rose and lay down. I lowered my head onto the car seat.

Rose eventually settled in. She hadn't been trained, so she didn't know anything about anything. Aunt Sonia brought a transparent kennel from the garage and put it in a corner to start training her.

"Woo-hoo!" I heard Anthony and Eric cheer as I got a drink of water. I walked over to the couch. They were watching a basketball game. Bulls vs. Lakers. The instant replay told me that Emil had just scored a lay-up. It was the fourth quarter and it was a close game. The Bulls were only winning by four points.

I don't understand, Rose said, staring intently at the TV.

You see that guy, number 21? She nodded. I continued, *That's Emil, Anthony's cousin.*

Huh, Rose said. *What'd he do?*

He scored, I explained. *Each basket is two points. Unless it's a free throw or a three-pointer.*

Why? Rose said.

I thought about this. *Good question.*

The night was peaceful, mostly thanks to Anthony's bass. He strummed to another old song by the same band, Queen. This one was called "Don't Stop me Now."

I sighed contentedly and fell asleep.

Chapter 20

· ·

My Goodness Gracious

I woke up very early to a crackling sound and jerked my head up.

Ugh, that cat is really getting on my nerves, I closed my eyes again. Just as I was falling asleep, I smelled smoke. *Impossible,* I leaped off the bed and ran into the kitchen. *My goodness gracious.* The curtains draped over the back door were on fire. It had spread to the couch already!

I sprinted to Anthony, barking in his face.

After what felt like a painfully long time, Anthony finally woke up.

"What the heck?" he mumbled. "Go back to sleep."

Fire! I screamed in his face.

"Wait, what?" Anthony sat up.

I ran to Aunt Sonia and Eric and woke them up. Anthony ran in.

"Fire! Get outside!" he said.

We sprinted through the front door.

"Anybody got a phone?" Eric asked.

Everybody shook their heads.

I froze as I realized something. I gasped. *We left Rose!*

Anthony and I glanced at each other and ran back inside. We were immediately surrounded by a roaring fire. We ran into Aunt Sonia and Eric's room just as the ceiling in Fabi's room collapsed.

Anthony fumbled with the kennel's knobs.

Get me out of here! Rose cried out.

You're going to be okay! I told her. *I promise.*

Anthony finally got the kennel door open and picked her up. We ran out of the hallway. The front door was blocked by the fire. Anthony ran ahead of me. Suddenly, the pillar beside me collapsed and landed on my prosthetic. I cried out. Anthony turned around. He was in front of his room. My eyes widened. The ceiling was cracking above him.

Watch out! I said as it fell. I saw him jump back but couldn't see any more. I heard him cry out as well. *Oh, no.*

Just then, somebody barked. *Clover.*

She jumped over the pillar and turned around to look at me.

Get Anthony, I pleaded.

But you're hurt, she protested.

Just go! I said. Clover hesitated but bravely ran through the fire.

I tried to get up, but to my frustration, I was quite stuck.

Come on, Oreo. You need... I grunted, still pulling, *to see...* my leg popped off and I winced, *the pups!* I stood up and took a deep breath. I managed to pick my way through the fiery rubble, managing to avoid the worst of it. When I got to our room, it was in flames.

Anthony was lying sprawled on the floor with his arm pinned by a burning beam. He'd blacked-out. Rose was panting but she was unconscious too.

I gently picked up Rose. *Clover, help!* I called, barely able to walk and on the point of passing out.

I am so grateful to Clover for being very brave and strong. She managed to push off the beam, wake up Anthony, drape me over her back, and howl for somebody at the garage door.

Finally, Eric appeared. I didn't see what happened next, because once I saw him, I allowed myself to pass out.

I wasn't out for long, because I could still hear sirens. The firefighters probably pulled Eric away. I was on the driveway, and Clover was a bit further away, passed out. Kate ran over to her. I limped over to them.

"You're gonna be okay," Kate rushed over to a truck down the street. She picked Clover and I up and put us in her truck. I passed out again.

I woke up groaning. I was in an incubator. Nobody was there to keep an eye on me.

I need to find Anthony and Rose… and maybe Clover, I pushed myself up on my paws, desperate to see my brother.

A vet pushed through the door. "Good, you're awake," her voice sounded muffled to me. She pulled me out and put on a new prosthetic.

Thanks, with my strength returning, I was able shake myself and stretch my leg.

The vet rubbed cream over my many burns. "I'll be right back," she walked out of the room, leaving the door open.

Bad idea, miss, I trotted out.

"Hey!" somebody grabbed my collar. "You're going to be staying with me for a while," Kate said.

Let me go! I struggled against her grip, but I was still weak.

"It's okay, Oreo," Kate reassured me. "Anthony will be just fine."

"Will be?" I repeated. *Lord, forgive me,* I growled and started running to the exit. Suddenly, a big, familiar hand grabbed me. *Eric, please don't do this,* I looked up at him.

Oreo, Anthony's fine! Clover told me. *You're staying with us until he wakes up.* But then she gasped and shut her mouth.

Excuse me? I exclaimed, my gut clenching.

N-nothing, Clover stuttered.

Your tone of voice isn't very reassuring! I said angrily.

I meant to say until he gets better! Clover argued. *I'm still weak.*

Yeah, yeah, I said. *What aren't you telling me?*

I promise, it's nothing, Clover said.

Promises, promises, I muttered. *I'll find Anthony later,* I thought to myself. *Where's Rose?* I asked.

The Yorkie? Clover asked.

I nodded.

With a vet, Clover replied.

Just then, a vet called Eric over. I followed him to the room. When I saw Rose wag her tail at us as we came in, I breathed a sigh of relief. The vet told Eric she was fine.

I'm so, so sorry we left you, I said, with my head bowed.

Rose bounded over to me and barked. *Don't be,* she nibbled my stomach gently. I smiled at her.

We left the room.

We should get home, Clover said.

Your home, I thought privately.

Kate grabbed our leashes, and we got into her truck.

It was *well* past midnight when we arrived.

"Crazy night, right guys?" Kate said.

I scowled at her. *Happy with yourself?* I started planning an escape. Kate was probably going to take us to what was left of

Aunt Sonia's house… I could run to the Jacobs' house… No, I didn't want to wake the pups or Lucky… Dad's house! *He* would let me see Anthony! I got ready to run.

We got out of the truck and walked to the ashes. I was going to pretend to be mourning everything that had been lost in the flames (some of the feeling would be real), and then I would run.

"Oh, it was *bad*," Kate exclaimed.

I walked through the ashes and rubble with her. I spotted Anthony's bass and went over to it. I whimpered. It was ruined. The strings had peeled off and some of it had melted completely.

"Come on, guys," Kate gasped quietly when she saw what I was whimpering at. "Oh, it's…" she didn't need to finish the sentence. Kate picked it up. I knew there was a chance Dad could fix it, so I set my plan in motion.

I trotted to the sidewalk, trying to look innocent and then started to run. Ignoring Kate, I just kept on running.

A car opened the neighborhood gate for me. Thankfully, Crystal Harbor didn't have a gate.

1… 37… 27. Here, I stopped at the house's front door and started barking as loud as I could.

"What the heck?" Dad muttered as he opened the door. Milo was with him. "Oreo?"

Hey, Dad. Milo, I nodded at my furry friend.

Hi, I guess, Milo seemed confused at my arrival (I don't blame him. It was probably around 3 in the morning).

"How are… wait, where's Anthony?" Dad said, looking around.

I whimpered. Dad went back into the house, and Milo and I followed him. He turned on the TV.

"Oh, my goodness gracious," he whispered.

Um, Dad? I wished he could hear me.

Dad staggered back onto the couch. *Um, Oreo?* he looked at me. *Any chance… this thing is genetic?*

It was as if the connection was breaking up. I guess it was stronger with Anthony. *You're breaking up.*

You... breaking what? Dad asked.

I only hear some of what you're saying, I said slowly.

Me too, Dad said even slower.

I ran… I decided to pause every two words or so, *away from… Anthony's… friend Kate.*

He looked at me. "You know I have to take you back, right?"

Milo had fallen asleep on the couch.

Do you though? I said.

"I'm sorry, bud, but Milo is more than enough," Dad whispered.

But you're… the only… one that… will let me… see Anthony, I explained.

Dad hesitated, but then said, "If they don't want you to see him, then there's probably a reason."

But there… isn't… They just… think I… will get… sad because… it seems like… he's… I gulped, *in a… coma.*

Dad looked startled. "Impossible. There's a reason," but I knew he wasn't sure.

You know… I might… be right.

"Look, Oreo, if Anthony's mom finds out I didn't let you go back with Kate, I'll be back to stage one. And maybe you, too," Dad said.

I sighed. To my frustration, I had to admit he was right.

We walked out to his car and got in.

Kate was sitting on the ground and staring at the ashes in shock. Clover wasn't with her. I barked as I jumped out of the car.

"Oreo!" Kate gave me a hug.

"Hello," Dad said. "I'm Anthony's father."

"Hey, Mr. Cane," Kate got up, and they shook hands. A car pulled up in front of us.

Clover and an elderly lady got out.

"Kate, Clover wandered over to my house, so I brought her back," the lady said.

"I figured," Kate said.

"Well, I should get going, 'bye Cupcake," the lady said. She left.

"Why did Oreo go to you?" Kate asked Dad.

"Um, he said you guys aren't letting him see Anthony?" Dad said.

Kate stared at him. "You have a…?" she gestured at me and then at Dad.

"Yeah," Dad replied.

"It's just…" Kate hesitated. "Anthony's fine, but, uh, the hospital said that Oreo, uh, can't go in."

Dad nodded. "OK…"

Seriously? I snapped at him. *She's lying!*

I know… bear with… me, Dad told me. "Well, do you mind if I take Oreo with me?"

"Yes," Kate answered, crossing her arms.

"Oh, okay," Dad said. *Sorry, bud.*

So, I went back with Kate. I tried not to hate her and Clover, but it was really hard.

I spent the night… Yeah, no. Did you think I would stand for that? You were wrong. I had an escape plan. (ANOTHER ONE!) I was going to sneak out that night.

I slept on Clover's bed because she slept with Kate.

Finally, I heard Kate and Clover snoring like grizzly bears. I pulled a blanket over Clover's bed and put some toys underneath. Hopefully, if they woke up and came to check on me while still a little asleep, they'd think it was me. I slowly crept out of the room, careful to step lightly over the wooden floor. Once I was out of the room, I relaxed. I had seen a doggy door at the front door when we came in, so I thought it would be easy to get out, but Kate had sealed it (smart girl).

I took a deep breath, hoped the girls were deep sleepers, and broke down the doggy door. Once I was outside, I didn't waste any time checking to see if I'd woken them up, I just ran.

I had been paying close attention on the ride here, so I knew exactly where to go.

In no time at all, even though I'd had to beg for water a few times, I was standing in front of Dad's house. He seemed to be... ready for me?

Don't be... mad, I begged.

To my surprise, he grinned. "We'll go see Anthony in the morning."

I barked quietly and licked him on the chin. Dad chuckled.

Dad let me sleep with him on his bed. Milo was waiting for us. We fell asleep in minutes.

If it was up to me, I would've gone to the hospital then and there, but at least I was actually going to see him.

I woke up on the bed, alone. I could hear noises coming from the kitchen.

"Good morning," Dad and Milo said at the same time as I trotted in.

Good morning, I said.

Dad had a different recipe for dog food, but it was pretty good. As soon as we'd finished, we set out to the hospital. Milo didn't want to go because he said he didn't like seeing sick humans, so he stayed home.

"Um, sorry, no dogs allowed," the receptionist said.

"He belongs to the owner," Dad lied.

"Oh, OK. Who are you here to see?" the receptionist asked.

"Anthony Cane," Dad's heart sped up.

"Room 77," the receptionist said after typing some things into her computer. "Floor 7."

The hospital was *huge*. Anthony was on the top floor. We found his room, and Dad knocked on the door. We both took a deep breath.

Amy appeared at the door. She had bags under her eyes. "Oh, hullo, Mr. Cane," she wiped her eyes. "Wait, isn't Oreo supposed to be with Kate?" she peered down at me.

"She said she had too much on her hands, something had come up at school and asked me to take him," Dad said. We'd agreed on the excuse beforehand.

"Oh, OK," Amy said.

We walked into the room. Aunt Sonia and Mom were in the room as well, but I was focused on Anthony. He was lying on a bed. I knew what people (and animals) smelled like when they were in a coma after what happened to Lucky, so I knew that he was just asleep. His arm was raised, attached to a strange contraption. Thankfully, his bed was pretty big, so I was able to jump onto it, which I did, very carefully. I plopped down next to him and sighed. I hoped he was okay…

"We didn't want him to be sad," Mom whispered to Dad. I let them keep thinking I couldn't hear them.

"I think he would rather be here with him and be sad then not be with him and worry," Dad said.

Mom started to look mad, but Aunt Sonia stopped her. "I think he's right, Holly," she said.

Mom sighed. "Very well."

Amy sat down next to the bed and held Anthony's good hand. I licked her hand. She smiled at me and put her other hand on my fur.

After a visit from a nurse, Anthony woke up. He grinned at us. Oh, how I love him. "Hello again, everybody. Dad," he smiled at him. *Hey, bud,* he said to me.

I lay my head gently on his lap. *Are you okay?*

I'm fine. But my arm isn't.

I let out the sigh of relief I'd been holding in since I was sprawled out on the driveway. *Okay.*

God's watching over us, you know that, right? Anthony told me.

Yeah, but I can't lose you, my gut clenched at the thought of losing my brother.

Anthony stroked my fur. *I'll always be with you.*

I held onto him. Dad came over and they talked for a bit. Then, Anthony fell back to sleep. A doctor came in and asked me to jump off for a second, so I did. He tended to Anthony's arm, which I didn't want to look at too closely.

After an hour or so, Dad said he should go check on Milo and maybe get him a babysitter (this was also so if Kate came to see if I was with him, she would think I ran to the hospital, which was partly true).

Later, in the evening, once Dad had come back, we went back home. I asked Dad if we could stop at where the house had been so I could pick something up (Anthony's bass).

Thankfully, it was still there.

"Hm, it'll be tough work, but I can fix this," Dad picked up the bass.

So we went back home, and he got to work. Milo passed him his tools, so I wasn't helping at all.

I looked around. We were in the garage. A convertible was parked next to us and a bunch of empty boxes were lying around.

"Hmm," Dad said thoughtfully. He was examining a big, burnt chunk of the bass.

Can it... be fixed? I asked.

"Pretty much, but it'll take a lot of careful measuring and hard work," he replied. Milo handed him a roll of flexible measuring tape.

What a relief, I said.

After a few minutes, I got bored. Dad noticed. "You know, I *do* have a very small backyard and maybe… I don't know… a football or two," he said casually.

I was very happy to hear this. It felt like forever since I had even picked up a football.

"They're in the attic," Dad told me.

I ran inside. I found the stairs. Oh… the *stairs*. I wanted Dad to fix Anthony's bass, so I didn't go running to him.

Lord Almighty, please help me run up these stairs without it being extremely painful. Amen, I prayed and took a deep breath. I ran up the stairs. I was fine. No pain, no anything. *Thank you,* I said to God gratefully.

In the attic, there were instruments, awards, pictures, and, best of all, several footballs.

Score, I picked one up.

The backyard was definitely small, but it was pretty nice. A pool took up most of the space, but there was grass next to it. A table and chairs sat in the shade of an umbrella. Dad, being the amazing man, he is, had a machine that could launch all kinds of balls into the air.

Perfect, I thought, inserting the football into it.

The machine launched it into the air, and it was going across the pool!

I quickly calculated where it would land, jumped, and caught it mid-air.

Woo-hoo! Anthony, did you see… my voice trailed off as I glanced at the machine. *Oh, right,* I sighed.

I played for a while, but soon got bored.

I was lying in the garage with Dad and Milo when I heard the doorbell ring.

Dad opened the door, and Mom and… oh, no.

"I knew it! What did I tell you, Mrs. Miller?" Kate said, crossing her arms. Clover was with her.

Close the door, I urged Dad.

You know… I can't, he said.

Mom sighed. "You know what? I should've let you bring him to the hospital," she told Kate.

"Wait, what?!" Kate and Clover said at the same time.

Hah! I said. *Best Mom ever!*

"Josh was right," Mom glanced at Dad. "I think Oreo was relieved to see Anthony again."

I ran around her legs and barked happily. She giggled.

"B-but…" Kate sighed. "Fine. I'll go," she walked back to her car.

Clover glared at me. *I'll get you some other day.*

I scoffed. *Sure, you will.*

"Um… thanks, Holly," Dad said once Kate drove away.

Mom smiled. "I'm trying out some new ways of doing things, so don't be surprised. Hello, Milo," she said as Milo came to say hi.

"We'll go visit in a bit. I just have to fix Anthony's bass," Dad said.

A few minutes later, I heard a string being plucked. I looked up. Then Dad played "Under Pressure," another old song by Queen: "Bum-bum-bum-bah-da-da."

You fixed it! I exclaimed.

"Yep," he looked at his watch. "Come on, let's go visit," he put the bass down on his worktable.

Then, I realized something catastrophic. *Oh, my gosh. Oh, no! Oh, NO!*

"What's wrong?" Dad asked.

Everything okay? Milo stopped chewing on his bone.

Anthony… Anthony can't… play football… or… the bass! I finished, my heart beating faster every second.

Dad froze, his mouth gaped open. "I-is he still studying music?"

Yeah, I answered, with a stone in my stomach.

Dad sighed. "Oh, no."

I gulped. Just so you know, Anthony was our *starting quarterback.* And he wouldn't be able to play his bass either.

We drove to the hospital having agreed to let him find out on his own. The doctor came in and told us he could give him a cast and a sling now that the burns had cooled down (yes, they were so bad that they took two days (or so) to cool down). The doctor also said that he could finally go... home.

Chapter 21

· ·

Sigh Lord Help Anthony's Substitute

"Julia said we can stay with her," Eric hung up. In case you've forgotten, Julia is Eric's other daughter, who couldn't make it to the Christmas party.

"Great," Aunt Sonia said.

I groaned. *You know your replacement is a spoiled brat, don't you?*

"Relax, it's not such a big deal. I'll be back by at least..., the playoffs." Anthony ventured cautiously.

"Son, we've told you over and over again that you're out for the season," Dad said.

"Yes, your health is more important than sport," Aunt Sonia glared at me.

By the way, once she knew Anthony was going to be okay, Mom went back to Nashville.

We just lost our starting quarterback! I barked at both of them.

"Relax!" Anthony told me. "Why are you so mad? *You're* still on the team, so we'll be fine!"

I stopped pacing around the room.

"Oreo?" Eric asked, waiting for me to answer Anthony's question.

I gulped down my frustration and anger. *I'm supposed to be the one who's always getting hurt… not you,* I looked at the floor. *And it's my fault… I should've gone in alone.*

Anthony laughed.

"What?" Aunt Sonia said. I was as confused as her.

Anthony repeated to them what I had just said. Then, the whole room erupted in laughter.

I'm so confused! I whined.

"It wasn't your fault!" Dad doubled over in laughter.

"Yes, *los dos son idiotas* for going in there!" Aunt Sonia giggled.

Translation, please, I said to Anthony, who had taken Spanish in high school.

The both of you are idiots, he said.

Oh, OK. I grunted at Aunt Sonia.

"Come here," Anthony calmed down and patted his bed. I jumped up. "It wasn't your fault," he reassured me.

"*And,*" Aunt Sonia added, "you have a substitute for him."

Right, Arran, I thought reluctantly.

Anthony stifled a laugh.

"You know, Arran isn't so bad," Anthony lied as we walked to practice.

Sure, I said, but I didn't want to think about what was coming.

"Okay, boys, let's get right to practice," Coach Dominguez said after we huddled. Anthony ran to the bench. "Arran, you're gonna have to step up and be our quarterback."

Arran... well, he only got into the team because he's the academic dean's nephew.

"Yes, coach," Arran said. He had a squeaky voice.

The whole team chuckled softly (well, not me. I laughed as hard as I could).

"You wanna laugh? GIMME TEN PUSH-UPS!" Coach Dominguez barked.

The team obediently completed 10 push-ups (and yes, dogs can do push-ups. Look it up).

"Okay, people, let's warm up," Coach Dominguez.

We warmed up by running 10 laps (Arran gave up before we'd finished), stretching, and doing some suicide sprints (he barely did three).

Once we finished, we started doing drills with our usual coaches. Kaleb and I went with Coach Likens; UM's assistant/wide receivers' coach.

"Excuse me, coach, but could I borrow Oreo for a second?" Coach Dominguez jogged over to us.

"Of course," Coach Likens said, nodding at me.

I followed Coach Dominguez to... Oh, no... Arran.

Seriously? I complained.

"Good luck," Joseph patted me as he ran by.

"Joe, you come, too," Coach Dominguez said.

Looks like you'll be needing some of that luck yourself," I said, even though nobody could hear me.

Coach Lashlee was talking to Arran.

"Oreo, be Arran's wide receiver," Coach Lashlee instructed. "Joe, you be the center."

Coach Dominguez stood by, probably waiting to see how bad our situation was. Joseph and I ran to our positions. Coach Lashlee took a few more minutes explaining to Arran what he needed to do.

"Oreo, I'm gonna be your defense. Just do your thing," he called.

Yessir, I barked.

"Hike!" Arran squealed once Coach Lashlee ran over to me. Joseph threw him the ball. Arran almost dropped it.

I started running around, trying to get rid of Coach L.

"Oreo!" Arran called unnecessarily. He threw the ball... somewhere.

I groaned, sprinting over to where I thought the ball would land. He didn't throw far but it was much too high. The ball was about to be in my reach when another football hit it right in the middle, sending it rolling on the grass. I was astonished. Whoever threw the other football had amazing aim!

The team burst out laughing.

Coach Dominguez was furious. He spun around to face everybody. "WHO DID THAT?!"

It was like Moses and the Red Sea. The team parted to reveal James, Joseph's substitute.

"Boy, get over here," Coach Dominguez said, turning around and heading to the locker rooms.

James took off his helmet and followed him, head down.

"Get back to what you were doing, everybody!" Coach Stroud ordered.

I hesitated. James had spectacular aim. I thought *he* should be our quarterback until Anthony got better. I glanced at Coach Lashlee. He was explaining yet *another* simple play to Arran. I snuck past them to the locker room.

"Did you have a good reason to do what you did?" Coach Dominguez asked James. I stayed by the entrance.

"No, sir," James muttered.

"Then, why did you do it?!?"

James hesitated, but said, "I don't know, sir."

Suddenly, Anthony came up silently behind me.

He should be our quarterback, we both said at the same time. We smiled at each other.

"Don't lie to me," Coach Dominguez stared right at James.

"I-I," James stuttered.

"Hey, coach?" Anthony walked into the room. I followed him.

"You'd better have a good reason for interrupting this conversation," Coach Dominguez snapped at him. He turned to look at me. "And *you* are supposed to be practicing."

"We have a good reason," Anthony said. "James has spectacular aim, and I- we," he gestured at me, "think he should be quarterback. If he wants to be," he glanced at James.

James let out a sigh of relief. "Yeah. I've wanted to be a quarterback for a long time."

Coach Dominguez seemed to be startled. "Oh… Well…" he sighed. "Everybody out onto the field."

We walked out to the field, and this time, Anthony stayed with us.

"Coach Lashlee, I need to talk to you," Coach Dominguez hissed. They went into the locker room. A few minutes later, once the team had practically gathered around us, they came back out.

"Arran, you're off the team," Coach Dominguez said.

The team cheered.

Arran tried to pull off his helmet and when he couldn't he ran back to the school, squealing, "Auntie! Auntie!"

I snorted. The team congratulated James, and I licked his chin.

"Let's get started," Coach Lashlee told him.

"Remember," Coach Dominguez said when we were done, "we have a game in two days, at 5 o'clock, at home."

"Yes, coach," the team chanted.

So, is Julia's house nice? I asked Anthony in the Uber.

She produces a lot of famous theater shows, so yeah, he replied.

Oh, OK, I said, expecting something a bit smaller than our house.

The Uber guy parked the car by a street. "I think y'all are gonna have to walk from here." Ahead of us was what looked like a forest.

"Thanks," Anthony said, and we got out of the car. The Uber guy drove away.

We found a path and soon the back of a house came into view. Then we rounded a corner.

Oh my… I stared in disbelief.

There were three separate buildings. The main building was two floors but very big. In front of us was a nice pool. There was a dock to our right. Beyond the second building, which looked like some kind of sporting venue, was the third, smallest building.

We walked to the main building, which was to our left. Steps ran up to the entrance, around a water feature.

Julia came out to greet us. I had never met her before. She had sleek, brown hair and brown eyes. "Anthony!" she exclaimed, hugging his good side. "Oreo!" Julia glanced at me. "Who's a good boy?"

Me! I jumped onto her legs and licked her chin.

Julia laughed. "Please, come in! Guys, they're here!" she called.

Aunt Sonia, Eric, and a young man came bounding in from different places around the house.

Wow, I said, amazed at the house. We were in a small lobby-type of room. It opened up onto a huge living room. It'd take forever to describe the entire house, so we'll move on.

"Philip, this is Anthony and Oreo. Anthony and Oreo, this is my husband, Philip," Julia said.

Anthony and Philip shook hands. I licked Philip's hand and he ruffled my fur.

"Philip, honey, could you show the boys to their room?" Julia told him.

Philip nodded. "Come with me."

Because I didn't have much experience with stairs, I slipped a little but got up pretty easily.

Philip and Anthony came up behind me.

"How the heck did you do that?" Anthony asked, panting a little. *Let's just say that I've had some practice,* I answered.

"You guys play football, right?" Philip said as we continued walking to our temporary room.

"Yeah," Anthony said. "Where do you work?"

"I help out with Julia's scripts and whatnot," Philip replied.

"Cool," Anthony said.

We turned a corner, came up to one of the many doors, and stopped.

"Here we are," Philip swung open the door, revealing a beautiful room. It had a king bed, medium-sized closet, and an indoor doghouse they'd prepared specially for me. There was even another toy football in it. We also had our own ensuite bathroom.

"Thanks," Anthony told Philip.

"No problem," he said. "One more thing: The bell is for meals."

"OK."

Philip left.

We flopped onto the bed. A few minutes later, Anthony's phone rang. "Hey, Kate… What…? Um, sure… No problem."

I groaned. *I know, I read your mind.*

Okay, explanation time:

Amy had had a lot of emergencies lately, and she needed somebody to take care of her cat. Obviously, she asked Kate (they're best friends). I'd never met her cat, but Anthony said she was very obedient. Anyway, what happened was that, uh, Amy's cat kind of flooded their house (they deserved it). Kate was still mad at Amy, even though she felt super bad and apologized like twenty times. So, they were staying with us… *sigh.*

I was practicing for my football game with Philip, even though we had practice. They had a huge backyard. Also, it turns out Philip played in middle school.

"Go long!" Philip called. "Longer," he added.

I went longer. He threw the ball toward me. I got in position to catch it. Just as it was about to hit the ground, I jumped and caught it.

"Yeah, baby!" Philip celebrated. "Another perfect catch!"

Yeah! I dropped the ball and barked.

After a few more throws, we went back inside. I immediately smelled Clover.

I sighed. *Here we go,* I followed her scent to their room. *Hello, Clover,* I grumbled.

She gave me an evil stare and growled.

Look, I'm not happy to see you, either, so let's just leave each other alone, I suggested, growling softly.

I told you I would get you, so this is me getting you! Clover pounced at me.

I rolled to the side and ran towards the stairs. Out of the corner of my eye, I saw Amy's cat as I ran out of the room.

You can't get down those stairs, buddy! Clover teased.

I sprinted down the stairs and started barking for Anthony. Instead, Eric came.

"Woah!" Eric grabbed Clover's collar. She tried to bite his hand but couldn't reach it.

"Clover, stop!" Kate ordered her. Clover obeyed her.

I shook myself. *You gotta learn to let go of grudges,* I told Clover. *The Bible says that revenge is wrong.*

Clover calmed down a little once I said that. *Fine,* she muttered.

I kept my distance from Clover. At dinner, Kate unnecessarily told us the whole story of how Amy's cat flooded their house (by accident). Anthony tried to defend Amy, but Kate just got madder. I found it ridiculous, to tell you the truth.

We didn't know where home was going to be from now on, so I was worried when I went to sleep. Would we be staying there forever?

Chapter 22

· ·

♪ Under Pressure! Pushing Down on Me, Pushing Down on... Coach Dominguez! ♪

Okay, I got to admit, I was nervous about the game. I had never, *ever*, played a football game without Anthony by my side. Also, if I didn't win this game, the school people would kick me off the team. The family could also have used a bit of extra money, so we could move out on our own.

The next day, I couldn't stop pacing around the house. I vaguely remembered Amy coming to pick up the cat and apologizing a *lot*, but I was too distracted.

"Oreo, come on!" Anthony suddenly called from outside.

Sorry, I sprinted out to the car and jumped in. We were riding in style. And by that, I mean a small limo (is that possible?). Kate and Clover didn't want to come, which I was happy about.

Fortunately, the limo gave me plenty of space to pace in. Julia and Philip's butler, Alfred (much better than Marth!) was driving.

"Why are you so nervous?" Aunt Sonia asked me.

I barely heard her.

"What did he say?" Julia asked Anthony.

"Nothing," Anthony answered.

Awkward silence…

You okay? Rose asked me.

Yeah… I lied.

"Who are you guys playing?" Philip said.

"The Wolfpack," Eric replied. "Not too hard."

I lay down in the space between Anthony's legs and the seat.

"You'll do fine," Anthony reached down to pet me.

Will I? I thought to myself.

The stadium was packed. Apparently, everybody knew about me. I could see a lot of friends from high school in the bleachers, not all of them from football.

"See you guys later," Anthony said before we entered the locker room.

"Oreo!" James sounded relieved.

Present, I said.

"Put on your uniform," Coach Dominguez tossed it to Anthony. I was number seven, and, obviously, it said "Oreo."

Coach Dominguez called a quick huddle after we warmed up.

"Okay, after the special team, these will be the starters; Joseph, James, Oreo, Josh, Carlos, Kevin, Kaleb, Ben, Chris, Xavier, and Leo" he said. "Go to your usual positions."

The crowd cheered as we ran out.

Please help me win this, I quickly prayed to God. "Captains!" the head referee called.

James and Joseph went up and came back with good news; we had possession of the ball. The special team went out to kick the punt to start the game. They got to the fifty-yard line, which is right in the middle of the field.

The starters were next. We planned on doing the Fake-Handoff Play, aka Code S.

"Hike!"

Joseph ran right next to James, making it seem like he had the ball. Only a few of the Wolfpack fell for it, but it was enough for James. He ran through a gap, and I followed him, so as to protect him from tackles. It worked. James and I sped up whenever I barked, which meant I thought somebody was going to tackle him. This made it so that they accidentally tackled me instead of James.

The crowd began to cheer.

Yes! I bounced up from the floor, knowing this meant James had scored. The team congratulated him.

"How-ell! How-ell! How-ell!" the crowd chanted. "Howell" was James's surname.

Next came the extra point. Jay, our punter, made it. The Wolfpack didn't manage anything. We huddled.

"Which play are we doing?" James asked.

Everyone looked at me. I wagged my tail in excitement.

"Code O! Hike!" James called.

I darted from side-to-side, getting rid of my defender. I barked. The ball came flying my way. *Uh, oh,* I said as the defender got in front of me. Thankfully, Kevin tackled him out of my way, and I caught it.

The crowd cheered. "O-re-o! O-re-o!"

The team came over to praise me.

Mr. Referee blew his whistle. "Time out, Wolfpack!"

"Good job, bud!" Anthony ruffled my fur.

Thanks, I said, drinking water.

"That was the perfect play!" Coach Dominguez exclaimed. "Well done everyone," he added. "Now all we need is a strong defense."

I'm going to skip this part, because they didn't score, and it wasn't exciting.

It was our ball next. Coach Dominguez put Johan in for me.

"W.R.! Hike!" James called. He threw the football to Johan, and he caught it. Johan ran. He almost made it, but something happened. A defender tackled him, and Johan's ankle... mmm, no.

I heard him groan. *Oh no, not again,* I said, running over to him. The crowd gasped, and Coach Dominguez, Likens, and Stroud followed me.

Johan's ankle was quite... uh, twisted. I whimpered.

"Oreo, clear the way," Coach Dominguez said as he and Coach Likens helped him up.

I barked and ran in front of them, *Move, people!*

A bunch of medics ran over to us with a stretcher.

"Oreo, go back to the bench," Coach Stroud told me.

I hesitated but followed his orders. The on-field players were already there.

"Well?" Joseph asked.

My tail drooped. *His ankle went...* I cocked my head to the side.

"That's how his ankle is," Anthony pointed at me.

Out of the corner of my eye, I saw Eileen, Johan's little sister, and his mom run over to the stretcher.

"Oreo can't play the whole game, so what now?" Chris said.

"I can always play."

Everybody looked at Hugh Rojas.

Okay, to be fair, Hugh is a pretty good receiver, but he's... well, he's short, and the Wolfpack were really big.

"We'll wait until Coach Dominguez comes back," Coach Hickson said.

"Johan has twisted his ankle, ladies and gents," the commentator announced.

The coaches came back. All of the coaches talked privately, until Coach Dominguez turned around.

He sighed. "One chance, Rojas, or Oreo's going in."

I panted innocently.

"Thank you, Coach Dominguez," Hugh said.

"Hugh Rojas is going in for Johan. Let's see how this plays out," the commentator said.

James quickly made the touchdown, and the extra point was next. Jay made it. James easily intercepted the ball.

"W.R, W.R, and pass it to Rojas," Coach Dominguez muttered into his microphone. "Listen to your coach!"

"W.R! W.R! Hike!" James said.

Hugh quickly got away from his defender and called for the ball. James threw it to him, but there was already another defender with Hugh, ready to intercept the ball. There was nothing Hugh could do.

"Intercepted by the Wolfpack!" the commentator declared.

You'll shut up if you know what's good for you, I grumbled at him.

"Sub! Sub!" Coach Justice called to the referee. "Oreo, get in there," he nodded at me.

I went in for Hugh. We stopped their run of luck pretty quickly, but by the third quarter, I was exhausted. Thankfully, we were winning 34-12, so surely Coach Dominguez would give me a break.

Break, I gasped, panting heavily. *Please,* I collapsed onto the grass.

Anthony crouched beside me. "Coach, he needs a break," he rested a hand on my fur and gave me my water bowl.

I lapped it up. *Thanks.*

"There, you got some water," Coach Dominguez said. "Now, get back..."

"Manny, he's been playing for almost three whole quarters," Coach Baker interrupted.

I whimpered. *Yeah, and all the other guys got subs.*

Coach Dominguez sighed. "Fine. Rojas, go in, but I don't want to sigh again today!"

"Yes, coach," Hugh said happily.

I didn't get up from my place on the grass for, like, twenty minutes. By then, it was the fourth quarter. Anthony gave me something for my leg, and I couldn't move for a few minutes. When I was finally able to move, the score was 40-35. We weren't winning by a lot.

"Oreo, please tell me you're ready," Coach Damian said.

Yeah, I got up and barked.

"Sub!" he immediately called.

I was back in the game. The crowd cheered. It was the Wolfpack's ball.

"Code K! Hike!" their quarterback called.

The wide receiver on Kaleb's side tried to get away from him, but Kaleb was too quick. On seeing his fellow wide receiver's failure, the one on my side tried to get rid of me. I let him think I was slow, and he called for the ball. I easily intercepted it.

The crowd roared, and the team came over to pat and praise me.

"Code red! Code red! Hike!" James called.

"Code red" was Joe's time to shine. James handed it off to him. Ben started following Joseph, protecting him.

I was holding off my defender when I realized that one of their safeties was out-running them. I barked, trying to let my team know.

Luckily, Leo, one of our running backs, understood me and quickly tackled him.

Yes! I cheered as Joseph and Ben crossed the end line. The crowd cheered with me.

The extra point was next. This time, Coach Dominguez let Mitch do it, and he made it. We cheered. There were 7 minutes left in the game. Both teams scored a field goal, so we won.

As we were leaving, we were treated to a lovely surprise.

Wait, is that...?"

"No way," Anthony said.

Aunt Sonia gasped.

"Hey, guys!" Fabi ran over to us.

"Fabi!" we all exclaimed at once.

I barked and leaped on her. *Fabi!!!* I licked her.

"Okay, okay!" Fabi exclaimed, gently pushing me off and standing up.

"Hi," Alex came up behind her. I licked his chin. He laughed. "Hey, Oreo."

We introduced Rose, and everybody said Hi.

"So, um, we have some news…" Fabi said.

"Yeah, um, maybe we should go over to the car," Alex said.

I tilted my head at something shiny on Fabi's finger. *Is that a rin… Oh!* I stopped myself. *You guys are getting married!*

"Wait, what?" Anthony turned towards me. "You guys are getting married?!" he said, realizing what I was looking at.

Fabi smiled. "Yes."

Aunt Sonia squealed and hugged her. Eric's jaw dropped. I barked happily and ran circles around the engaged couple. Rose followed suit.

We took Alex's car. Eric drove, with Aunt Sonia next to him. Fabi and Alex were in the back seat, and Anthony, Rose, and I were behind them.

While they were talking about the wedding, I asked Anthony, *Where are we going?*

We're going to go visit the pups, Anthony replied.

Yes! I exclaimed.

Chapter 23

· · · · · · · · · · · · · · · · · · · ·

Here Comes the Bride...

As soon as Alex opened the car door, I jumped over him and rang the Jacobs family's doorbell.

Jackson appeared in the doorway. I barged in, Rose behind me.

Daddy!!! all seven pups came flying at me.

I laughed. *Hi, guys! Lucky!* I said as she nuzzled me. I licked her.

The Jacobs were strangely quiet.

"Everything okay?" Anthony asked.

Aiden whispered something into his ear. Anthony's eyes widened but not in a good way.

What's going on? I glanced at Lucky.

I don't know, she said.

"Can't somebody else do it?" Anthony asked the room. Fabi, Alex, Aunt Sonia, and Eric now seemed to know the news, too.

"You do it," Jackson muttered at Anthony.

Anthony, what's going on? I asked, getting worried.

He took a deep breath. "Oreo, buddy, friend, brother, man," he stammered. "Don't overreact, but... um, well... they have to... uh... the pups have to get adopted," Anthony blurted quite suddenly.

THE ADVENTURES OF OREO

At first, I chuckled. But I realized he was serious. *No,* I said sternly, stepping in front of the pups. Lucky followed my lead. This gave me a terrible flashback to the time when my sister was getting adopted. Then, I remembered that that had led to the pound.

Anthony read my mind. "I promise you, that won't happen. They'll have very nice families."

Aiden picked up a basket and walked towards us. "It's okay, guys."

Lucky and I growled.

Mommy, what does "adopt" mean? Spot said.

It means getting taken away from us, Lucky answered.

The pups whimpered.

Don't worry, we won't let that happen, I growled again as the humans crept closer.

"Come on, guys, you'll see each other!" Fabi said. "*Ohana!*"

That one word triggered a memory.

Okay, so Fabi watches a lot of "original" and "classic" movies. This one was called "Lilo & Stitch."

"Ohana," said one of the characters.

What does "ohana" mean? I asked Cookie.

It means family, and family means...

"Never leave anybody behind," the character said at the same time as her.

Huh, I said. Wait, but doesn't that mean that adopting is kind of wrong?

Cookie thought about that for a moment, and then said, Well, then, I'll add my own definition to it. Family also means "a group of people who will always be in your heart," Cookie said.

That's very true, I cuddled next to her. Fabi joined us.

This memory led to a very different memory...

Why are those pups getting taken away, mommy? one of my sisters said. I glanced over to where she was looking. Three pups were being carried away by one of the humans.

Well, sweetie, they're getting adopted, she nodded at her fellow mom.

What does that mean? I asked.

They're getting a human family, my mom replied.

Are they going to see their mommy again? one of my brothers said.

Our mom hesitated, No, sweetheart.

Will that happen to us? I was getting worried.

Yes, but it's a good thing, mom said.

We whimpered.

Won't you forget us? one of my sisters said.

No, sweethearts! Never! mom exclaimed.

We want to stay with you, I said.

My mom sighed. You can't. It's a dog's destiny to be with humans.

What if we forget you by accident? another one of my brothers said.

May I sing another song to you? our mom asked.

Yes! we all practically screamed.

Mommy giggled. Okay, then.

We all cuddled close, and she started singing.

♪ Come stop your crying. It will be alright. Just take my hand; hold it tight. I will protect you from all around you. I will be here; don't you cry, ♪ she licked us. For one so small, you seem so strong. My paws will hold you, keep you safe and warm. This bond between us can't be broken. I will be here; don't you cry. 'Cause you'll be in my heart. Yes, you'll be in my heart, from this day on, now and forever more. You'll be in my heart, no matter what they say. You'll be here in my heart, always…

I yawned sleepily. My mommy licked me one more time, and I fell asleep.

I stopped growling.

Lucky glimpsed at me, still snarling. *What are you doing?*
Lucky, stop, I told her.
Why? she said.
Trust me, I said.

Lucky stopped. The humans seemed confused. Aiden crept towards us, but I growled softly.

I looked at the pups. *Do you know what* ohana *means?*
No, they all said.

Ohana *means family, and family means "never leave anybody behind,"* I began.

That's why you're protecting us! Go-Go said.

Yes, but there's another definition, and I learned it from a very wise dog, I glanced at Cookie Jr. *Family also means "a group of people who will always be in your heart,"* I finished. I looked at Anthony and then back at the pups. *And take it from me, you can have more than one family.*

The pups and Lucky thought about this for a minute.
Will we still see you? Max asked.
Absolutely, I said, having quickly consulted with Anthony.

Mr. Jacobs's phone chimed. "It's Hunter's owners. We'd better get going," he stood up.

We said goodbye (for now) (Rose joined us), and Alex and Fabi told the Jacobs' the news.

Lucky and I insisted on meeting the pups' owners. They all turned out to be really nice.

You okay? Rose asked me in the car.
I'll get over it, I said, quite honestly.

"So, when and where is the wedding going to be?" asked Aunt Sonia.

"Mexico City. Alex's dad was a missionary there for a while, and he says he fell in love with the place, right?" Fabi glanced at him.

"Yeah. *Y hablo español,*" Alex said.

Huh? I said.

He speaks Spanish, Anthony told me.

Oh, I said.

"Muy bien!" Aunt Sonia exclaimed.

Translation, please.

Very good, Anthony replied, and then, "Okay, can we talk in a language that the dogs understand?"

Everybody laughed.

"Anyway," Fabi giggled one last time, "we don't know when yet. 'Cause our family's huge."

"You're right," Eric agreed. "It would have to be convenient for as many people as possible."

"Well, your *abuelos* are always free, so that's no problem," Aunt Sonia said. "You also need a wedding planner."

"Way ahead of you, *mama,*" said Fabi. "We already got one," she added.

"We're going to check out some houses, aren't we?" Anthony said.

"Yep," Eric answered.

Aunt Sonia and Eric found a house, but we were planning on moving out. We dropped off Fabi and Alex at their place and went to see the houses. We were in Dad's neighborhood.

As we walked along the sidewalk, we were stopped by a boy who looked about eleven.

"Wait, are you Oreo?" he stared at me.

I tilted my head. *How do you know my name?*

"How do you know him?" Anthony translated.

"From football, of course!" the boy exclaimed, like it was the most obvious thing in the world. He unzipped his backpack and pulled out a piece of paper and an inkpad. "Do you guys mind?"

Wait, what? I was extremely confused.

Autograph, Anthony told me.

Oh… OK, I said.

The boy opened the inkpad and put it and the piece of paper on the floor. I pressed my paw against the inkpad and onto the paper.

"Thanks!" the boy put everything away and ran across the street.

"That was…"

Weird, random, amazing? I tried to finish Anthony's sentence.

He chuckled. We all kept walking.

You're famous! Rose said.

Yeah, I guess I am, I admitted.

We stopped at a really nice house, and Anthony and I agreed that it was perfect. We walked up to the salesman.

"How much for this house?" Anthony asked.

"$400,000," the salesman replied.

"We'll take it."

So, Anthony signed a bunch of papers. Blah, blah, blah.

Once he was finally done, we drove back to Julia and Philip's to pack.

I'm going to miss you, Rose told me.

She and I were lying on the couch. A few hours had passed, and the moving truck was here.

You'll still see lots of me, I reassured her.

Ooh, you're right! Rose exclaimed.

"Oreo, come on!" Anthony called.

I sprinted outside and into one of Julia's many cars.

We got to our new house. I helped Anthony unpack. We still had to buy furniture, so we slept on a cot in our new bedroom.

The next day, Anthony got online and bought some furniture. He also bought two or three Roombas and cleaning robots.

We walked to the grocery store (I had to sign a few more autographs) to get some food. By the time we got back, the furniture people were there.

"Thank you!" Anthony called after them at noon. I was lying down on our new couch, watching a replay of the game on the Samsung television.

So, the layout of our house:

The living room, where I was, was by the entrance. If you walk down a hallway by the entrance, you come to the kitchen. Keep walking, and you eventually push open a door to the lounge area. Take a right at the entrance, and you'll find our bedroom. In front of our bedroom door, there's a guest room. We also have an ensuite bathroom. The garage was to the left of the entrance, where Anthony's new navy-blue Jaguar was.

I watched as Joseph scored a touchdown, and I couldn't help but bark.

We drove to the dog park. Anthony was able to drive now (kind of, don't ask). We picked up Amy and Sky on our way.

I haven't seen you in a while, I said.

Yeah, Sky replied. *I missed you.*

I smiled. *I missed you, too.*

"Is Kate still mad at you?" Anthony asked Amy.

"Yeah," Amy frowned. "She hasn't changed."

"I'm not surprised," Anthony admitted.

"Anthony!" Amy punched him gently. "People can change…! Sometimes…"

"Mmhm," Anthony said.

I sniffed the air. *Nah, I must be tired.*

Nope, Sky said in a panic.

Code K! I warned Anthony. *And C!* I added.

THE ADVENTURES OF OREO

"Uh, oh," Anthony said.

"Don't tell me."

Anthony nodded.

"Bloody hell," Amy buried her face in her hands.

Suddenly, a bunch of people surrounded us: instead of Kate, it was football fans.

"Out of the way!" a familiar voice said after we'd been jostled for a while. They didn't move.

"Dad!" Anthony exclaimed. He and dad hugged.

"Hey, son," he said. "Scram!" he said, yelling this time.

"Oreo, say something to your fans," a shoved a microphone into my snout.

I barked, not knowing what else to do.

"Oreo, bark again if you love your team," said someone else with another microphone.

I barked.

"Do you plan on continuing your career? Bark if so."

I barked again.

"Did you think you were ever going to become famous?"

I stayed silent this time. A vicious bark scattered the people. *Oreo!* Clover ran over to me.

I assumed we were good. *Thank goodness,* I said. *Fame is annoying.*

"Hey, Clover," Anthony said.

Sky, where are you? I mumbled out of the corner of my mouth.

Hiding, she answered from her hiding place.

"Kate… Hi," Anthony said.

Kate gave him a curt nod.

"So, how was the wedding?" Anthony asked her. Maddie (the horse girl) had had her wedding.

"Fine, I guess," Kate replied.

Amy slowly and cautiously walked our way. Kate all of a sudden seemed annoyed. Yep, that's Kate!

You know what, I think I see a friend. Ima bounce, I escaped the scene.

"I should go with him!" Anthony said a little too loudly. He quickly followed me.

I actually wasn't lying this time. I had spotted some friends. Shelby and Enzo, a Boston Terrier and French Bulldog, with their owner, Mia. She was Joseph's little sister.

"Hi, Anthony!" she had her hair pulled up in a ponytail.

"Hello," Anthony said.

I licked Mia's chin.

She giggled. "Hey, Oreo!"

I dropped back down to the floor. *Enzo! Shelby!*

Oreo! they exclaimed in unison. They tried to tackle me, but I was much bigger.

"So, how's music?" Mia asked.

"Great," Anthony answered. "How's baking?"

"Amazing."

They kept chatting while us dogs roughhoused.

"Well, I'd better go. See you around," Mia walked away.

I saw Sky run over.

What happened? I asked her.

Kate ignored us, Sky answered.

Ah, a new stage of Kate's stubbornness, I saidm imitating a wildlife reporter. *Fascinating.*

Sky chortled.

We settled down in a café for a while and then we left.

That night, I had no trouble getting to sleep.

The wedding came in a flash. About three months had passed and we'd got everything ready.

Anthony woke up with a little help from yours truly. He got dressed in casual clothes, and we ate breakfast.

Anthony picked up my bow tie and called me over.

Yes! I love *bow ties!* I happily trotted over to him. He wrapped it around my neck. I ran to one of the bathrooms, jumped onto the ledge of the sink and looked at my fancy self. I barked, my tail wagging. Anthony laughed at the door.

We left at ten o'clock in the morning.

I stuck my head out the window. The playoffs started in two days, and a bunch of people waved to me. I barked back.

We finally arrived at the airport, and were treated to a pleasant surprise.

"Emil?" Anthony said.

Emil turned around. "Anthony!" he exclaimed. They hugged and patted each other's backs. Emil peered down at me. "And Oreo! I don't know why I wasn't expecting you guys," he said, patting me. I wagged my tail.

"Same here," Anthony confessed.

"I finally got the boarding passes," Brooke walked over from the registration area. If you don't remember, she's Emil's wife. "Oh! Anthony and Oreo!" she hugged Anthony and stroked my fur. "You're a great addition to the team."

Thanks! I licked her fingers. Brooke grinned and stood up.

Anthony looked at his watch. "We'd better go."

"Of course. See you guys later," Emil said.

"Yeah," Anthony and I walked away.

A few very nice fans asked for "pawtographs" (yes, it's a thing now), and we trotted outside to a private jet area.

We have a jet? I said.

No, but Mom does, Anthony said.

Just then the jet landed near us. A few moments later, a familiar figure stepped out. I sprinted to Mom and lightly pounced on her.

She laughed. "Hey, Oreo! I missed you guys!"

"Mom!" Anthony hugged her.

Mom laughed in delight. "Hey, sweetheart," she kissed his cheek. "Quickly, quickly," she rushed us into the jet.

We rode in luxury. It was a three-hour flight from South Florida to Mexico City. I was kind of tired once we landed, and I couldn't sleep on the jet, so the rest is a blur. I remember sleeping in a car, though.

Anthony gently shook me awake as the car parked in front of a hotel. I collapsed onto our suite's bed.

"It's your birthday tomorrow," Anthony whispered as he turned on the TV.

I yawned. *Cool,* I said sleepily before drifting off.

In the morning, I was treated to a quick vanilla ice cream. I was surprised that the wedding was on my birthday.

Anthony, Mom and I got ready and headed to the church.

We sat near Amy, Sky, Rose, Eric, Emil, and Brooke.

Any idea how weddings work? asked Rose.

No clue, I said.

Same, Sky replied. *I do know they, like… you know… kiss.*

Rose groaned. *Ew.*

I will protect your puppy… -ish, I nodded at Sky, *minds.*

They giggled.

The wedding started. The first people to walk down the aisle were the groom (Alex) and his mom. Next came the bridesmaids followed by the bride (Fabi) and her dad.

Here comes the bride… I sang to the tune.

I love her dress… Sky continued.

That color looks so pretty on her, Rose finished.

Fabi was wearing a pastel blue dress with beautiful flowers all over it.

The wedding went on very smoothly. First, they completed the civil ceremony, then the religious one.

"I now pronounce you husband and wife," the priest said. "You may kiss the bride."

Us dogs groaned and turned away. Everybody cheered.

After this, we went to the reception, which is basically a party. We danced and ate dinner. Thankfully, it was outdoors. All in all, it was a pretty great wedding. I was hoping to stay in Mexico for a while, but we packed up and went straight to the airport.

Come on! I complained. *Just let me stay for* one *day! Even Mom's staying! And she has work!*

"And *we* have playoffs," Anthony dragged me along the floor of the airport.

I don't need to practice! I'm very experienced! I argued.

"Practice this week is mandatory," Anthony said.

"Practice this week is mandatory," I mocked.

Anthony rolled his eyes and continued dragging me.

Mom had let us borrow the jet again. It was a pretty good flight. While I was falling asleep, I realized that I was slightly nervous about the playoffs.

Chapter 24

· · · · · · · · · · · · · · · · · · ·

The Championship

Sadly, after our first playoff game, we held a funeral for Moldy (Jaylee's chinchilla). It was very sad. We helped Jaylee out by watching anime with her and by putting up with her endless anime nerd talk.

Then, we were off to our next game against the North Carolina Tar Heels. We beat them 21-14.

To my relief, I got to see the pups regularly. Their families were very welcoming and the pups were happy.

Also, the team's new director of nutrition and performance, Noelani Rodriguez, was the perfect fit.

Three days after the Tar Heels game, Lucky and I officially got married. Best day of my life.

"Oreo, do you take Lucky as your wife, to love forever and ever?" Dad said at the Jacobs's house.

I barked. *I do.*

"And Lucky, do you take Oreo as your husband, to love for all eternity?" Dad looked at Lucky.

She barked. *I do.*

"I now pronounce you husband and wife," Dad announced. "You may kiss the bride."

Lucky and I nuzzled and licked each other. Anthony, Amy, Sky, Aunt Sonia, Eric, Rose, the Jacobs, and the pups cheered behind us.

Yeah, go dad! Spot called.

Yay! All the girls said.

I will hunt down anybody who tries to separate you! said Hunter, and he probably meant it.

And I'll help him! Max added.

We had our wedding party. It was AMAZING.

Two days later, we beat the Virginia Cavaliers 24-21. I was getting kind of scared that one of the teams was going to win. *Groan.* Great, now I was thinking negative thoughts.

One day, we were chilling in Anthony's room when his phone rang.

"Hi, Dad…" Anthony sighed. "Are you trying to taunt me, or did you forget about the arm…? Special lessons…? Just tell me… Fine, we're coming over," he hung up.

I tilted my head at him. *He didn't tell you why these lessons are special?*

"No, but we'd better get over there."

We drove to Dad's house. Anthony rang the doorbell and Dad opened the door.

"Hey!" Dad sounded excited.

We walked in and said "Hi" to Milo. Then, we went into the living room.

"Anthony, this is Ryan," Dad said, introducing a man who was setting up some stuff on the carpet. "Ryan, this is my son, Anthony."

"Hello," Ryan said. He was a middle-aged man with brown hair and glasses.

"Hi," Anthony said. They shook hands. "What's that?" he gestured at the contraption on the carpet.

"This is going to help you play," Ryan patted it.

"What does that mean?" Anthony looked at Dad.

"Ryan helps people play instruments when they're injured," Dad explained.

"Yep," Ryan confirmed. "This is for bass players like you."

Anthony widened his eyes. "Really?"

"Yeah," Dad said. "You did bring it, right?"

"It's in the car," Anthony rushed outside and brought in his bass.

"Okay, just stand right here," Ryan tapped his foot on a spot on the carpet. Anthony followed his instructions.

In a few minutes, Ryan had set the contraption up on Anthony's bad arm, so it supported it, but also helped him play. Ryan handed him his bass and told him the best way to play.

Anthony started slow by playing "Burn the House Down," a song by an old band called AJR. Halfway through the song, he winced and stopped. Ryan then told him how to fix this problem. The next time, Anthony was able to play the song all the way through.

I barked. *Yay!*

Everybody chuckled.

A few minutes later, Dad, Milo, and I went outside and played football for a bit. Milo thought it was normal fetch, which it kind of was, since I'm a wide receiver.

The lesson was an hour long and by the end of it, Anthony had gotten really good. Ryan said he would be glad to give him the contraption for free.

"Thanks so much, Dad," Anthony said as we got into the car.

Dad grinned. "No problem. He'll go over to your place every Tuesday from now on."

"Okay, see you at Oreo's game," Anthony said.

"Yeah," Dad glanced at me. "Practice hard, champ."

I barked. *Roger that.*

We drove home and Aunt Sonia invited us to dinner a few hours later. It was delicious. After this, we went home and fell asleep.

The next day was Monday, which meant school (and practice). Anthony brought his contraption, and his teacher actually knew Ryan, so everything was pretty much perfect. I just waited anxiously for practice.

"Football team to the front office, please," the PA said in the middle of Anthony's Business class. Business was his minor, and music his major.

Anthony and I exchanged a glance, and Anthony got up from his seat. He picked up my leash, and we headed to the front office. On the way, we met up with the rest of the team.

James knocked. The Vice-Dean Dr. Lips, opened the door. She looked a bit… nervous? Wow, that was new. The only other people in the room were Coaches Lashlee and Baker. No Coach Dominguez, though.

Where's Coach Dominguez? I asked.

Listen, Anthony said.

I nodded.

"So, we've, um, got some disappointing news," Dr. Lips said.

We waited expectantly.

Coach Lashlee sighed. "Coaches Dominguez and Stroud have both come down with the flu."

The whole team immediately groaned.

What?! I exclaimed. *At the same frickin' time?!?*

"At the exact same time?" Anthony translated calmly.

"Yeah," Coach Baker confirmed.

"But it's fine," Dr. Lips. "Because Coach Lashlee and Coach Baker have offered to be your head coaches."

Coach Lashlee raised his eyebrows at her. "Huh?"

Dr. Lips glared at him.

"Oh, right!" Coach Lashlee lied. "Right…"

I groaned. *That's convincing.*

"We're still going to the playoffs, right?" someone asked.

"Yes," Dr. Lips reassured us. "And your coaches should be better soon."

So, Coach Lashlee and Coach Baker took us for training on Monday. It was… different, but we were kind of used to them, since they're the coordinators, so it wasn't that hard.

I haven't told you this, but Anthony and Amy hadn't gone on a date for a *while*. It was weird. Every time Anthony called her, she said she had an emergency. And Anthony was afraid to ask her… again.

The next day, Amy asked Anthony to watch Sky for the night. We agreed.

So, I said after she had dropped off Sky, *what are all these emergencies about?*

Sky froze and dropped her bone. *Um… nothing. Just… family business,* she stuttered.

What kind of family business? I tilted my head.

Whatever, um… Whatever Amy's dad does, Sky said.

Just tell me, I urged.

Sky hesitated. *I… I can't. It's a secret.*

What? I was very confused.

Suddenly, the doorbell rang, cutting our conversation short. We ran to the door, and Anthony opened it.

"Hey," Ryan said.

"Hi," Anthony moved aside. "Come in."

Ryan and Anthony set up the contraption, and Ryan handed over the bass. Anthony started playing "I Feel Good," which was originally called "I Got You." I pulled Sky into our room.

What? Sky complained.

Do you trust me? I questioned her.

Yes! Sky said skeptically.

Then, why won't you tell me your secret? I said.

Sky gulped. *It's supposed to be a surprise.*

The Sky I know would be excited about a surprise, I was starting to worry.

It's just… Sky paused. *Amy's not sure about this surprise yet.*

Oh… OK, I said. Sky went back to the living room.

I paced around the room wondering what this "surprise" could be. Amy was studying architecture, so maybe something to do with her career? No, she would be excited to tell Anthony. Sky also said she wasn't sure about it. Maybe… No, I was stuck.

I ran back to the living room, where Ryan was handing him some sheet music. Anthony started playing a song I had never heard.

What song is this? I asked as he finished it.

A really old one, Anthony replied. *It's called "Billie Jean." It's by this dude, Michael Jackson.*

Oh, I said. *I'm going to go practice for my game.*

Our next game was on Thursday, which was two days away. I picked up a football from my toy box outside. Our backyard was simple with a small pool and grass beyond that.

I inserted the ball into the launcher and pressed the button. I ran backwards, following the path of the ball, jumped, and caught it. After a few more throws, I practiced my tackles on the dummy. I almost ripped its head off by accident.

I was doing suicide sprints when Sky came outside.

Wow, you're fast, she complimented me.

Thanks, I said, panting. I realized she had her tennis ball. We played Chase-the-Ball for a bit and went inside once Anthony's lesson had finished. Then, we went to visit the pups.

Dad! Max nuzzled me. His owners came out from the kitchen. They were a nice couple, Jasmine and Sam.

"Hey, guys!" Sam said.

We traveled to see the rest of the pups and then went to the Jacobs' house.

Did you see them today? I asked Lucky.

Yes, she said. *I heard your coaches are ill.*

Two of them, I confirmed. *The head coach and the assistant head coach.*

Wow, said Lucky. *At the same time?*

Yep, I said.

I was hoping to see at least Coach Stroud the next day, but he was still sick. Coach Dominguez, too.

Later in the afternoon, Amy picked up Sky. She looked very tired.

Anthony noticed this, too. "You wanna come in?"

"No, it's fine. Thanks, honey," Amy kissed him and left.

"You talked to Sky the other day, right?" Anthony asked me at dinner.

Yeah, I answered.

"What did she say?"

That the reason Amy's having so many emergencies is a secret/ surprise, I said.

"Why?" Anthony took a sip of water.

Because Amy's not sure about it or something like that.

"What?" Anthony's nose scrunched up.

That's what I said, I glanced at him. *I'm going outside.*

I practiced a bit. Anthony told me that Fabi and Alex were moving to Miami, which was splendid news. Our game was against the Pittsburgh Panthers. They were good.

In the morning, I paced around nervously. We went to school, but I was very distracted.

Finally, it was time for the game. I knew we had to defend our record at home.

The Panthers got the ball first. They made it to the sixty-yard line. Not too bad.

"Hike!" their quarterback said. I saw him hand it off to his center. He got past our tackles, but not our ends. They tackled him. The center had gotten to the forty-yard line.

First down.

"Code W! Hike!"

The quarterback threw it to the wide receiver that I was guarding. I immediately tackled him.

Long-story-short, they got to the twenty-yard line before Ben stopped them. It was our ball next. The special team got to our forty-yard line.

"Code O! Code O! Hike!" James grunted.

I ran as far as I could before James threw it to me. I had to go forward a bit to bypass my defender, but I successfully caught it at the Panthers' thirty-yard line. I ran towards the end line. The safeties loomed in front of me. Everybody else was too far away to help me, so I let them tackle me at the thirty-five yard line.

The crowd cheered.

First down. We agreed to do the Hand-off play.

"Hike!" James immediately handed it back to Joseph, and Joseph started running. Ben tackled their middle linebacker, clearing a path through the middle for Joseph. I sprinted to the safety on my side of the field, knowing he would be able to tackle him. I barely reached him in time. Out of the corner of my eye, I saw Johan tackle the other safety. If the rest of the team had done their jobs, Joseph would have an easy path to the end line. I tried to hold off one of the cornerbacks, who was making his way toward Joseph.

The audience roared as he reached the end line. We congratulated him.

Thankfully, we ended up winning 31-27. It was a very close game. We had had to make a field goal so they wouldn't catch us.

Our next game was against the Syracuse Orange. They were pretty good, but not great. Thankfully, it was at Miami. Turns out they have a lot of fans, though. The stadium was full to the brim.

"Okay, team, let's do this," Coach Lashlee said.

"Captains!" the referee called. James and I hurried over to him. I tried not to fixate on Syracuse's very buff captains. We shook hands (and paw). "Heads or tails?" the ref asked them.

"Heads," the one on the right said.

The Ref flipped the coin. It landed on heads. "Ball or side?" he turned to look at the captains.

"Ball," the other one replied.

So, we ended up with the same side, without possession of the ball. The special team went out for the punt and stopped them at our thirty-yard line. I was very happy with them.

"Hike!" their quarterback grunted.

I ran to the wide receiver I was supposed to guard. The quarterback faked a hand-off to his center, and Ben was the only one to fall for the trick. The quarterback sprinted up Johan's side. My eyes widened as he jinked past him. I ran to help, worried that he would get past Chris, one of our safeties. I was right. He did. I was now just about within reach. With one great leap, I tackled him. We went rolling down the field. I heard the Ref blow his whistle. I slowly got up and shook myself. It was just the first down, and I was already covered from head-to-toe in dirt.

Johan ran over and helped the quarterback up. Then he patted me and said, "Thanks, boy."

I barked at him. *Yep,* I glanced down and realized we were at their forty-yard line. We could still do this.

"D! D! D! Hike!" the quarterback called.

Once again, I ran to the wide receiver. He sprinted toward the end-line, and I followed, knowing this probably meant he was going to call for the ball. Suddenly, he ran away from the end-line

THE ADVENTURES OF OREO

and did just that. He caught it, but I was there to—Ouch. I'm just remembering this part—stop him. Or so I thought. He had thought he had left me behind and didn't see me behind him. He tripped over me, and I yelped, stumbling onto the floor.

"Ooh," the crowd winced collectively.

Josh ran over to check on me, followed by the rest of the team. The Ref blew his whistle several times. Coach Lashlee and Baker came to me. I saw Anthony struggling to get past everyone.

I'm fine, I'm fine, I muttered, trying to get up. I heard the wide receiver groan.

Josh pulled me up carefully and grabbed my collar to keep me upright. "Take it easy, bud."

Anthony finally got to me. Josh handed me over to him. I leaned against his chest, being gentle with his arm.

"Anthony!" Carlos called, handing him a pack of ice. Everybody was standing around me, and the quarterback was limping over to a stretcher. Anthony gently put the pack of ice on my side, and I winced.

"Relax, bud," Anthony stroked my fur. "Coach, help me with him."

Coach Baker, who was the closest to us, picked me up. We jogged to the bench, where Amy was laying out soft pillows (don't know where she got them) on the floor. Coach Baker put me down on them. The whole team surrounded me.

"Give him some breathing space!" Coach Lashlee ordered. They backed up a little bit.

"Here we go," Amy laid a larger ice pack on my side.

I hate getting hurt, I mumbled. I glanced at Coach Justice, who was pulling a roll of bandages out of a first-aid kit. He tossed it to Anthony.

"Lift him up for a second," Anthony said. Joseph and James did this. In a flash, Anthony wrapped a bandage around me. "Okay," he said, signaling for them to put me back down.

"Looks like Oreo will not be going back to the field," the commentator announced.

I slowly lay down on my stomach and winced.

"Kaleb go in for him," Coach Baker instructed. Kaleb nodded.

"Kaleb Grooms will be going in for Oreo, and Justin Hay for Hills," the commentator said.

I watched as they set up at our ten-yard line.

"Code red! Code red! Hike!"

James aimed to tackle the quarterback, but the quarterback quickly handed it to his center. The center ran, getting past James. Luckily, Xavier caught him not a moment too soon.

It was second down now. They had made it to the seven-yard line.

"D! D! D! Hike!" the quarterback said.

This time, it seemed like he was going to throw it to Johan's wide receiver. Right before James tackled him, he threw it to him. The wide receiver sprinted backward, which was not smart of him. Johan easily intercepted the ball.

We cheered. The players on field congratulated Johan.

Next, it was our ball. The special team went ahead and did the kick-off, getting us to our thirty-yard line.

From what I heard; the team was going to do the Hand-Off play again.

"Hike!" James called. In a flash, he handed it to Joseph. Joe sprinted as fast as he could. One by one, Ben, Chris, Tony, and everybody else stopped the Orange from tackling him. Unfortunately, one of them got through a gap and was able to bring him down, but we had gotten all the way to their twenty-yard line!

"Turn! Turn! Hike!" James said.

"Turn" meant that James was going to fake a pass or a hand-off and score.

THE ADVENTURES OF OREO

James faked a pass and ran to the end-line. The middle linebacker had fallen for it, so he had a clear path there. He threw the football to the ground as he passed the end-line.

Everybody cheered.

The special team went out for the extra point. Luke made it through a millisecond before they stopped him. We cheered some more.

I wasn't able to go in, but Kaleb was pretty good, so we won. Anthony was going to take me to the vet afterwards. Oh, the score was 21-13. I was very relieved.

"Can you walk?" Anthony asked me as he stood up from the bench.

I stood up and took a few steps. *Yeah.*

I had to sign a few things first, so we ended up staying longer than planned.

The last to want autographs was a group of three: a young lady with light brown hair, a man who seemed to be her boyfriend, and a miniature golden doodle with black-brown fur.

Hello, I said to the puppy.

The pup looked awe-struck. *I-I can't believe I'm meeting Oreo!*

I chuckled. *Thank you,* I looked at the humans and barked. That's what they usually like best.

"Hi!" the lady said. "May I pet you?"

I barked to indicate she could. She stroked my fur. The man followed suit.

"It's an honor," the man shook Anthony's hand.

"Thanks," Anthony replied.

"Do you know Kate?" the lady said. "Because I think she mentioned you."

"Oh, yeah, we do," Anthony said. *Okay then,* he told me privately.

Yeah, I guess we're doing this, I smiled.

You know Clover? the pup asked me.

Yeah, I answered. *What's your name?*

Mocha, Mocha said.

Well, nice to meet you, Mocha, I told her.

Mocha squealed. *It's amazing to meet you!*

I smiled even wider. *Thanks.*

"I'm Brooklyn," the lady told Anthony. "This is my boyfriend, Daniel."

"Nice to meet you," said Anthony.

Mocha barked at Brooklyn. She laughed. "Alright, here," Brooklyn handed her a piece of paper and set an inkpad down on the floor. I pressed my paw against it and made my mark. Then I handed it to Anthony, who had a pen. He signed it, too.

Thank you, thank you, thank you! Mocha exclaimed; her tail was wagging very hard.

Of course, I said.

"Thanks so much," Brooklyn said to Anthony.

"No problem," Anthony said.

Bye!!! Mocha called as they walked away.

Bye, I said, grinning. *I love our job,* I glanced at Anthony.

Anthony chortled. "Yeah, me, too."

We went to the vet. Jackson, Lucky, and Dad were already there.

You okay, honey? Lucky asked me immediately.

I'm fine, I reassured. *Just a little bruising.*

"How do you feel, bud?" Dad knelt down and studied the bandage.

Good, I said.

The vet called us into the room.

"He should be fine if he takes it easy," he said after checking my injury.

"No medicine or anything?" said Anthony.

"Nope," the vet stated. "Unless you count rest as medicine."

I barked and licked his hand. He chuckled.

So, we got home, and I rested. I was chewing my bone when Anthony's phone rang.

"Hey, Amy… Oh, OK, great…! Yeah, I'll meet you there," Anthony hung up and grinned at me. "She's free."

Finally! I bounced up.

We drove to the Starbucks nearby where we met Amy and Sky.

"Hey," Anthony kissed her.

"Hi," Amy nodded to me. "How's he feeling?"

"He's fine," Anthony replied. "All he needs is rest."

That was scary, when you got hurt, Sky told me.

I'm fine, I said, barking at her.

Sky wagged her tail. *Okay.*

"Oreo, stay out here," Anthony said as they entered the Starbucks.

Got it, I sat down.

They came out a few minutes later with all of our drinks and food. Of course, Sky and I each got a Puppaccinno.

"So, how's architecture going?" Anthony asked.

"Great, actually," Amy said. "Um, you can't play music, can you?"

"Actually, my dad found somebody who specializes in injured musicians, so I can," Anthony said.

"Splendid!" Amy exclaimed.

"Hey, what are your minors?" Anthony questioned.

"Uh," Amy hesitated, "pediatrics and paedology."

"Oh," said Anthony. "Cool."

They talked for a while, and we went back home.

Anthony had a doctor's appointment the next day, and I insisted in going with him.

"So, I've got some good news," the doctor said. "You can play."

My eyes widened. *What?*

"You're kidding, right?" Anthony was just as astonished.

"I'm not. A new treatment has recently been developed," the doctor grinned.

"Yes!" Anthony and I both exclaimed.

Long-story-short, we won the rest of the playoffs and were in the semi-finals two weeks later. The vet said I could play in that game. And now, Anthony didn't have to play the whole game, because James was his substitute! Also, to Coach Lashlee and Coach Baker's relief, Coach Dominguez and Coach Stroud were back.

I wasn't surprised about the fact that we were playing against the Florida State Seminoles. They didn't like us, for some reason. It was at their field, which wasn't a very long drive away.

"Let's show these people how it's done," Coach Dominguez said.

We ran out of the locker room, and the crowd roared.

"Captains!" The Ref called a few minutes later.

It felt so good to go up there with Anthony.

"Heads or tails?" Mr. Ref asked us.

Tails, I recommended.

"Tails," Anthony translated.

The Ref flipped the coin. It landed on tails. "Possession or side?"

"Possession," Anthony replied.

The game started. The special team's kick-off got us to our thirty-five-yard line, which wasn't bad at all.

"Set! Hike!" Anthony called.

We were doing the wide receiver play. Coach Dominguez said it was to see how I was feeling.

I immediately sprinted towards the end-line and found that my defender was pretty slow. I barked. Anthony threw the ball to me, and I caught it. I ran as fast as I could. I still had to get past the outside linebackers and the safeties. I swerved past the linebackers, but the safeties were eager to get me. I knew we would be fine either way, so I let them tackle me.

I looked across to the marker. *Fifty-yard line. Not bad.*

We quickly agreed to Anthony's specialty, the Leap Day play. *Chuckle* This was fun.

"Leap Day! Leap Day! Hike!"

Everybody except Anthony immediately got to work with clearing a path for him. As soon as there was a gap, Anthony ran through to the end-line. Out of the corner of my eye, I saw somebody slip through our grasp and head toward Anthony. Thankfully, Josh saw and stopped him.

The crowd cheered as Anthony passed the end-line. I ran over to him and barked.

Do I even need to tell you? The dream team was back, and we won 35-17! Back at home, Anthony played "I Feel Good," and I hummed along.

A few days before the championship game, Amy told Anthony to come over. This sounded suspicious to me.

Anthony rang the doorbell. Amy was still living with her parents, since her house hadn't burned down…

Mrs. Mullins appeared at the door. "Anthony! Come in!"

Amy immediately appeared and didn't give me any time to admire her house. She rushed us into her room, which was pretty nice. Pink bed, closet, and a chest of drawers.

"What's up?" Anthony asked her. Sky had followed us.

"You remember all those emergencies I had?" Amy said.

Anthony's shoulders slumped. "Yeah."

"It was supposed to be a secret, but," Amy hesitated. "I've decided I can show you before it's finished."

"What is it?'" Anthony asked.

"Just… follow me," Amy walked over to her nightstand. On it was a lamp and nothing else. Suddenly, she pressed a hidden button, and I heard a whir somewhere below us. Suddenly, in one of the corners, the floor opened up like a trapdoor, revealing a fireman's pole made of a material you could grip onto with your mouth.

Sky slid down it like she did it every day.

Uh, what just happened? I asked, shaking myself out of my stupor.

"What is that?" Anthony pointed at the trapdoor.

Amy grinned. "Follow me," she followed Sky.

Anthony and I looked at each other and went down next.

Woah! I backed into the pole. The room we'd come into was pretty big! It was probably actually even bigger than it looked, but it was filled with architectural sketches, tables, and several lamps.

"Welcome to the home of 'The Project,'" Amy said casually.

"Huh?" Anthony and I both stared at her.

Amy giggled. "'The Project' is the reason for all the emergencies."

"Huh?" Anthony and I said again.

"Just… come over here," Amy waved us over. She was standing at a table strewn with sketches.

We jogged over. Sky was on the other side of the table.

"This," Amy gestured at the messiest sketch, "was the first."

I don't know much about architecture, but to me, it looked like an ordinary building. It was labeled "The Project."

"But what is 'The Project?'" Anthony asked impatiently.

Sky barked. *Come,* she had moved to a covered board. Once we trotted over, she pulled a rope and the cover dropped down, revealing a lot of stuff.

The first thing I saw was what looked like the finished sketch, which had been copied from somewhere else. Besides that, all there was on the board was a bunch of question marks, statements, and reminders.

My eyes wandered to a word that had been circled.

Orphanage

Suddenly, everything made sense. All the emergencies were her trying to get approval and that kind of stuff. She must've had to go out of town to either meet people or inspect land. Or both. She'd studied pediatrics and paedology for this.

She's building an orphanage, I said.

Anthony's eyes wandered over to the word. "Oh. You're building an orphanage." He looked at Amy.

Amy was fidgeting nervously. "Well, what do you think?"

Anthony looked around the room and then back at her. "I think it's amazing."

Amy breathed a sigh of relief. "Good."

"Are you still trying to get approval?" Anthony questioned.

"Yes, that's why I wasn't sure about it," Amy explained. "I also need letters of support."

"How's it going?" said Anthony.

"Not very well," Amy frowned. She walked over to a monitor on a wall and turned it on. "These are all my fails."

I glanced at it. On the screen was her inbox. A lot of the emails were from planning and funding organizations saying that her application had been denied. I counted at least twenty.

"Why aren't they giving you approval?" Anthony asked.

"Because I'm still in college," Amy answered. "And they don't think I've studied enough or that I have enough experience."

"Hmm," Anthony said. "Have you told your parents?"

"Besides Sky, you and Oreo are the first to know about anything about this," Amy said.

"So, you built all this yourself?" Anthony asked skeptically.

Amy laughed. "Of course not! Remember when I went 'out of town?'" she made air quotes with her fingers.

"Uh-huh."

"That was so I could get people to come in here and do it," Amy revealed.

"What about your folks?" Anthony said.

"They were on a business trip," Amy said.

"Clever," Anthony complimented her.

"Why, thank you," Amy kissed him. "But that's it."

"OK, this is pretty cool," Anthony crossed his arms.

Did I do a good job keeping the secret? Sky asked me.

Definitely, I said.

Over the weekend, we went to an NCAAF event, which is basically like the NFL experience, but for college. It was at Clemson University, in South Carolina. I slept half the flight, so I can't tell you how long it was. We had to get there a little early to get our schedules, but we didn't even stay at a hotel.

I'll just tell you Anthony's schedule and then mine:

> From 10 o'clock to 2 o'clock, Anthony was stationed at the signature booth.

> He had a one-hour lunch break.

> From 3 o'clock to 4 o'clock, he was going to pass a football to his fans.

> From 4 o'clock to 5 o'clock, he had a Q/A session.

> And from 5 o'clock to 6 o'clock, he was required to help me with my Q/A session (turns out everybody believed in the physic-connection thing).

Here's mine:

> From 10 o'clock to 2 o'clock, I was stationed at the signature booth.
>
> I had a one-hour lunch break.
>
> From 3 o'clock to 4 o'clock, I was supposed to catch passes from my fans.
>
> From 4 o'clock to 5 o'clock, I would be holding races with my fans (good luck with that).
>
> And from 5 o'clock to 6 o'clock, I had my Q/A session.

So, we had pretty busy days.

"Okay, players due for signature booth, if you could follow me," somebody said. We followed him to a backstage area. Beyond the curtain were our booths.

"This'll be fun," Joseph told us.

"Yep," Anthony agreed. The three of us were the only ones from the Canes who were starting with the signature booth. I spotted one of the players from the Clemson Tigers, which was the team we were playing against in the final.

I met a lot of very nice fans. Most of them were either as enthusiastic as Mocha or even more so. I was pretty tired after pressing my paw onto inkpad after inkpad and paper, shirt, or whatever they wanted signed, so I was extremely thankful for the break.

Next, came the passes. That was also very fun. A lot of the people who signed up for it were pretty good at throwing. And if they weren't, I made up for it and caught the ball anyway.

Then came the races. That was probably my favorite activity. I found that some people were very fast. Sometimes, I thought; *You should be a wide receiver.* Other times, it was a piece of cake.

And finally, the Q/A. This was… interesting. To me, anyways. I had never been asked many questions. It was one question per person.

"Do you have a wife and/or child?" one of my fans asked.

"He has a wife and seven pups," Anthony replied.

"Do you remember your genetic family?"

Like it was yesterday, I said.

"Like it was yesterday," Anthony translated.

"Do you think you have a good chance in the finals?"

Yes.

"Yes," said Anthony.

"How did you get your prosthetic?"

"Truck accident."

"Have you had multiple owners?"

Anthony glanced at me. *Two, right?*

Yeah, you and Fabi.

"He's had two," Anthony said.

"What was the difference between working with James Howell and Anthony?"

Only the physic connection, I chuckled at my answer.

Anthony smiled. "Only the physic connection."

We were all very tired by the end of it, but still flew back that same evening.

The period leading up to the championship was kind of tense. Usually, Coach Dominguez tells one or two jokes at practice, but now, we were all silent. Even at home we practiced. For example, one time, while Anthony was cooking, he passed me a football, and I caught it. We continued this until he finished cooking.

Are you nervous? Milo asked me. We were at Dad's house.

No, I said in a squeaky voice. **Ahem* No, definitely not.*

I'll take that as a "yes," Milo went back to chewing his toy.

I glared at him; he chortled.

We'll be cheering for you, Rose promised at Aunt Sonia's new house.

I know, I'm just… nervous, I admitted, *and scared.*

That's how I felt in the cardboard box, Rose sympathized. *Until you came along.*

I smiled. *Thanks.*

Amy and I made a sign to wave around with the cheerleaders, Sky told me. Anthony and Amy were talking at the Starbucks table above us.

Really? I tilted my head at her.

Yeah. I mean, you need all the support you can get, right? Sky wagged her tail.

I grinned. *Yeah.*

I'm not a fan of sports or dogs, Emil's cat, Iris, said from her perch on the windowsill. She was a white cat with blue eyes. Emil had invited Anthony to play football with him, since he played in middle school, *but I think I can make an exception for you,* Iris finished.

You guys are coming? I asked.

Iris purred. *Of course, pinhead.*

I chuckled. *Thanks, I guess.*

You know, we've had some rocky times in our friendship, but I wish you the best of luck, Clover said at the dog park. *We'll be cheering for you.*

I smiled at her. *Thank you.*

"You're going to do great," Fabi reassured me. She and Alex had come to one of our practices.

I barked at her and licked her chin. *You guys will be there, right?*

"Of course they'll be there!" Anthony exclaimed.

"Did you really think we'd miss it?" Alex asked, raising his eyebrows.

I barked at him. *My apologies.*

I'll be there, Lucky told me. We had finished visiting all the pups. They had promised to be there, too.

Thank you, I licked her.

The championship game came far too soon, it felt like. It was at Clemson.

"Okay, pre-game speech," Coach Dominguez said in the locker room. "Everybody, sit down."

I put my rump to the floor.

"I know you're nervous, and that's understandable, but I need you to remember one thing," Coach Dominguez said, "no matter what happens, I'm proud of the men you've become."

I barked.

"And dog," Coach Dominguez added. The team laughed. "Let's do this!" he finished.

We walked out of the locker room. The crowd cheered. I quickly scanned the bleachers. I saw Mom, Dad, Brooke, Mocha, Kate, and everybody else who had promised to be there.

I took a deep breath. *I can do all things through Christ, who gives me strength.*

We warmed up and did some short drills. Then, it was time.

"Captains!" Mr. Ref called.

Anthony and I went up to him. We shook hands with the other captains.

"Heads or tails?" The Ref asked.

I wagged my tail.

"Tails," Anthony said.

The Ref flipped the coin. Bless the Lord Almighty: it landed on tails. "Possession or side?"

"Possession."

The special team went out. They did the kick-off pretty well and gave us a forty-yard start.

"Hike!" Anthony called.

We were going to do the Hand-off Play again. Anthony handed it to Joseph. We immediately tried to clear a path for him. He got to the forty-five yard line before getting tackled.

Second down.

"W.R! W.R! Hike!"

Johan and I ran towards the end-line, trying to get rid of our defenders. I saw Johan confuse his and get ahead of him. He called for the ball, and Anthony passed it to him. Thankfully, Johan caught it and started running. I rushed over to try and help with the safeties, but they tackled him at the fifty-yard line.

First down. We quickly agreed to do the Fake-Handoff play.

"Hike!"

I got ready, just in case. I watched as Anthony slid by Joseph but didn't give it to him. One or two of the Tigers fell for it. My defender was already charging toward Anthony.

I barked. *I'm open!*

Anthony immediately passed it to me. I sprinted forward, never daring to look back. The safeties were still there, but Johan was fast, maybe even faster than me. He tackled the one on his side, but the other safety was still too far away.

I braced myself as he tackled me at thirty-six yards.

Johan helped me up once the Ref blew his whistle. "Time out, Hurricanes!"

Second down.

"Leap Day! Leap Day! Hike!"

In a flash, each of us was pushing back a defender. Coach Dominguez had ordered Johan and I to go for the safeties instead of the cornerbacks, so we did. It was the right call. The cornerbacks weren't as fast or well-prepared as the safeties. Anthony made good progress to the twenty-yard line before one of the cornerbacks got to him.

"Code B! Code B! Hike!"

I don't think I've ever mentioned Code B. This was for Ben. He was our tight end. Anthony handed it to him, and Ben ran. He made it to the fifteen-yard line.

Second down.

"Turn! Turn! Hike!" Anthony faked a pass to Johan, and he ran. To my disappointment, the middle linebacker tackled him at eleven yards.

Third down.

Code O! Code O! Hike!"

"O" is for Oreo. I ran to the safety making it seem like we were doing a different play. The cornerback fell for it. He ran up to help his team. I called for the ball and caught it at the seven-yard line. I saw Josh tackle one of the safeties, but the other one was right behind me. He tackled me at the three-yard line.

First down.

"Code S! Code S! Hike!"

Code S was… well, code for the Fake-Handoff Play.

Anthony faked the hand-off to Chris and ran. Johan and I simultaneously tackled the safeties. Thankfully, Xavier tackled the cornerback closest to Anthony.

I barked as he scored the touchdown. The crowd roared.

Jay made the extra point.

The Tigers made it to their thirty-yard line.

"Code Red! Hike!" their quarterback called. He handed it to his guard. I made sure to check his hands for the ball, but I was right. I sprinted to help as he eluded Anthony, Ben, and Chris. Luckily, Joe caught him at their forty-yard line.

Okay, fast-forward to them being at our thirty-yard line. It was third down. Coach Dominguez had put in Samuel for Carlos, who was a safety, and Kian for Kevin, who was an outside linebacker.

"W.R! W.R! Hike!"

Somehow, the wide receiver on Johan's side tripped him.

Oh, no, I thought. I started sprinting to their side to try and help.

The wide receiver jinked past Samuel, but luckily Johan had gotten back up and tackled him at our twenty-two-yard line. It was now the fourth down. They did a hand-off play and their center saved them by getting to the eighteen-yard line.

First down.

"Code blue! Code blue! Hike!" the quarterback faked a pass to my W.R. and sprinted toward the end-line. Anthony tackled him at the sixteen-yard line.

Second down.

"Behind! Behind! Hike!" the quarterback handed it to his fullback. The fullback started running. His team cleared the way for him. They were doing a good job. I got past my defender and tackled him at our eleven-yard line.

Third down.

"Hike!" the quarterback ran to the left (Johan's side) and sprinted forward. The cornerback cleared out Johan, but Kian tackled him at the nine-yard line.

First down.

"Code Y! Code Y! Hike!" the quarterback quickly passed it to the wide receiver on my side. The halfback got behind him to protect him. I tricked them by panting harder to make them think that I was getting tired so maybe they'd go slower. It worked. I sped up and tackled the wide receiver at the seven-yard line.

Second down. We stopped them at the six-yard line.

Third down. Anthony tackled the quarterback.

Fourth down. They went for the field goal. The special team went in, but they scored it.

The special team went in and did the punt. Theo did really well and made it all the way to their forty-eight-yard line.

Coach Dominguez put in Kaleb for Johan and James for Anthony.

First down.

"Code G! Code G! Hike!" James called. "Code G" was code for "Turn." He faked a pass to Kaleb and sprinted toward the end-line. He swerved past the outside linebacker on the right (my side). I pushed the cornerback back so he wouldn't be able to tackle him. Xavier tried to rush to the safety, but the safety tackled James at their thirty-four yard line.

First down.

"W.R! Right! Hike!"

Now, you're probably thinking that you've worked it out and that James was going to pass it me. You're wrong. "Right" actually meant "left." Got it now? Good.

James faked the pass to me, and I helped out by jumping into the air. Then he passed it to Kaleb. Not everybody had fallen for it, but Kaleb's cornerback had. Everybody (except me, since I was supposed to fake it) had already been making their way to the safeties. Carlos tackled one, and Joe tackled the other. The cornerback had realized what was going on. He tackled Kaleb at the twenty-one-yard line. But we had made massive progress. It was one of our best plays ever.

The audience cheered. We congratulated each other, especially Kaleb.

First down. James made it to the twenty-nine yard line.

First down. I made it to the twenty-four-yard line.

Second down. Ben made it to their twenty-yard line.

First down.

"Code O! Code O! Hike!"

I jogged towards James, and then sprinted to the end-line. I called for the ball at the fifteen-yard line. James passed it to me, and I caught it. I started toward the end-line. The safeties were basically the only thing between it and me, since I was faster than the cornerback. I avoided one of them, and Kaleb helped me with the other. I scored the touchdown.

Everybody cheered. I barked and wagged my tail.

The special team made the extra point.

Fast-forward to the fourth quarter. We had somehow ended up tied at 24-24. There were five minutes left in the game. It was the Tigers' ball. Third down.

"W.R! W.R! Hike!" the quarterback called.

I stuck to my W.R. like glue. The quarterback faked the pass to Johan's W.R. and then passed it to mine. He probably thought I would fall for it. He was wrong.

I backed up a bit, sprinted in front of the wide receiver, jumped, and intercepted the ball.

Everyone cheered and patted me.

Our ball. The special team went out for the punt and made it to the forty-eight yard line. Coach Dominguez put the starters in.

"D! O! Hike!" Anthony called.

"D! O!" stands for "Dog Oreo." I got past my defender and caught the ball. One of the ends tackled me at the thirty-nine yard line (I had feinted past the safety).

First down.

"Code S! Code H! Hike!"

That meant that we were going to fake the Fake-Handoff Play.

Anthony faked the hand-off to Joe and then handed it to Xavier. Xavier started running. I focused on the safety. He got to the 32-yard line before the middle linebacker tackled him.

Second down. We agreed that Anthony would pass it to Johan.

"Hike!" Anthony said. I started heading toward the safety but still kept an eye on my cornerback. Johan called for the ball. Anthony passed it to him; Johan started sprinting. Ben tackled one safety and I tackled the other. They were already starting to get up when Kevin tackled the cornerback. I quickly tackled my cornerback and went back to Johan. I couldn't believe it. Were we going to do it?

The crowd burst into a roar as we all reached the end-line. Everybody else had caught up with us by now.

Coach Dominguez smartly called for a two-point conversion. We agreed on doing Leap Day.

"Hike!"

We all started clearing the path. I held my cornerback. Scanning the field, I saw an open space for Anthony. He saw it, too and ran through it. Just when you thought he was going to make it, somebody got through and tackled him. Here's the thing: the ball didn't stay in Anthony's hands, he threw it up, probably by accident, and sent it flying.

Somehow, I knew exactly what to do. I leaped over the prone Anthony-Tiger tangle and caught the ball. I skidded to a stop, turned and set out headlong for the end zone.

Everybody cheered. I was astonished with myself. The team patted and praised me.

From the punt, the special team stopped them at their 43-yard line, which was amazing.

First down. All we needed was a strong defense (or an interception).

"Hike!" their quarterback called. He handed it to his center. A second later, Joe had tackled him.

Second down.

"Code red! Hike!" the quarterback faked a pass to my W.R. I fell for it at first but recovered. He then passed it to Johan's W.R., and he caught it. Johan somehow managed to tackle him a few inches further on.

Third down. They made it to their forty-yard line.

First down.

"Hike!" the quarterback handed it to his fullback, who started sprinting to the end zone. He made it to the thirty-five yard line before getting tackled by Carlos.

The Tigers called a time-out.

Second down.

"Code M! Hike!" the quarterback handed it to his tight end. Kevin tackled him at thirty-three yards.

The Tigers called a time-out.

Third down. They reached the thirty-one yard line.

Fourth down.

"Hike!" the quarterback handed it to his center. Joe got juked; I started to panic. But then, Anthony tackled him, giving us the game.

We cheered and jumped up and down together. The whole bench ran out and celebrated. The crowd screamed.

A few minutes later, the Ref had each team shake hands. Then, he gave us our trophy.

"The winners of the 2035-2036 NCAAF ACC Division League are..." the director of the league stopped for a dramatic pause, "the Miami Hurricanes!" he handed Coach Dominguez the trophy. We cheered some more.

UM held a party the next weekend to celebrate. It was a lot of fun. We got congratulated by a lot of people.

A few days after the championship, Amy told us that she got approval for the orphanage.

"Are you planning on telling your parents?" Anthony asked her at "The Project's" headquarters.

"Yes," Amy said.

"Anybody else?"

"Just them until I get enough letters of support," Amy explained.

"Okay then," Anthony kissed her on the cheek.

All in all, everything was going great.

Excited for movie night? I asked Molly as we drove to pick up the rest of her siblings. We had rented a limo.

Yeah! She exclaimed. *What are we watching?*

The Tale of the Century, I said.

Okay, Molly nuzzled me. Her owners, Dave, Kacey, and their baby son, Geo, were with us.

We picked up everybody else and met at the Jacobs' house. It was nice being together again. The rest of the year was going to be pretty uneventful, which meant that we would get to see each other a lot more. The pups loved the movie.

"This is nice," Joseph said in our living room. We were watching a replay of the championship, "just being lazy for once."

"Yeah," Anthony agreed.

I watched one of the Roombas whir around the room and agreed. *Definitely,* I said, laying my head on my paws with a sigh.

Epilogue

· ·

Well, that's it. That's my life. It was pretty… eventful (that's an understatement, but you get what I mean). And no, I'm not dead. I'm alive and well. Fourteen years old. I retired a couple of months back but I still get fans coming to my door every now and then.

Anyway, let me tell you a little about how things turned out.

Amy's orphanage was a huge success, and visiting the kids there is one of my favorite parts of the day.

Now that I'm retired, I have much more free time. I use it to visit my family, answer letters from fans, and sometimes just to be a normal dog.

Anthony got invited to play for the Miami Dolphins. He accepted. All he has to do is finish the year and he's going to be in the NFL.

Fabi and Alex are having a baby boy in a few months. I gotta say, I'm excited to meet the kid.

Dad finally found a band for himself.

I'm going to be cast in a movie about sports dogs soon. I'm pretty excited.

All in all, life is pretty normal now (I know, shocker). I hope it didn't make you too sad. Oh, and that you get the signed edition.

The End

Acknowledgments

· ·

Thank you, dad, for being such a great agent.

Thanks to my mom, who is always excited for me.

Thanks to my editors, Kit and Ziomara, for doing such a great job.

Thank you to my illustrator, Diego.

Thank you to my brother, who wasn't as excited but let me bother him with questions.

Thanks to my partner-in-writing, Maddie. Especially for letting me collaborate with her.

Thanks to Eileen, who started late, but I see great potential in her book.

Thank you, Mrs. Todd, for giving me the idea of writing a book. I would've never started without you telling me.

Thanks to my fifth-grade class, who never judge me for being an overachiever.

Thank you, Cookie, for never minding that I'm on my computer a lot.

Thanks to my family, who seemed to enjoy me telling them about my book.

And finally, thank you Lord, for helping me complete this.

Biography

Fabiana Salgado Vazquez is an 11-year-old. She was born on January 26, 2009, in Mexico City and became an American Citizen one year later after lots of trouble, thanks to the stubbornness of her father, a saga that deserves another book to tell the story. Her hometown is in Pembroke Pines, Florida. She attends Potential Christian Academy and is in middle school. This is her first book. She has a brother, 2 stepbrothers, 2 stepsisters, 2 stepparents, a beloved dog sister, Cookie, and a beloved dog stepsister, Alexandra. She loves to play soccer and basketball, for which she has won several trophies. She also likes the piano and is taking lessons presently. She loves to travel and understand other cultures and languages. It seems she likes to write, a lot. But most importantly, she loves, she gives, and she knows how to be grateful when someone has both love and knowledge to give. Congratulations baby, I love you.

A very proud Dad,
Javier Salgado Marin

Lightning Source UK Ltd.
Milton Keynes UK
UKHW010634080321
379980UK00001B/154